The Promise of Heaven

Hazel E. Pinder

Editing/Interior Book Design/Layout/Publishing Assistance
CBM Christian Book Editing
www.christian-book-editing.com

Printed in the USA

ENDORSEMENT

"The Promise of Heaven offers an epic journey into the very pages of history and the Bible that come to life before your eyes."
~CBM Christian Book Editing

Acknowledgements

When we understand the dynamics of a God who supports us as we navigate the rocks of life it is awesome.

I have also felt His touch through family and friends on my journey and I am grateful for their encouragement and love.

To Barbara, Rory, Francis and Elaine thank you for laughter, it has certainly helped me to come out of the shadows and fly.

Hazel

Dedications

To those I treasure.

Special thanks to my family; all so unique and precious, who keep me grounded and loved, the young ones and the old, the future is yours. To my husband, for his encouragement, whatever the weather, I love you all.

And I said to the man who stood at the gate of the year:

"Give me a light that I may tread safely into the unknown."

And he replied:

"Go out into the darkness and put your hand in the Hand of God That shall be to you better than light and safer than a known way."

So I went forth, and finding the Hand of God, trod gladly into the night. And He led me towards the hills and the breaking of day in the lone East.

King George V1

"A new year is at hand. We cannot tell what it will bring. If it brings peace, how thankful we shall all be. If it brings us continued struggles we shall remain undaunted."

Minnie Haskins' poem "The Gate of the Year" (1908).

CONTENTS

.

Foreword Curtain Up ～～～～～～

Within the journey of this small book of stories, is a desire to understand and contemplate a minuscule glimpse of the heavenly realm of God. It is radical in its approach, gazing at the world seemingly through heavenly eyes. **The Promise of Heaven** is a work of fiction in which I have endeavoured to honor the Word of God.

Cameos of the Bible, simplistic in presentation but at times extreme in content, with other works announcing the coming Messiah, or **The Promise of Heaven.** One could say this is a considerable endeavour, which seems on the surface to be unrealistic and hugely intrusive. My hope is it will help us ponder on our God of creation and meditate on His colossal depth of "being."

In my radical approach, the facet I want us to reflect on is the hidden world, that is behind everything we do. The level of activity of supernatural beings all around us, is a reality, not to be feared but respected.

It is obvious, in writing in this way, it could become vast and complex, which a study by academics would cover in a great depth, which is not quite what I had in mind. My thinking is to hopefully whet the appetite of the reader, to believe that beyond our understanding, there is so much more. To this end, I write snippets that will encourage us to look far beyond the written text. To contemplate events around us through the eyes of faith and delve deeper when we read the Bible.

A question I ponder on is: Is it a possibility that we have become resistant to the essence of much of what we read, ultimately without noticing, possibly gliding over facts? Maybe blasé to a degree, we practically dismissed the nub of what is written; and lose the authenticity that is there? These are mere thoughts to inspire us to go deeper with our God, to recognize the wonder of Heaven and consider the reckless enemy that is always trailing us. Thus, I write, endeavouring to paint a picture and to search for a reality of "being there," that has often escaped our grasp.

Possibly you may disagree with some of my thoughts, that is quite inevitable. But probing into the things that we read is healthy, invariably throwing light on the whole picture. Combined with meditating on the "Word", kicking the leaves and pondering about events, may help to keep perspective. Musing in this way, it is conceivable that this may encourage us to see how miraculous Heaven is...while considering, how incredible is "**The Promise of Heaven**" and Christ's sacrifice?

All of this, some may consider wild imagination, not worth anyone's time. My thinking is that behind the scenes there is much more, in our own lives and the heavenly sphere! God the great designer, gave us creative minds and expression when He created humanity and this glorious world. So, what about Heaven? Is it worth considering that Heaven is brimming over with an active force of supernatural beauty, colour and action? It could not possibly be otherwise when we look at the creation that God designed for us, here on Earth. How much more beauty surrounds Heaven and all that is God?

Therefore, can we agree, that the power majesty and radiance of our triune God must be breath-taking? Together, let us then take a peek through the keyhole of Heaven. Of course, it is also vital to be realistic and keep our feet on the ground and avidly read Scripture. Accept God, **The Mighty One** as the supreme authority powerful, formidable and immovable. Accept too, that lurking behind the devastations in the world, an enemy awaits, who wants to triumph.

By living God's way, we walk protected, by defying God we leave ourselves vulnerable. The reality of a supernatural war happening is real, and our Defender and defence is God. Once we accept all this, isn't it entirely conceivable that beyond the logical, there are things that happen that are beyond our understanding, in a balanced and wise way.

Accepting and investigating this thinking can facilitate our faith, in many ways, especially in our prayer life. We have a truly dynamic and awesome God who has all authority and can wield the influence of a phenomenal kind. If in understanding this, it brings us closer to perceiving Him a little more, brilliant! If I can also awaken in us the reality of a Savior, who radiated love to such a degree, it made the angels ecstatic with joy, then I am pleased.

If on the reverse you see evil as frightening, I have failed. On knowing the Lord Jesus Christ as our Lord and Savior, we are "more than conquers" and live in a privileged position. As our Savior, we carry the name of the Lord Jesus on our foreheads; and become His invincible army.

It is quite frankly this: He fights our battles. So, come with me, let us look behind the scenes and see the producer while imagining just a little of "how things may have happened", putting faith into action, approaching everything with expectation and joy…a fantastic adventure. In this aspect, it is refreshing to look through a different prism on our journey of faith. Naturally, elevating events to the extent that they become more important than the "Giver" of those things is wrong. Sensationalism gives a platform to darkness and is reprehensible. Even so, disregarding the supernatural, because behind this "seeming unreal place", lurks a hive of activity is naive.

We worship our God in spirit and truth, so having a spiritual awareness is essential. Embrace this fact and the necessity to experience the anointing of the Holy Spirit, absolutely vital to our growth in Christ; it is fabulous. Therefore, without seeming to be too over-imaginative, let me take you on a journey to highlight some of the things we rarely think about and unquestionably never talk about, reflecting, that we mustn't embellish God's Word. It is critical that we do not change the Word of God, but is it not sensible to realize that as our grandfather clock has hidden workings, so has Heaven?

Let us contemplate and meditate on our God and yearn to grow closer to Him. To help us have an even better understanding of our relationship with His Son. I ask that you read with an open mind and as you gaze on the pages, see "**The Promise of Heaven**" revealed in all of His beauty.... while we... "Run the race in the certainty of the high calling of the Lord Jesus Christ."

The Reality of Heaven to Earth

It was a void, a deep penetrating blackness, completely consuming that hung silently around. Suddenly...He appeared. A compelling, captivating startling vision, brooding over all, exuding a commanding presence of strength ...The Spirit of God.

The light of His intense, spectacular presence was

extraordinary; it radiated a gleaming and impressive impression of power frightening to behold! With Him, there appeared two others, one on His right and the other on His left, set apart and beautiful. The three connected but not adjoined; individuals working as a trio of one, exuding a strength that was breath-taking, incredible.

It was splendour beyond words, a fantastic expression of beauty that the eye could barely conceive. As an aura of holiness not contemplated, surrounded their presence. It was a place of wonder, this heavenly realm was brilliant in magnitude, as seven flaming torches, encircled these powerful beings. Creating a place of breathtaking awe, illuminating everything around it in mystery.

In the centre, a golden stairway led to gleaming thrones, dazzling, exquisite, with sparkling diamonds, emeralds and rubies that reflected light and glittered. It was remarkable in its grandeur, awesome to gaze on, and seemed to go on and on. Around this area, the wings of thousands of delicate, fragile angels fluttered in the phenomenal atmosphere. The whole scene was hardly translatable into words. Powerfully transmitted, was the extraordinary feeling of power and presence of peace everywhere. Around the centre of the thrones, seraphic beings praised **The Mighty God** in an undulating wave of worship.

At the same time, millions of magnificent creatures amassed from all directions. Everywhere, color movement and beauty, filled the heavens as millions of angelic beings made homage to their Creator. Others stood by, as natural guardians, upright and immovable, ferocious adversaries standing ready to serve their "Supreme Being", in any way that was required. The strength in all of the assembled beings was colossal, diverging from their natures, a sense of resplendent nobility and power.

It was a unique scene of light that was sensational. While a never-ending act of worship, like droplets of pure rapture, could be heard, of wonderful exuberance everywhere. Angelic voices were heard praising their majestic Creator with joy, thanksgiving and worship. A purposeful tribute, of honor at His presence, declaring His extraordinary worth with sanctified endless praise.

The scene was an incredible testimony, of supernatural beings' earnest devotion to their Creator. It was devotion of an extraordinary strength and power. It was the beginning of all things! Suddenly without warning, it happened, the Supreme Being, lifted up His arms and communicated to the void. All waited for His voice, intent on seeing, the fantastic God of creation's authority and power demonstrated to all.

It was the biggest cataclysmic proponent of force the universe had ever heard, and all listened in breath-taking silence. "Let there be light." The authority of His voice resounded out in the heavens with formidable strength. It was a time of wonder, as the Creator of all things stood radiant, as a crescendo of lights appeared into the blackness.

It happened ... God created and divided the light from the darkness! The world of the future was happening, and it was good, holy, mystic and beautiful. Not a sound was heard except His commands, as His authority overshadowed all. His thunderous voice echoed as a wave of sound through the silence, resonating everywhere, as light appeared at His bidding. This symphony of lights was every place, translucent illuminating flickering lights, that danced and became stronger, surging powerfully in all directions. Gradually a symphony of sound could be heard as soft as a snowflake but as beautiful as a trickle of a mountain stream, bells of rapturous joy greeted Him everywhere, declaring His

Majesty.

This was **The Mighty One**...who brought a possibility, into a reality! The light continued, spectacular in its depth, as it soared over all. As the angelic beings watched, anticipating that there was, so much more to come! The Earth with its infinite void of darkness, also waited, as to what **The Mighty Ones'** expectation for the future was to be.

The beginning of all things had started. The mighty triumph that was to continue, as the author of the plans, proceeded to initiate them. Swiftly, daylight swept across the firmament, as God showed His power to a world waiting. While all of Heaven watched, holding its breath.

Instantly, it happened, suddenly there was evening and morning, the first day! God then said, "Let us divide the water, and separate these elements. The sky and the water divided, and that is how it was, and God called the summit sky. The air was beautiful, its purity and lightness, almost fragrant! So, there was evening, and there was morning the second day. The beginning of all things had started. Directly it seemed to be a sign for the celestial beings to explode with joy. While all around a gradual crescendo of praise increased and increased. The pleasure was esthetical as the songs of Heaven resounded around the Earth.

Here began the journey of creation and a display of power that the universe had never seen before. A great adventure was occurring, as life was created in all forms. Tremendous excitement around the world was almost palatable, as all waited expectantly, looking to see the plan unfold!

The Creator's Plan!

The vision was to bring life into being. Like all visions, it had to become a reality. Quickly **The Mighty One** set about working to create not only the environment for life, but life itself.

Strength and power conveyed to all, as the three majestic beings stood strong and resolute, each supporting and encouraging the other. All around the rapturous chorus of Heaven resounded, as adulation continued hand's raised in praise and worship.

It was a scene of breath-taking joy everywhere, as eternity waited for His plan for the world. Life was spectacularly revealed in all its fullness, as the power of God declared creation. Oceans, vegetation, animals and life in all forms, appeared.

The Creator had begun. His plan, to bring into being, a world of wonders, had started. The angels watched with anticipation and joy, except for one. He was defiant and gazed on, waiting for his opportunity to try to undermine **The Mighty One** to take "power."

Audacious plans, organised by **The Mighty One,** to create a world of beauty were all in place. Radical and amazing, with provision for eternity, all thoughtfully promised. Possibly, the moment that He made provision, for Sheol to deal with evil? Knowing the future and understanding all things, He is a Creator and a visionary. The enemy will never out smart Him! Consistently active, **The Mighty One** can deal with all matters, as His eye is everywhere. The heartbeat of creation lay in His hands, as He lovingly announced each piece. It was a time like no other when at the thrones of Heaven, an impressive selection of power unfolded, and creation began. Heaven and Earth were created in splendour as all of Heaven rejoiced. It was not only a grand plan but a beautifully orchestrated adventure for life where all beings, have their rightful place. The finale for all of this fantastic scheme was the creation of people. It was the culmination of all, when from the dust of the Earth, Adam the man was created, the friend of Heaven.

At this feat all of Heaven rejoiced, as all of Heaven revelled at the presentation of this magnificent creature. God was activating His plans, and it was going to be tremendous, a time for joy. **The Breath** and **The Beautiful One** used their mighty powers together with **The Mighty One** in the creation of man. It was a time like no other, never to be experienced again, and all gazed on in excitement.

Moulded by the hands of his Creator, the man stood visible, and all of Heaven was in awe. The man smiled, with joy on his face as he gazed around. It was a unique time, peaceful and happy as **The Mighty One**, **The Breath** and **The Beautiful One**, laughed together at events. The pinnacle had been realized, man created, and it was the start of all things...

It was a friendship that **The Mighty One** was to enjoy spontaneous and instinctive. Sensitive to all things, **The Mighty One** discerned the need for Adam to have company and discussed it with him. Adam agreed, and **The Mighty One** and **The Breath** put him to sleep, to bring forth another miracle.

The God of creation was mindful of all things, and from out of Adam's body they formed Eve, the companion for him, woman. Heaven watched, thrilled at the new events occurring, with joy and expectation all around. The future had started, an exciting journey, when everything was to become bigger and more complicated. All of this firmly on **The Mighty One's** plans for the future. While

The Promise of Heaven was teetering on the horizon.

Beginnings

All Heaven was excited, keen to understand, what the three powerful beings had planned for the future. Confident in their Creator, they knew that the adventure was going to be amazing. The Triune God had all matters in hand for the future. When Adam and Eve were set to embrace a more significant role in the Kingdom.

The angels watched in readiness for the bidding of their supreme being. These magnificent beings continually worshipped the God whom they adored. Around them was the Godhead like no other, seated together, **The Mighty One, The Promise of Heaven** and **The Breath,** a formidable trio. Possibly frightening in their might and power, as victorious, immovable, beings!

These are three distinctly different persons, but one in everything. It was these three that the angels worshipped day and night, giving them praise and adoration. A mighty God, an incredulously powerful being, timeless, knowing all, a holy God of creation, evoking praise. All of Heaven was watching, waiting eagerly, anticipating that more was to happen in the Garden of Eden.

As the seventh day approached, it was an exceptional time. **The Mighty One** had decreed was to be a day of peace and tranquillity, after the activity of Creation. As a day of worship, God blessed the day, declaring it holy, and walked the Earth looking over all. It was a beautiful world, produced by **The Mighty One** for humanity's enjoyment. Excited, all of Heaven celebrated with praise and worshipped Him. Later, the three dominant beings stood enjoying the river that watered the garden and flowed onwards, surrounded by beautiful trees. Joy, peace and happiness seem to be inherent in these mighty beings, viewing the beauty of creation. **The Mighty One** knew that it would not last, but for this moment, Heaven overflowed with joy. On the threshold, challenges, and a battle in the future. Although all were confident of the winner. He stood resplendently and all around bowed to this fantastic Godhead.

Broken Friendship

A slight breeze gently wafted the vegetation as **The Mighty One** and Adam walked in the garden. Their routine, adopted as their friendship deepened, and they met together to talk. Adam, God's friend, continually named the animals as they walked, and the two enjoyed each other's company. It was a walk of benefit, evoking questions the man Adam might have to ask **The Mighty One** after work, in the garden. Standing nearby, angels stood watching, listening to the dialogue as the couple walked together. The astoundingly beautiful angels and archangels were always ready to do the bidding of their commander, to serve Him in any way they could. Silent beings, they waited, hidden away mostly, following Him. Suddenly, another figure appeared on the scene, with a tiger walking alongside her, it was a woman. **The Mighty One** held out his hand in greeting and smiled as Eve arrived. The three continued their walk, stroking various animals on the way in the sweetness of the evening hour.

The air was fresh and still, silent as if even nature bowed to the presence of the mighty Creator, as He walked through the lush grass. The created beings shared a bond of unity with their Creator, and in each other's company. **The Mighty One** pointed out trees and shrubs, while Adam named the animals, consequently laughter was often heard in the garden as they viewed all the different things around them.

It was the beginning of time, and the creation of all--when humanity walked in harmony with God. It was their routine each day, to meet in the evening time, a favorite for the three of them. On one of these excursions, he reminded them of all the excellent vegetation in the garden to eat but prompted them again, that there was a tree not to touch. The tree in the centre of the garden was the Tree of Life, and the other the knowledge of good and evil. **The Mighty One** warned them that death would be the outcome if they touch the tree of understanding good and evil.

It was a tranquil time in the garden, with the couple happy, secure in the life they had, in an environment that was peaceful. In fact, peace and holiness seemed to permeate everything around them. The perfect backdrop of a beautiful world portrayed with animals and lush vegetation that gave a sense of tranquillity. In this place, animals and people found sanctuary and were secure together. It was a huge garden, so Adam and Eve roamed everywhere, enjoying life in all its fullness. Contented, with a sense of belonging, they played with the animals, laughed, and lavished, in the breath-taking beauty of this place, Earth.

Daily, Adam worked in the vast garden, while Eve had a sense of adventure and enjoyed investigating, to share later with Adam. An extraordinarily beautiful woman, with warmth about her and a curiosity for all things. In her wanderings, she came upon the trees that **The Mighty One** had told them to avoid and gazed upon one of them for a time. As she did so, the serpent sidled up to her and spoke to her, telling her very quietly that there was no reason for them not to eat from the tree. Hearing the serpent speak made her jump and she responded by stating firmly that **The Mighty One** had said to them that they mustn't eat from this particular tree. The serpent laughed, and craftily said! "The only reason for this is that you will have an understanding of right from wrong. At present, you beings know little!" He said with a sneer!

"But I know **The Mighty One** said we were not to eat that fruit," said Eve. "Will you live your life being dictated to by **The Mighty One**? Wouldn't you like to become as knowledgeable as Him...go on and try it, I assure you it won't hurt?" He laughed again knowingly, and turned his head away from the woman, so that she couldn't see the contempt in his eyes.

The woman turned her head and looked at the beautiful tree and the luscious ripened fruit. Prompted by the serpent to try the fruit, she considered what he'd said. *No one will find out,* she thought, as she put out her hand. She took the fruit that hung temptingly, waiting to be consumed and took a bite. By this time Adam had joined her, and she passed it over for him, to take a bite of the fruit too. "Isn't this the fruit that **The Mighty One** said not to eat?" He asked. Eve brushed his concerns away.

"Oh, it's only a little fruit, it tastes delicious," said the woman.

The serpent scampered away chuckling. He had a massive plan of defiance that had been masterminded well to overthrow **The Mighty One** and it was working! Lucifer was knowledgeable, a trusted servant, intelligent and he had a prominent place in Heaven. Dressed to deceive he knew what he wanted and was out to get it, using any method he could. The serpent, a decoy for this most beautiful of beings, was useful and had served his purpose.

Angelic beings created to worship their Creator never hankered for notoriety and praise. Except for Lucifer who was exalting himself into a place of importance. The "glistening one", adorned with magnificent beauty by his Creator, embraced pride and wanted to use his power to raid Heaven.

On this day everything was significant, and as evening arrived, **The Mighty One** came looking for Adam and Eve, which was His custom. He called to the man and woman. The two heard **The Mighty One** walking in the garden, sadly on this day they had gone into hiding. Adam and Eve knew that things had changed! A hesitant Adam eventually came out from the place he was hiding, reluctantly. He had gathered an array of leaves over his body, and lowered his head as **The Mighty One** spoke to him.

"Adam, why have you hidden from me?" Adam flushed and said," I know that I am naked, and I am ashamed."

"Adam, did you eat the fruit from the tree I told you not to touch?" **The Mighty One** asked. "Well...the woman gave it to me!" said Adam and lowered his eyes. At this, the woman came close to Him, and pointed in the direction of the snake and said.

"He told me it wasn't a big crime, in fact, he said it wasn't significant, and I believed him."

The Mighty One looked sad and put out His hand to the two in front of him. "Dear ones, I gave you both the opportunity to make choices, as to how you could live and what you could do. I wanted to see if your love was strong, and that you'd trust me implicitly, unquestioningly in everything. It was necessary for you to prove that to me in obedience. It seems that you both decided to defy me and do things your way. Dear ones, I concluded that this would happen, and prepared, but your actions have grieved me. You disobeyed all I said, sadly it has consequences and the future will be uncomfortable. Through listening to another voice, and acting opposite to my words, you have caused a chasm between us. It has blighted our friendship; I am unable to associate with you as we have done in the past.

Your decision has broken trust and put in place another value, unrighteousness. We are divided in our intentions, so our friendship takes on a new role. This event and the outcome especially will have repercussions on all life forms. Everything will be tainted and blighted, damaged by your defiance and disobedience. Once you decided that your will was better than mine, it affected all things. Evil has been unleashed to operate, endeavouring to get power, through your deliberate act of defiance. All creation will feel its effect.

Sadly, I must remove your dear presence from here and send you out to live in the harshness of the world. The blight of evil will always try to attract and solicit your attention. My love was ever yours, and it is still that way, but we must separate and live in different worlds. I love you, but you have made a decision to follow a way that is opposite to holiness.

From the sweat of the ground Adam, you will cultivate food, working to survive in a world caught up in a battle between evil and good. Moreover, for you Eve, all of your offspring will be born in pain, and the future will be lonely, although, if you dear one's search, you will find me! Our relationship takes on a different role, but I will know your thoughts and when you cry out to me, wherever you are, I will answer your spirit.

My dear children, I send you away from this place of security, out from my presence, with colossal pain and sadness. Unfortunately, it was imperative, that you realized that trust and piety must be implicit in our relationship. I gave you free will to make choices, so that we could be equal, but you decided to do things your way and to ignore my words. Therefore, your spiritual journey through life, will be tainted by your actions. From this time on we must separate and go our different ways. Through the folly of listening to the serpent's deception, you must leave here, and life will be harsh and painful in the future.

I am grieved with our parting, our intimate friendship was personal, and I know that you are sad too. I promise that in the future, I will send a Savior for the world and deal with all evil, be watchful!

Come my children; it will be a cold and harsh on your journey, I will ensure you are clothed for protection from the elements out in the world. From today all things have changed, even death has entered the garden. I must kill an animal for your covering, which is a sad time for us all. All must be done quickly to prepare for your leaving and provide for your new environment."

The Might One continues, "Because of your actions, a new order has had to be put in place, that has changed everything. From dust, I brought you to life and in due time to dust you will expire. Always remember, 'dear ones,' I gave you life because I love you, and mankind was created because of you…"

Adam and Eve realized from these words that through their folly of listening to the whispered voice of the snake, they had acted opposite to God. In deciding to do things their way, they had

23

gone the way of Lucifer, who had tricked them. Blighted by disobedience, they had opened the floodgates of evil, that was now laughing with glee. Realizing that their Creator was kind and good and loved them made their hearts sorrowful. They were grieved that their action had been used to manipulate a battle, against **The Mighty One**. Comprehending fully, that their decisions had consequences, frightened them as they realized their stupidity!

"The evil snake is cursed for his part in this dreadful debacle and will forever crawl in the dust of the world. While Lucifer and all his plans are cursed, and in due time "**The Promise of Heaven**" will come into action. Evil will not win this battle, and his head will be crushed by **The Beautiful One**, who will bruise his heel!"

The voice of "**The Mighty One**" thundered out, stating the future, in a declaration that resonated all over Heaven!

"Now my children, we must go and prepare to send you out, as your future life awaits, with all its difficulties and joys. Come let us give you some covering for your journey and make the first sacrifice!"

The Mighty One stood gazing as the pair walked from the security of His presence, He wiped a tear from His face. Turning now to the angels by His side and the cherubim on His left, He ordered flaming swords to be set up at the entrance. "**The Promise of Heaven**" had begun, and Adam and Eve were now fending for themselves!

Adam and Eve in the World

Denton and Heaton had been summoned to support the children of God as their guardian angels. The angels walked close to Adam and Eve, as they trudged across the land, seeking to help them where possible. Sadly, the remembrance of the time in the garden was gradually becoming a faded dream. It had been a breathless and sad farewell, as **The Mighty One** gave them a coat to wear and hugged them. While the vision of the cherubs gleaming swords, protecting the entrance of the garden, was seared in their memory. Although, it was a remarkable departure they thought they would never forget, nevertheless that was not entirely true. Consequently, the longer the pair wandered away, thinking about the future, the past seemed to diminish even more, with each step. This world was so different from the beauty and security of the garden, covered with weeds and brambles in profusion. There also seemed an air of heaviness that permeated the atmosphere, making everything harsh. It was entirely different for their angels, Denton and Heaton, who looked around the world with particular interest. Although, the two humans' memory of the garden had faded in the garden. It was impossible for the angels to forget the scene earlier, as the two had departed.

The Mighty One's sadness, standing with The Beautiful One at the entrance, as the couple left. Although, the many angels watching, were confident in the future plans held by the God head. It had also been a new experience, hearing **The Mighty One's** voice raised, alerting the cherubim to protect the entrance with their flaming swords, ensuring that there was no way back for Adam and Eve. Watching the two dejected beings, walking along battling with the elements around them, the angels observed their vulnerability. It was not going to be easy for this couple in the world. Consequently, angels had been assigned to protect the couple in the future. The pair were to be supported in their lifetime by angels. It was **The Mighty One's** plan for all people. Denton, and Heaton obediently endeavoured to fulfil their master's wishes. As the coupled battled the strong winds around them, Adam held out a hand of support to Eve.

Adam gazed around and looked for shelter away from the elements and pulled his fur coat tightly to him for protection, "This looks like a good place," he motioned to Eve, as she struggled with her footing through the undergrowth. The two angels, Denton and Heaton supportive of the pair, went ahead and disturbed frightened wolves from their dwelling. The animals raced away, frightened, on seeing the humans. A boulder was hiding the opening of a cave. So, the two angels endeavored to clear it and encourage the pair towards the entrance. Although, Adam and Eve could not see the angels, the two were helping them, aiding them on their journey. Denton also bent back the foliage around the area so that Adam could have a better view of the ground and see the cave adjacent to them. The two angel's role was in protective permanency, through life's adventure, to support the couple on Earth in any way they could. In the world, angels will always be restrained by the character of the people and governed by Heaven in everything.

Sadly, Adam and Eve's decision to disobey **The Mighty One** had other consequences. Not that the pair understood any of this at the moment, but their choices had ramifications; in fact, on the world's sovereignty. Leaving the safety of Heaven, meant that they had to live in a world where evil could progress. The choices and decisions that they made would also be entirely through their own will. If they chose a pathway of sin, and deliberately flouted

The Mighty One, the angels would be powerless to help. Thankfully, after some time, Adam and Eve eventually found the cave and crept inside, away from the cold wind to contemplate on their next course of actions. Looking around him, Adam found some brushwood, although his fingers were cold and stiff by this time. Searching outside again for something to make a fire with, he was confident that he could make a spark. The couple required warmth, and Adam had an idea, that if he struck two stones, against each other, he could create a spark. Carefully, the angels tried to help, by pushing the right type of rocks into Adams direction; eventually, he found some quartz. It was not an easy job to create a fire, but after much enduring, he made a spark, and the brushwood caught alight. The pair sat in the cave and warmed themselves; it was very smoky, but they were warm and safe. Realising that life was going to be difficult, they clung to each other for protection, uncertain of the next move.

"Well, we are safe here, but we must have food and a place to lie down," Adam said to Eve. "If you try and find a suitable place inside here and make it flat, with something that is soft enough for a bed, I will search for food."

Eve nodded, she was tired and felt very strange in this dark place and wondered, how they could survive. Adam went outside with Heaton following him. He had seen some berries hanging from a bush nearby, which he thought were edible. Heaton pushed the branch further away, knowing that this sort of fruit was poisonous. Fortunately, as the fruit was hanging out of reach, it proved difficult for Adam, so he gave up trying to get them and went further into the forest.

After a while, Adam found some ripe fruit hanging on a tree, and picked that. Putting the fruit into a giant leaf, he found mushrooms and some nuts, before noticing that the sun was setting and that the evening was beginning. He felt dismayed, as thoughts of the past came to mind, of walking with **The Mighty One** in the evenings. A feeling of sadness overwhelmed him, and he knelt on the forest floor and lifted up his head and spoke aloud. In an anguished voice, he cried out, "Oh my God, forgive us, we have made so many mistakes, by not doing your will and we are sorry. **Mighty One** we ask for help to trust in and serve You as our God, please give us protection." Heaton stood watching Adam; he knew that **The Mighty One** always answered prayer, and sure enough to Adam's spirit flowed God's voice.

"I understand my dear one; you are my child. Adam, I see your heart. I feel your sadness and I go with you, trust me." On hearing this, Adam brushed a tear from his eye as he bowed his head motionless. He then stood up and searched for an offering of love to give to **The Mighty One**, just something to tell him he loved Him. He did not have anything, so he lifted up his eyes to the heavens and raised a hand and said out loud.

"Thank you, my Father!" He felt right after this and knew for sure that they were never going to be alone. They were starting out on a journey through life, but God would be with them. It was not going to be easy he understood, but the more he learned to trust his God, they could achieve anything. Turning to go back to the cave, he saw a deer grazing near to him. Once the animal caught sight of Adam, it ran away. Sadness came over Adam as the realisation dawned on him, that nature too was in rebellion. The enmity between him and the world was real, no longer could he expect peace. The world seemed very dark to him at that moment, as he remembered the past. However, the night was coming down fast, and he needed to get back to the cave.

Although now (after eating from the Tree of Life), his thinking was even darker, as he struggled back to the cave and considered their position. Holding his food tightly he negotiated the entrance of the cave and went in to find Eve; this was their first night together. It was an adventure that was going to take them on quite a journey, the start of their life together on Earth.

Thankfully, Adam knew that they were not alone, and that **The Mighty One** went with them. While also silently watching them, waiting to cause them problems, was the enemy. Contriving, to cause trouble by any means. He aimed to bring them destruction, ridicule them, and cause them offense. These were **The Mighty One's** people, these weak human beings; it was farcical! Resolute, **The Mighty One** had said He would not abandon mankind but give a precious gift of restoration and salvation. Forever caring for the world, He was allowing people a choice. Free will to elect to have a relationship with Him or to wilfully disregard His provisions.

Behind the Scenes

In most stories, there is often an individual who is a bad guy, the one who makes the story compelling and active. In the reality of Heaven, the individual is called "Lucifer."

He was no ordinary villain; this was a creature who was going to try to bring the downfall of all. This angel was the most beguiling of creatures. Full of beauty and occupying a pivotal role in God's plan. He is the angel that so many looked up to because of his position in Heaven. It seems privilege, authority and power, was not enough for this beautiful one; he had to have more. Lucifer, a fascinating creature, thought of himself not only as necessary but a beautiful leader, so why not more? Deciding the position, he was going to take, he worked out a plan, to gain control! Lucifer knew it was an act of defiance to go against **The Mighty One** but reasoned that many who looked up to him were on his side. He had powers, why not use them, he was better than all of the other beings in Heaven?

At the very beginning, he thought that God's plan for creating humankind was foolish. Create people, befriend them and allow them free will. Why the idea of it, was a positively flawed plan? Although, then he reasoned...for him, hmm, all this could be an advantage! A strategy...which was quite straightforward, that could make him powerful was what he craved! Lucifer had reasoned that this humankind could be coerced easily into doing his will in the future. Confident that in their naivety, they will believe anything he deceitfully fed them. He decided that he should play his hand and decided to act swiftly; this was the opportunity he had been waiting for...to make him the leader of all. Speaking to the serpent, to play his part, all so relatively easy to accomplish. It had worked! He had shown his hand and couldn't go back! He was a dominant leader, who could be very persuasive, acutely aware of those he could coerce to fight with him!

While the Godhead watched, recognizing his wilfulness, they waited for his next move, and allowed him time to reform. Having insight to all things, they were conscious that he was going to use his power to harm. They were also incredibly grieved that such a distinguished being was set to become so evil.

It was a testing time for **The Mighty One**, although He could not lose, and had knowledge of the future. He patiently waited, allowing Lucifer at least an opportunity to change. Obviously, He realized Lucifer's planned intentions; it was straightforward! His ambition was to rule the world, to have dominion over his creator. Pretentious and vigorous his aim was to control all, and to become the supreme being with his cohorts in Heaven.

Lucifer was one of God's most beautiful created beings, a meaningful angel who had retained such a prime position. Unfortunately, his self-importance was his undoing; a most ingenious and manipulative angel, who endeavoured to become more important than God. Disdaining all things pure and holy, he embraced an arrogance of pride believing he was greater than all. **The Mighty One** with all wisdom allowed him to continue, knowing that over time, his wilful behavior could be used to help people understand right and wrong. There was to be possibly, mayhem in Heaven for a while, as others chose to go with Lucifer. Pride is always a downfall and to stand up against God, astonishing! Doubtless, making the other angels distraught with disbelief, at such wickedness.

Since the beginning of Creation, there had been a war behind the scenes with Lucifer out to make trouble. This amazing angel was intelligent and held an excellent understanding of all matters. He knew with clarity the damage he was causing all of Heaven and the triune God. An essential angel to the mighty ones, he had been privileged and trusted in his duties. Therefore, because **The Mighty One** had allowed him a platform to show himself off, it somehow made his disobedience worse! His downfall was all the more astounding and grievous, rooted in arrogant pride. Going against the Godhead had changed his position forever.

Therefore, once he had stationed himself on Earth, with his army of supernatural beings, he took on a new identity and became Satan. Scheming and with a new facade, he was now a beguiling angel of light, always pretending to be encouraging and harmless to manipulate people. Successfully, he wooed them, and led his array of powerful supernatural beings to entangle them into a web of deceit and darkness. These angels were smart and empowered to promote evil, endeavouring to be defined as truth. The disguise led unsuspecting people into the corruption of all kinds, ultimately to worship demons. Of course, this domain of darkness contrived to remain hidden, endeavouring to discredit **The Mighty One** and those who loved him. It was a deception that was relatively subtle, that often seduced the world's people, so that evil prospered.

A battle has begun. Evil, intent to resolutely spread their powers, set up strongholds everywhere, as humans allowed them a foothold through their lives. Principalities, influential forces of darkness all immense, determined to influence everything down the ages. In time, nations, the media, churches, countries, politics and people will be seduced, by an array of evil beings. A variety of strength far-reaching in its magnitude that is astounding. A colossal battle, but understood by **The Mighty One**, prepared. Evil is no match for the wisdom might and power of **The Mighty One** and will not be allowed to win! His season of freedom will eventually end! God understood all and was prepared for this holy war, effectively using His people to thwart evil. His plan, to battle for holiness, nurturing a nation that would seek out His will in love, choosing His identity to live by and honor Him. They would have protection and aid provided by His laws and covenants, with His great promises for the future. A way of life, inaugurated by **The Mighty One**, reasonably easy to understand and accept, based on love and obedience. In the future, the people of this nation were to give **The Mighty One** allegiance and love. These were to become His peculiar people, "the apple of His eye." It was a massive adventure of faith for many who realized the wonder of a God who knew their hearts and loved them. The world was beginning, life in all its fullness, exciting and mysterious.

As a supernatural creative God, His other plans were also far-reaching, possibly hard to comprehend-a spiritual awareness to strengthen people. He planned to use angels, discreet guides, bringing **The Mighty One's** aroma to Earth, not to be worshipped but to do His will. Holiness was the **Mighty One's** way. Amazing plans, complex for some to understand, but all wrapped up in an intricate plan of support for people. Therefore, as a holy God, **The Mighty One's** expected His people to also adopt and embrace holiness through life. After bringing life to humankind, He wanted people to walk hand-in-hand with Him, and to do things His way, in a loving relationship. In the Garden of Eden, He had declared this. His prophetic utterance of a future sacrifice providing an escape from evil, free for all who would accept it, was heard by all. A Savior was to come, to bruise the head of this irritating angel of evil and rescue the world! Evil had to be separate from God's holiness.

In the future **The Promise of Heaven** would arrive as a Savior for people, to deal with and successfully break the power of darkness. He was the Messiah ready to make an entrance at the right time, with Heaven's complete protection. A very creative plan proposed by **The Mighty One**. In everything it will be the people's decision, their choice to decide where their loyalty and fidelity is rooted. The beginning had started, and through time, there was to be a finale. The future one day was to become the present, and to a degree, it began with a man called Noah. He was a man for the season, who listened and did not do the will of the people, but only the will of **The Mighty One.**

Noah

A man called "Noah" arrived on the Earth. He was an esteemed man, who had been on an incredible journey. The way he had arrived in this place on Earth was a miracle, and he stood now amazed, breathing the fresh air! Like no other time in history had so much happened to the planet, and Noah had played a part in all of this. In a tiny vessel compared to the might of the engulfing oceans, Noah, had sailed to safety. The seas had roared, and the deluge of rain had come down on the Earth when everything drowned and was swept away. It was a time of cleansing for the Earth, from the deluge of evil that had engulfed it. Nevertheless, Noah and his ark were safe through the power of **The Mighty One**. What an experience, a miracle that all in the ark were safe, when all of the past, everything had gone, disappeared in Flood.

Although, this was all in God's plan, it had not been easy, Noah thought of his family and the experience they had come through. How at times, they had clung to each other as the ark had drifted and the wind had sounded so loud. His wife had cried, and the boys had thought, *that this is it, we are all going to drown,* as they heard dreadful sounds all around them outside. The rain continually, beating down, as the family had listened and wondered what their future would be? It had been a terrifying ordeal, and yet they had ended up safe and secure, it was utterly unbelievable! The whole Earth, everything was gone, lost, and here he was with his feet on dry land safe from harm. Noah felt old, possibly the journey in the ark with all the inconvenience attached to it had made him aged. He did not know, but he had not slept during the time, supporting everyone, to ensure everything was going well. Amazingly, they were safe, so there must be a purpose, thought

Noah! Nearby to this extraordinary man Noah, Denton, his angel stood silently watching to see if he could help Noah in any way.

He was not the only observer, un-be-known to Noah, **The Mighty One** was observing him too, "his special man", not forgotten at all! Noah had been a man who had loved his God and worshipped Him all his life. **The Mighty One** saw this and took a keen interest in Noah, and his journey through life. Once events happened during the flood, He watched to ensure Noah's safe passage.

Noah, happily freed from the confines of the ark, looked around and breathed in the clean air. Admittedly it was not home, as he'd once known it, and he had no idea where he was, but frankly, any place apart from the sea was marvellous. It had undoubtedly been a miracle, which had brought them this far, to this place, wherever that was? He grinned suddenly, thinking about all the animals shuffling out of the ark, what an incredible adventure! Moreover, yes, there was much to discover and think over, for the future, plus so many unanswered questions, but they were safe.

Noah reflected on his past, those who had gone before, like his father, Lamech, a man who had walked God's way. He would have known what to do about everything. As a child, he had listened to his father's tales of the old world, handed down to him from Methuselah, Lamech's father. Such tales, extraordinary glimpses of the past, that Noah remembered so well. Hearing tales of godly Enoch and his disappearance were amazing. He was another genuinely fantastic man of God. Everyone believed at that time in God and respected Him. Although the amazing event on Enoch's death, when God had taken him straight up to Heaven was unique. Noah remembered the many conversations he had with his

35

father, as they sat around the fire as a small boy. Precious and beautiful memories, his father Lamech had instilled in Noah. Speaking truth had been one of his lovely qualities and encouraging Noah how to live. Constantly reminding him how vital it was to be guided by the Almighty at all times.

Noah remembered it all as if it was yesterday and the warnings that Lamech had impressed upon him. Evil in all forms must be avoided, be pure in life he'd said. Sitting together, he had reminded Noah regularly about the prophecy on his life when he was born from **The Mighty One**. His father had not mentioned it to Noah's siblings; as they did not have the same beliefs. Noah felt a stab of regret that he'd not listened more intently at the time, to all that he'd said. Too late now to wonder about all that he mused, his father had died long ago, and memories are all that was left.

Although, the world that he had known, people places, had all disappeared. Noah felt grieved; even his siblings were no longer alive. Sadly, they had all laughed at what they considered to be, Noah's "cracked pot" ideas! Why couldn't they have listened, where were they now, all gone he thought, dead? Although, as Noah reflected, his father had been right. He had told Noah, that the way evil beings had taken over the Earth, "no good will come of it!" It had been alarming, as over the years, around the land, the oddest people had somehow arrived. Extraordinary people, mighty, giants, who practiced all the arts. It had been apparent that they had supernatural powers, as they did strange things and wanted sexual gratification constantly. Silly women, beguiled by them, were impressed. It was very unpleasant and astonishing things happened.

Rebellion to God was apparent everywhere, while evil was practiced openly in every place. It was hard not to be swept along by its powers; it was so prevalent and intriguing. Evil deeds very evident, allowing supernatural powers to be imminent everywhere. It was a time of great darkness over the Earth. Lamech viewing this declared to Noah, God will not allow it, and he was right, the past weeks had shown this to be true. Lamech had told Noah years before; evil people will not mock God, he is too powerful. Noah had never forgotten these conversations with his father. Consequently, Lamech had died. Noah had grieved, not sure about so much, wondering as to what he should do. There was no one to talk about **The Mighty One** anymore, in the way his father did. Still, God's presence was there helping him! Little did he know that **The Mighty One** had planned every detail of Noah's life. Amazingly too, **The Promise of Heaven** was on the way. Not only that but he, Noah, had been an intrinsic part of **The Mighty One's** plan. While by his side, his angel endeavoured to guide him, whenever Noah was ready to listen.

Powerful Beings Talk

Watching all that was happening on the Earth years before Noah's journey, **The Mighty One** had said, "Enough." He had created a beautiful world and watched over it. **The Mighty One** was sad and disappointed, as people turned their back on holiness, permitting Satan to come in and desecrate everything. The Earth changed, as its inhabitants became wicked. Evil was taking over, as most of society embraced evil in all forms. Spirits of darkness were apparent everywhere, as sin took hold and strongholds were set up. It was obscene that these powers had taken over the world, that had begun so amazingly. **The Mighty One**, **The Beautiful One** and **The Breath** decided, enough, it had to be challenged.... evil had to be purged away and cleansed from the world. As **The Mighty One's** talked, they decided how things might be accomplished to rid the world of evil. Speaking quietly together, they spoke about the antics of Lucifer, or Satan, as he was on Earth. His evil beings had tried to gain control, with cohorts imported from the heavens, to desecrate the Earth. Evil had proved resilient to challenges, so they must do something about it! Once the fiend of darkness had discovered that he could woo people with his corruption, it abounded. Satan had laughed, he was going to see the world over-run with sin, he would make sure of it!

The Mighty One knew all of his thoughts and was angry and sad at the way evil had multiplied. Society had embraced a way of life that was despicable, forgotten their roots. He knew this could not continue. His plan was drastic, as evil in this form had to be purged and uprooted from the Earth. Emphatic that they had to act to stop the continuance of evil, the trio decided on action. **The Mighty One** had to rid the Earth of rebellion, and forceful measures were needed, although they were hard decisions. Planning the strategy for the future, they searched the globe for godly people to implement their plans. They found only one man who was upright, a descendant of Lamech, a conscientious man who loved God. The radical decision they had made was to flood the Earth and purge away the tremendous evil that had corrupted it. All of Heaven watched, confident in the judgement of **The Mighty One**, to see its fulfilment!

God had scrutinized Noah and knew he was upright and went to speak to him. He warned him of the dangers to come and told him of His plan, for Noah to build an ark of safety. The ark was to be God's sanctuary, a place of holy protection and peace for those **The Mighty One** elected to be there. Explaining that He was going to flood the Earth and that Noah was the one man to expedite His plans for the future. **The Mighty One** had planned all in great detail for Noah to understand, and in time through his diligence, the ark had gradually taken shape. Observing all, **The Mighty One** was confident, looking at this godly man's heart, pleased everything was going to plan.

Noah and the Future

Noah and the family were safe, which was the main thing after the ark experience. The clean, fresh air all around was a delight after the ark, with its smelly atmosphere. Noah strolling on the mountainside was happy feeling the ground under his feet. Reassured, he wondered about the future, what was to happen?

Suddenly, something caught his eye and he noticed an extraordinary phenomenon in the sky forming. A prism of colours lit up the sky, as a brilliant rainbow glistened overhead. It was as if even the heavens welcomed Noah to this place. Not at all sure of what this beautiful natural rainbow was, he walked on contemplating and thinking over everything. Watching all, **The Mighty One** looked down on the Earth; the past had been complicated, by so much interference. He was grieved how evil had taken over the world, trying to force holiness out. Ridding the world of immense evil had to be accomplished. The action of the Flood had ensured that this happened. Acute and dangerous, dealing a tragic blow to the world's inhabitants, immensely alarming to feel power demonstrated in this way! Once He had flooded the Earth, **The Mighty One** realized consciously, that in the future He was never going to flood the Earth again. To ensure that this was known to all, He used a distinctive sign. Across the sky in the form of a rainbow, His seal of promise was on display for all to see, as a sign to honor His word for the future. Attesting to this, He also made a covenant of promise for all people. Declaring that He will never allow the inhabitants of the Earth to be annihilated in this way again.

Noah, although a God feeling man, did not comprehend the enormous grief God felt, killing the world's population. While the past remembrance of God speaking to Him, about building a boat seemed, such a long time ago.

In the past he had been ridiculed for his wild scheme, when he had discussed plans with the family. The people in the neighborhood had also mocked him, hurling abuse when they saw him. They had watched with disdain, making a jest of all he was doing and called him a fool! Buying the timber, selling their home and his wife's disgust, at making them penniless. It had taken so long, and the thought of all that had happened terrified him again.

He had been so earnest in telling people, trying to make them understand about God, but everyone had called him daft; ridiculed him openly. Often over time, people stood, shouting obscene things at him, as he built! Why couldn't they have understood and saved themselves, he wondered? Noah himself had not entirely perceived everything, about the measurements and the plans that God had given him at first. It was hard, complicated trying to undertake the plan, but he trusted God and accomplished it well. When **The Mighty One**, had informed Noah that a flood was coming that would decimate everything. It had seemed incredulous. Although, once the rains started, it became a reality. It happened as God said, a total outpouring engulfed the Earth, but with Noah and his family safe in the ark. Pondering at the sheer miracle of animals coming into the ark with such obedience, amazing! There were so many, and he questioned where to put them; it was an incredible experience. Of course, the journey was uncomfortable. Continual fearsome rain, hurricanes, and the shaking of the boat, was challenging and frightening. At times, the family were all scared and wondered if they were going to survive, as they felt the banging of things colliding with the ark. Noah was frightened too, but somehow.... he knew **The Mighty One** was with them, and they were going to be safe!

It was a miracle. The buildings, homes, everything was gone. It was as if **The Mighty One** was building a new world. Lamech had been so right about so much! Sitting now on a rock Noah remembered the beginning, how everything had taken so much time, constructing the ark. It had not been an easy task, and his boys had helped, although they had been ridiculed too by their peers and the society around them. It had been different later, when the animals had arrived, everyone had been watching and were flabbergasted. The family themselves had been overwhelmed, surprised wasn't the word, they were all amazed! What was also unbelievable, was how they had coped in the ark! Such a long time in the ark cooped up, invariably feeding the animals, it was all too much somehow, what a nightmare! So many thoughts, what a jumble, he pondered in his mind, considering the people who had died, and knew in his heart why.

It was a matter of disobedience, waywardness, not caring about God's will or purposes, in fact, evil! Evil had been everywhere; it was coarse, unyielding and dark, so something had to happen!

Everything at the time had been a jumble in his mind, until eventually, the sea became calm and receded, that was when the birds went out! Although, after sending out of the dove twice, and seeing it arrive back with nothing, alarming! Noah had become fearful and anxious at this time. He had a constant dread that **The Mighty One** had forgotten them, quite foolish, but real at the time! Everything had worked out all right eventually, just as God said it would. Noah remonstrated with himself, and as to the future, well they must wait and see! Feeling secure with his family around him and the sun on his back, he realized that even at old age, life was an adventure, an adventure of faith, but where was God taking them? His thoughts turned again to God's providence towards them, and he was thankful!

The Mighty One had brought them through such a profound time of trauma, and he wanted to say thank you. Noah had brought his offerings with him, with which to worship his God and that is what he intended to do. Finding some large stones, he started to make an altar out of them, and then he bowed low. Noah loved the Almighty and had worshipped like this all his life, but today, a new era had begun. Kneeling on the ground in worship of **The Mighty One**, he lay his sacrifice of thanksgiving on the altar and felt so humble. His God, **The Mighty One** had brought them down into the pit of darkness; and then out, leaving evil behind them. The dawn and safety of a new life awaited them; tears drenched his face! So many miracles, to thank God, his savior for; he had saved them, his voice cracked with emotion as he knelt down. He was speechless, no lengthy platitudes, just him and his Creator. It was Noah's obedience and love that had saved him and his family from death. Kneeling silently on the ground in worship, the intensity of the situation overwhelmed him. Tears once more flowed down his cheeks, and he cried out! "Thank you, Father God, for your protection; you brought us through. Show me how to live according to your purposes." Silently, with his face wet with tears, he bowed his head in humility and thanks. In reality, he did not understand very much. Nevertheless, he knew that his extraordinary God had special plans and had saved them. It was the Almighty's hand of provision extended to Noah's family. His forefathers were right. They had remembered the history of creation in detail handed down over the years. Sitting silently in the place where he had made his altar, he heard a soft voice in his spirit, speaking to him, saying.

"Noah, you have found favour in my sight, because you trusted and loved me, and kept clean from evil. I want people to love me and to have faith, and to understand that I love them." Sitting perfectly still, Noah listened. "This is my covenant with humanity; look upward, I will never flood the Earth again. My promise is sealed by the rainbow in the sky." Noah wept with gratitude. Saved by God's grace, His unmerited favour.

Continuation of a Plan

Noah was a humble man who loved God and listened to Him. Noah was also part of **The Mighty One's** intrinsic plan. He was to make mistakes in the future, just as Adam and Eve had done. The consistent fact that encouraged Noah was the knowledge that **The Mighty One** was always going to be there for him. The truth is, **The Mighty One** never sleeps. He and **The Beautiful One** and **The Breath** watch and care for the world all the time, as the evil one attempts to cause havoc. After Noah, there would be many more, Abraham, Moses. No surprises, about anything because **The Mighty One** knows the future. His plans exist, and down through the ages, they will continue. Because ultimately, He is in charge and the winner. His timing is unimaginable, and **The Promise Of Heaven** is on target and one day, all will be revealed to the people of the world.

The life of Noah was an example of what will happen thousands of years later when people will be deceived into acute sinfulness once again. In Noah's generation, they lived in rebellion against God, encouraged that nothing was going to happen, and disregarded **The Mighty One**, at their peril! At that time the people were swept away, drowned! All excruciating to a sovereign God, who could not allow evil to control the world. The story of obedient Noah is such a fantastic adventure. Many may question its relevance today, as it happened so long ago. The answer must be, yes, it is most certainly relevant today. The God of creation's plans were voiced through His prophets at that time, when all was revealed, completely through them. Because **The Mighty One** has a season and time for everything to happen. In Noah's time, the beautiful rainbow was a sign of God's covenant, His promise. In later years, He was to show His children other wonders, as He guided them. The Bible lays everything out clearly, and those discerning can find His plans out by searching. Even now, the last pages of the book of Revelation are arriving, being accomplished and things are being put carefully into place; are we ready? The future and the present gradually become one as time goes on and judgement waits for us all. It is dangerous to ignore its message, as the people found out at the time of Noah, as the water rushed in. It was just too late! Later there would be other prophets in this new world, like Moses, the man who became a fantastic leader. The man challenged, and changed by **The Mighty One**, to be the one who led a nation through the desert to the promised land.

With **The Mighty One**, there is always another adventure

for someone around the corner, waiting to happen!

Moses

Standing motionless on a terrain that was rocky and barren, a man gazed back at the landscape, from where he had come from. Finding himself alone in this wilderness, all for a principle; the question was, whose principle had he stood up for, and what did he genuinely believe about anything? Why he asked himself again, climbing up into the mountainous area around him, why couldn't I have been like everyone else? Here he was, a product of a mixed culture with a messed-up head, he sighed with irritation! He thought of his Egyptian mother and then his nursemaid, who turned out to be his birth mother. It was a unique situation, bizarre having two cultures vying to indoctrinate him. The point was, whom did he represent, was he an Egyptian or an Israelite? The two cultures that had once worked together were now in conflict with each other. The years had long gone since the patriarch, Joseph, had worked for the Egyptians. It was a different story now. The Egyptians decided they must have control. Determined that the Israelite nation be reduced, they decided to make them into slaves. Unfortunately, this did not decrease the population, so they resorted to other subtle ways to deal with the situation. Cleverly, they contrived a program to decrease future generations, right from birth. Once a boy baby was born to an Israelite woman, the Egyptian midwives were given directions to kill them. The mothers tried to secrete the babies once they were born, away from Egyptians eyes. Moses' mother had endeavored to hide him inside the bulrushes, hidden in a small basket lined to keep out the water!

Possibly, it was the best way of protecting Moses she thought. The tiny bundle, vulnerable in the water, was torture for her to watch. Fortunately for Moses, he had not been long in the water, when a princess found him. Ordering a servant to rescue him and to take him into her home for safety. She sent for a maid to find a wet nurse, to look after him. It had been a considerable gamble for Moses' mother, which had quickly paid off, as her offer, to nurse the child for the princess was accepted.

Consequently, Moses grew up as an Egyptian on the outside, dressed and designed to look the part in the court of Pharaoh. Although, spiritually an Israelite, taught and raised by his mother. He was also accepted into the life of the court of Pharaoh, where a daunting array of power and cunning was prevalent, became educational for Moses. It was here that he saw cunning and power depicted constantly. As a culture, the Egyptians were heavily involved in black magic and plans that involved using the slaves, in a measured way. Decades ago, Joseph had arrived and saved Egypt, he had eventually brought all of his Isracli family to live there. Life had been very different for the people at that time. Joseph's strategy was clever, allowing Pharaoh to boost the economy and gain power, as people bartered for food as the famine increased. These extreme plans when famine had dominated the nation had been well documented, but quickly forgotten once Pharaoh died. Joseph's considerable amount of descendants, had now become a nuisance to the Egyptians. There were just too many Israelites and they had become a liability. Which was why they used the Israelites as slaves. The nation had grown in size over the years and Egypt could not cope economically. Consequently, the obscene law to kill the Israelite babies at birth, happened regularly.

As Moses grew older, he saw the regular abuse of the

Israelites by the Egyptians, which bred resentment and anger. It was apparent everywhere that they were hated and severely treated. When he had lifted his hand against the Egyptian, he had not meant to kill the man, but seeing injustice displayed so blatantly had made him mad, and he reacted. Through this, a man died, by his own hand! Although the sneering voice of the Israelite standing nearby, asking if he was going to kill him too, was perhaps as difficult to stomach. He had been insolent, speaking to Moses like that, but that was how people were, especially if they were scared of what the future might hold! What was clear now, without a shadow of a doubt, was he had to escape far away from Egypt, as he had undoubtedly burnt all his bridges! By now he had travelled a long way up on the mountain, still musing about the history of the Israelites. Curious as to how the Israelites had got into this mess.... possibly, it was Joseph's fault, he reasoned. He was the man who had brought all his family to Egypt. It was here that the tribe had grown strong.

Why then, would a God who had rescued people, then let those same people become slaves? Why allow them to live in such a way, it did not add up he mused? Whatever he thought, it does not concern me now. In any case, the Egyptians could not do without the slaves, they did all the nasty jobs, and to his mind, it was a no-win situation! As for **The Mighty One**, well if He was the God of the people, why hadn't he considered rescuing them? What was it his mother had said about all this? Indeed, his mother had told him much about his ancestors; and also, something about **The Mighty One** who was going to use him too; what nonsense! Moses frowned; he knew for sure that **The Mighty One** would not use a killer! Moses was versed in all of the requirements of His God, which his mother had ensured, especially, about the covenants. She had taught him well, in any case, that was all in the past. A holy God was not going to have anything to do with him now, he argued. **The Mighty One** will not use a killer, he repeated to himself. He felt sad and disorientated, what was he doing here, running away, yes, but to end up here was madness. If he did not die in this wilderness in this heat, it would be a miracle! Why hadn't he gone with his brother Aaron's suggestion, that he hide him away? He sat down on a rock and looked about him, a complete wasteland, nothing growing for miles, a dry arid place that was just rocks and mountains.

Sitting motionless, Moses was now a sad, disillusioned man tired of living, torn by culture and circumstance. He knew he had no future, and he was a failure. He was not an old man; in fact, he had his whole life in front of him, but he was disillusioned! Realizing that he was hated by both cultures he had represented, he understood that there was no way back! It would have been better if they'd let me die at birth he thought. I'm one mixed up man, who can't fit in anywhere! Not really an Egyptian, although educated that way, not an Israeli either. A nomad, who will never be accepted, wherever I go. Remembering was uncomfortable, the thought that he, Moses, had killed someone. He shuddered at the recollection. The Egyptians would never forgive him.

As for the Israelites, they mocked him, which was why he had run away and now found himself, alone with no hope. Sitting contemplating, he wondered how he had got here. Walking away from Egypt was not difficult once he realized, he'd been detected for his crime. However, to walk this far and find himself out here in this wilderness, where he knew he had little hope of survival. Of **The Mighty One**, what did he know, gods? The Egyptians had so many there were loads to choose from, out of their assortment? The Egyptians had influenced his life greatly, although his nursemaid mother had always told him he belonged to Jehovah. His mind was disturbed, alone, afraid and exhausted and contemplating **The Mighty One**... how stupid was he?

Satan smiled nearby, the future of the Israelites, why they had none. As for this young man, he'd soon make sure that he died of thirst. **The Mighty One** must be very hard up for support if he thought he could use this stripling. He was going to rule and reign on the Earth, Satan, and nothing was going to stop him; he was the best! Calling to one of his cohorts to oversee Moses' death, he flew off happy at the outcome he perceived would happen! Angels also stood quite near to this dusty, tired man and looked at him with interest. **The Mighty One** was coming and was going to use Moses in the future. Denton had been sent to await his coming. He was Moses' guardian angel and stood next to this weary man, looking after his welfare when he could. Denton had distracted the guards at the city gate, on his escape from Egypt, so they had not noticed his departure. He then encouraged him away from the city on to the pathway that **The Mighty One** wanted him to travel on.

Moses' Future

Moses, unaware of all this, lay quite still now on the ground. Fear was his companion, contemplating death, while around him the deserts arid atmosphere, was stifling. He was weary and had no water; it was time for him to give up, what was the use? His mouth was dry; he knew that this was the end! The angels moved near to this man so that their holy presence of hope would influence him. After a while, Moses got up and started walking. Purposefully, walking into the valley, he moved forward.

Not questioning his energy to walk or his companions, unseen nearby; giving him strength and encouragement.

Eventually, he came to a well in the land of Midian and sat down by its side. He managed to let down a leather bucket and refresh himself and sat there resting. After a time, women came to water their father's flocks in the troughs and then shepherds came too. They were angry that the women were there first and tried to push the women away. Moses was sitting a little way off, intervened, helping the women to get the sheep watered, quickly. The women were grateful to Moses and returned home with the sheep.

A short while later the women returned, asking Moses to join their father Jethro and eat with him. The angels still by his side, watched over this man, always ready to do **The Mighty One's** business. The enemy of God was displeased, the man had survived, but Satan was in no hurry, time was on his side. He will kill off this ambassador of **The Mighty One**. Moses stayed with the family and was refreshed after his ordeal, happy that he was accepted. He felt safe, knowing he was away from the Egyptians and his people.

His discussions with Jethro and the company of the women were all a delight to this man, added to which he helped with the sheep. He was in the land of Midian and decided after a great deal of thought and discussion with Jethro, to work for him. Happy in the company of these people, Zipporah one of Jethro's pretty daughters, eventually became his wife.

Moses' life took on a different direction, as he spent his days on the mountainside, looking after Jethro's sheep. Eventually, Zipporah, his wife, became pregnant and it was a peaceful, happy time for Moses. His wife gave birth to a son, and they called him

Gershom, and he felt his life was complete. The past had become a distant memory for Moses by this time, but **The Mighty One** had not forgotten about him. He had a plan to use Moses to free and save His people who were slaves in Egypt. The people had cried out to God regularly to protect them from the burden of slavery. Moses, entirely unaware that he was going to be used by **The Mighty One**, worked hard for Jethro for many years. His daily task was to look after the sheep and ensure that they found useful grazing. Of course, it meant as a shepherd, Moses regularly took the sheep for miles in search of grass. He travelled far, even up to Mount Horeb.

One day after traveling a long way grazing the sheep, he sat alone on some rocks gazing about him and noticed something odd. A short distance away he saw a bush on fire. Becoming very curious as to what was happening, he went over to the area to investigate. Getting closer to the burning bush, he saw that it was real, but the bush did not burn up, and Moses was even more curious. Standing very close to the fire now, he heard a voice saying, "Moses take off your shoes; this is holy ground." Fear rushed through his veins; it was a frightening experience for Moses as he heard!...

The Voice!

The Mighty One, the ageless one that Joseph and the patriarch had known, was it possible? Thoughts and fears came flooding in, tears prickled his eyes, the voice, what was he to do? Suddenly Moses faced the reality of all that had happened in his life and realized that he had made a complete mess of everything.

Whomever **The Mighty One** was, He was hardly going to be interested in a liar, a cheat and murderer like him, and yet, The Voice!

This encounter was awe-inspiring, something was happening to Moses that was having far-reaching effect. His mind questioned, doubted, but deep in his spirit inside, he hoped that the voice wanted to meet with him! He stood hesitating, wary. A man who thought he had no future with **The Mighty One,** the Creator of the universe. For one second his mind challenged his actions; He cannot know what I've done and then chided himself, of course, **The Mighty One** knew everything! This encounter with the burning bush, it was a challenge. Little did he know, that this meeting was going to change his life. He took off his sandals and stood, vulnerable, looking at the bush. The voice spoke to him again.

"I am the God of your Father, the God of Abraham and the God of Isaac and the God of Jacob." Moses was even more afraid and hid his face, scared to look at **The Mighty One**, God, although something continued to happen deep inside him. **The Breath**, the Spirit of the living God, was working, and Moses was being touched and changed.

Gradually the past was being washed away, and he was being sanctified, cleansed and made ready for service. He fell to his feet, weak but strengthened in the Lord. This was no chance happening, The Lord had a plan and was going to use him in the most spectacular of ways! The arrogance, that had been part of the man who fled Egypt was challenged. He knelt now in homage and humility. Silently **The Breath** anointed Moses ready for service and he changed, the arrogance and anger disappeared. God's power fell upon him, and he was a man released, as the past was stripped away. While this happened, **The Mighty One** continued to speak to him, telling him the plans not only for him but for the Israelites. The cries of His people had not gone unheard **The Mighty One** said, He had heard their agony of spirit. The people were going to be set free from the stranglehold of the Egyptian authority. Telling Moses that he was the man chosen for the task, to rescue His people from their prison. Moses, an alien in many ways to the Israelites, working as a shepherd was dumbstruck. He was a murderer, a man as far away from **The Mighty One** as it was possible to get, yet God was about to use him? He continued, saying that Moses was to be His instrument, to free the people miraculously from the Egyptians.

After hearing all that **The Mighty One** pronounced, Moses became frightened, having to go back to Egypt. It sounded unbelievable, and he stuttered. Feeling unequal to the task, he muttered that he was no good for a job like this. It could not be him; someone else must be found to go on the mission. He was no speaker, and he had no voice, no eloquence of speech. Apart from that, he had run away; he could not go back, he had given up that life for a peaceful life here, with his family. He was no leader! **The Mighty One** ignored his comments and commanded Moses to throw down his crook. The miraculous always present with **The Mighty One**, He transformed his crook into a serpent. Jumping out of the way, Moses looked astounded.

"Pick it up," **The Mighty One** said!

Carefully Moses picked it up by its tail, and it had reverted to his crook.

"Put your hand inside your cloak," said **The Mighty One**.

Putting his hand under his cloak, he then removed it, and it was leprous. It was a defining moment for this man who had run away in great fear; this was amazing. Weak and frightened Moses realized that **The Mighty One** was bringing him home! He stood a murderer, a man who had been broken by his circumstances, a failure in many ways. An individual who had settled for the most menial of job; who was now chosen, for a massive adventure of faith! Moses still doubtful, stuttered and trembled as he voiced his concerns that he did not meet the criteria needed. With a quavering voice, he said.

"My speech is poor, and I am weak, I cannot be your mouthpiece to speak to the Egyptian authorities; I am not good at speaking, others are better than me. I am not suitable. Isn't there anyone else who could do a better job?"

The Mighty One looked at **The Breath** and sighed. "I have chosen you for this task Moses. I am with you, and through you, many miracles will happen. I will make the hearts of the Egyptians hardened, so they let my people go! I will turn the water of the Nile into the blood. Inflict devastation upon these people and kill their first born. At that time, they will give my people all of their riches to rid the nation of them! Trust me, Moses, I will use you in a mighty way."

Moses, being a timid man, doubtful of his capabilities, remonstrated once again. "I know this is a great task, but …"

"Oh, Moses....you are frustrating...I have chosen you to fulfil my plans; because of your hesitation, I will allow your brother to assist you. Go now and prepare to leave!" **The Mighty One** disappeared.

Moses stood in the same spot for some time, thinking, amazed and aghast all at once. He had thought that his old life was quite finished. The effective escape from Egypt that he had made, and now to return, how will his family react? It was all quite overwhelming, the God of the past, really was the God of the present. Remembering how he had considered that **The Mighty One** had forgotten the people when nothing could be further from the truth! Realising that he had to go and speak with Zipporah about this meeting was slightly daunting. More importantly, her father's reaction to his plans? What was he going to think? Aaron was going to help him, that was good, but everything was going to be a challenge. Calling to his sheep to follow, he started to walk back, pondering about the future. At the back of his mind, Moses questioned his reaction to **The Mighty One**. How could he have said that he did not want to do His will?

With all of the recent happenings quite unnerving him, a slightly bewildered, and anxious Moses walked on. Gradually he smiled, whatever happened, he realized, that wherever he went he was never going to be on his own. On his return, he shared openly with the family, which to his surprise, were all very helpful. Jethro was a priest and had realized during their first encounter that Moses was an extraordinary man. He understood this even more, as Moses explained the meeting in the desert. Urging Zipporah and her sister to get the children ready, he helped the couple pack. He questioned Moses, about the wisdom of taking the family with him immediately, as he realized his son-in-law had a job to do. While Zipporah had always listened intently to all Moses had told her about his culture and the laws of his God. As a Midianite, she understood holiness and the need to respect **The Mighty One**.

As her husband was an Israelite, she tried to understand all the requirements of his faith too. After hearing all Moses had to say on his return, about his encounter with **The Mighty One**, she was in awe of all that had happened. It was at this time, **The Mighty One** considered his plans for Moses. It was very evident that Moses had not been diligent with the teachings handed down from Abraham. He had left Egypt and his past life, not considered the requirements his mother had instilled in him. Ignoring **The Mighty One's** covenant with His people, with a disdain that was quite arrogant. Why should **The Mighty One** save this man Moses, others could be used? As **The Mighty One** came to this conclusion, Zipporah realized her husband might have done wrong. Appreciating his culture and in awe of his meeting with the holy one, she questioned if he had been diligent about the way he lived. Remembering all Moses had told her, of the customs and laws he lived by, for his religion. She knew obedience was **The Mighty One's** way, and that while they had been together, Moses had not honored his culture!

Zipporah realized that all was not in proper order! He had not circumcised his son and fulfilled all that Moses had been taught to do. Zipporah, contemplating all of this, as to what was required by Moses' God, was frightened!

As an intelligent woman, her foresight was clear, **The Mighty One,** the God of the Israelites could also use His judgement upon them. Moses had shamed them, and not taken full responsibility for his family as he should. Finding a flint that was sharp, she took the child aside and carefully circumcised him, dropping the bloodied foreskin on Moses' feet. Startled he looked at the blood on his feet, and at that second, realized his wife had protected them.

"We are right in the Lord your God's eyes, as a husband of blood," she cried. "The blood has protected and anointed us; we are all one!"

Moses gazed at his wife with thanks. He realized with misgiving his error. **The Mighty One** required obedience, and His covenant adhered to; because of his lax attitude, Moses had nearly thrown it all away. As **The Mighty One** looked down and viewed the blood, He saw cleansing, honor and obedience were in place. An intimate relationship was what God wanted, and circumcision was by itself a confirmation that worked two ways, God and man. It was a covenant of love, for Moses' future mission, everything had to be in place. Recognizing that all had accomplished in obedience, **The Mighty One** knew that the future was safe, and that Moses was the man he could trust.

It was going to be a task stretching Moses to the limits, a job that would take him far beyond the boundaries of Egypt. It was a relationship with Jehovah, **The Mighty One** that he never dreamt of and it had started with humility and obedience. It began with Moses taking off his shoes humbling himself, to allow the holiness and the power of **The Mighty One** to work. He was going to be a man who not only heard God, but was intent on doing His will, a friend of **The Mighty One**. A leader of a nation and God's chosen vessel, to be used in the miraculous. Moses was now a man a resolute leader, filled with **The Breath of God**.

The Mighty One's plans for the future were unique and required people. The plan was to continue, as He conceived a nation that **The Promise of Heaven** would one day appear from. He had spoken to Abraham years before about the future and destiny of His people, and He was continuing to build a nation that **The Promise of Heaven** would one day appear. A considerable nation governed by His laws and decrees, a particular people, known as His people. The "apple of His eye," and from these people He was to give out a message to the world, that He was a

God who loved and cared for all. Tremendous plans that had started through Moses' ancestors, which the enemy had tried his utmost to destabilise. However, now He was to establish these people through Moses' leadership. A journey that was to try His patience, but that was to take them to their own promised land, that **The Mighty One** had planned for them. The journey of a lifetime was beginning, a massive adventure of faith, where the miraculous happened, and people became aware of the might and power of their God.

Quite soon, Moses would lead this army of **The Mighty One** to freedom from their prison with the Egyptians, to an escape. Certainly, a miraculous journey, starting with the obstacle of the Red Sea, as they fled from the Egyptians.

What an adventure, as Moses in obedience, the man of God, lifted up his staff and the water divided. This was the beginning, of an astounding adventure of faith, for the Israelites. When Moses boldly announced to them, "People, The Lord will fight for you; turn to Him and wait!" This was the feeble Moses, whose life was touched by the might of God. A giant of a man, who encouraged people and revered **The Mighty On**e.

It was a terrifying time, with the Egyptians chasing them, the people of God, stood frightened on the shoreline of the Red Sea. Where were they to go, fearful with water in front of them, and soldiers behind? It was as the waters parted, they saw the mighty miracle, of their God's power. It was just one of the many miracles that, **The Mighty One** was to do for them in the future. A covenant-making God, His plans for His people were terrific. A future unbeknown to Moses, after his encounter with God, as he started out towards Egypt with foreboding, as to what he was to encounter when he arrived.

While **The Mighty One** gazed down at Moses' heart, He knew that He had chosen wisely; this man was honorable. The adventure was beginning for Moses, yes, it was going to be stretching, through trials and tribulation, he was to face in the future. Amazingly, **The Mighty One** uses the most extraordinary of vessels for His glory. Those like Moses who walk in obedience, love, and humility, are the qualities He is looking for time and time again! Confident, **The Mighty One** smiled; Moses journey had started, and the Israelites were soon to be escaping from the Egyptian's clutches. Never again to be yoked to slavery.

While His grand plan for **The Promise of Heaven** to arrive one day, was starting to become clearer. Moses' future was going to be astounding! This incredible man even featured hundreds of years later meeting **The Promise of Heaven** on a mountain in Israel. No one can plan like the God of creation, **The Mighty One,** past, present and future, He holds them all in the palm of His hand. Moses was unique and godly, a man who was to follow **The Mighty One** through difficult circumstances, a man loved by His God. However, for now, Moses full of trepidation stepped forward in faith as **The Mighty One** supported him. This adventure was going to be the most challenging and miraculous of journeys, that everyone would hear about in the future. There were going to be others too who would follow on with the baton of faith. Although, this man Moses, is possibly a challenge to those reading about him, who may wonder, how the timidest man became a mighty leader. Completely, through the power of God! Others will arrive, weak people discarded by society but used by **The Mighty One**. One of the men like this was David, a man of the people. A shepherd boy who would become king one day and lead the nation. He was a weakling who became powerful, until he forgot to focus on **The Mighty One's** plans, and terrible things happened.

Satan and David

While the enemy of all, Satan, behind the scenes was more than a little disturbed, he thought that he'd got rid of this... Moses! He was supposed to die in the desert, and now he would have to find other means of getting rid of him, another headache to find the solution too!

All humans were weak, yes, he would get rid of godly Moses somehow, Satan sneered. Why, with the people he was leading, there was going to be plenty of opportunity. Another bunch of human weaklings that **The Mighty One** was going to use, what a farce!

Whatever Satan, the enemy thought, eventually the nation of Israel was to emerge into its land. With power and confidence, **The Mighty One** would protect and lead His people. Moreover, many leaders were to become apparent in time, prophets who took **The Mighty One's** truth forward. Although, Satan put many obstacles in the way as he did for David, determined that he would trip him up.

David was a man of integrity, a godly man who became king and who was honored by **The Mighty One**.

Although, for such a long time, Satan, had worked to discredit all of God's people, and especially this extraordinary man. It had been difficult as David had high standards, but he had accomplished it eventually; and now he had him!

David had integrity and it was difficult to find fault with him, but the enemy had eventually snared him well! Satan had figured out anyone could be caught in the spirit of lust, and David had proven him right and given into his desires. He was finished as God's servant, washed up, a broken man, no one was going to think highly of him now. A killer and adulterer, no way was David going to be a part of **The Mighty One** after all that had happened. Satan's plans over the years had been frustrated, fraught with difficulty, although using more of his evil spirits everywhere had helped.

Since Noah's time, it had not been as easy. The Flood was catastrophic to his empire, as much of the evil he had nurtured had been swept away in the water, not, of course, his demons. Fortunately, he was patient; corruption was increasing, and men and women were fallible. Satan had learned much, turn all the "God things" the opposite way. Create darkness, war, hate, murder everything that could separate people. Confusion in everything that was the order, he was going to mastermind the evilest treachery he could, time would show! The spirits of darkness were terrific and ready to do all of it! Sodom and Gomorrah had been a setback, but they were again on track, and this man was part of that plan. David, **The Mighty One's** man, Satan snickered... not for long, that was for sure! He was going to fall so far from righteousness even his troops will be ashamed of this "mighty warrior!"

David the Adulterous King

David lay distraught, face down in anguish, realising that he had damaged his relationship with **The Mighty One** forever. Nevertheless, he still called out to Him, imploring Him for help as he realized that a child's life was in the balance because of his behavior! His eyes wet with tears, distraught at his actions as a leader and disgusted for all the lies and deceit. Laying now prostrate in the dust on the ground, he thought of his disobedience. He remembered what he had done, and how far he had fallen from accomplishing **The Mighty One's** will.

Having discarded the way of righteousness, the path he had lived by since a small boy, God's way, he was out on a limb. Moreover, he had thrown it all away, what had it been for, a thirst for lust and gain? Prostrate before **The Mighty One**, he pondered on his life, as to how it had happened? He had contrived to have a man killed to cover up his act of adultery, how evil was that? The point was, had it been only because he had been caught, that he was so remorseful? David lay still, he certainly needed to consider that thought! Stricken with the sadness he felt, where was he to go, what should he do? Nearby Denton stood as a sentinel next to this broken man, a king caught in a web of deceit that had wrapped itself around God's man.

One Year Before

It had been some time ago, that David had persuaded himself, that he deserved a life of ease. Tired after fighting so many battles, he was worn out from war; and needed to take a rest, possibly put his relationship with God aside. Not that he had considered the matter in that way. A matter of feeling older, to a degree he had felt disillusioned and angry that he had missed out on life. Although musing about events, especially those of the last months, he questioned himself about so much. Why steal another's wife? Wasn't it a fact he could have had any woman? Irresponsible and reckless, how could he be swept along by passion in that way?

It had happened so quickly, taking time out for himself had been easy, and the months had been uneventful, relaxing away from the army, serene; in fact, although after a while he got bored. He enjoyed spending his days writing and singing songs and sitting on the roof at the end of the day. He was often found lying in the cool of the evening, in this exceptional haunt. Although, as wars continued to become extended, he realized that the time was coming when he must re-join his men. However, this was his time, and just sitting on the rooftop, he was going to enjoy it! Gazing around him, he noticed that someone else had the same idea, enjoying the evening sojourn.

From way off, he could see a woman who also enjoyed the cool of the evening. He noticed her ritual, it happened regularly, and David enjoyed watching the woman. It was her daily bath time in the cool of the night, on the rooftop. He thought little of it, as a leader, wasn't he entitled to view anything he wanted? He was not doing any harm. Also, it was a distraction, from the mundane things around him, a little light relief. The woman was gorgeous. David was attracted, and it became a habit to arrive on the roof at the same time every day. He enjoyed the scene and argued with himself that watching from afar didn't hurt anyone. He quickly justified his actions that he was lonely and asserted that he was not doing anything wrong to appease his guilt. As time went by, he decided it was a neighborly act to meet with the woman. Excited, and thinking that this was a sensible plan, he sent a servant to invite her over to have hospitality with him.

On meeting Bathsheba, which was her name, he was overwhelmed by her beauty and decided that he wanted more. She was lonely as he was, as her husband was away. Naturally it seemed a like a good idea to give her support and comfort her.

Convincing himself that there was no harm, the relationship became a sexual one. David knew by this time he had stepped out of line and that as a leader, this was not how he should live. Appeasing his conscience, he came up with the idea, that with a bit of negotiating he may be able to offer the husband recompense and buy her. It all seemed to be straightforward; it was not going to harm anyone, and he was influential and could sort it all out.

Once the idea had formed in his mind, he was content. It had just been a stupid slip, but he could wheedle out of the predicament. After all, it was a little harmless entertainment, and he was not going to worry, no harm was done, or was it? Having found out that her husband was a very faithful and trusted officer, he did feel a slight pang of guilt for his actions. To compound the matter, sometime later the woman sent a message to David, saying she had become pregnant. David found himself in a predicament. He had to get out of this mess and wheedle himself out of this sticky situation quickly. Sending word to the commander of the army for her husband Uriah to come back from fighting to meet with him. The man came dutifully to visit David, who questioned him about the war and then deceitfully sent him to spend time with his wife. On the following day, David summoned him and interrogated him. Cunningly, he asked if he had enjoyed the company of his wife. The soldier said that he could not lay with his wife with a clear conscience, while his men continued fighting. David was dismayed. He realized that this man was full of honor. In his mind, he questioned as to what he should do.

Finding himself in an awkward position, David felt cornered. His reputation at stake, he realized he needed to be smart. The question was, how should he handle this predicament? Inviting Uriah to his home on the following day, he asked him to eat with him and plied the man with alcohol. Hoping that the man in a drunken stupor, would go and see his wife while he was drunk. Nothing happened. It did not have the effect that David had hoped. David was then forced to take more strident action and sent Uriah back to the war, with a letter to his commander.

He ordered him to send Uriah to be detached; with the soldiers into the line of fiercest fighting. This honorable man was to serve on the front line, the place of most action, where he was sure to be killed! David reasoned that no-one would know about his secret scheming! Disregarding the dreadful truth, that he had schemed to get a man killed. David felt confident that he had handled the situation to the best of his ability. After a short time of mourning, it was easy once her husband had died, for David to officially take Bathsheba as his wife. He had used cunning for his sole purpose and murdered one of his most loyal officers. Audaciously he pretended later, that he was supporting his wife after her husband had died, but he knew his secret, and so did **The Mighty One**! Not the stance of a godly king, to be involved in murder and deception, and then try to cover it up and pretend he was an innocent party!

David's Time of Reckoning

Restless, David's head had all the answers, but in his spirit, he was in a place of crisis and understood that he had let his God down. He had tried to worship God, but his actions got in the way of his relationship. He had broken his friendship with **The Mighty One**, and realized, that he was far from God. A king with a fortune and a future, who had worshipped and sung praises to his God, now lay distraught! Feeling lost, hidden from holiness by his own indiscretion, his tears of self-pity fell easily, finding himself embroiled in circumstance of his own making. He was angry at his folly, as he sat anxiously contemplating the mess he had caused, wondering how he was to deal with everything.

At this time, David had a visitor, a seer. David came from his chamber with a heavy heart and wondered why this holy man was calling on him. He had known Nathan over the years, as a friend. Although, on this day, David felt foreboding as he went to greet him. After a few words of greeting, he told David he wanted to tell him about an injustice perpetrated in the land and find out what his thoughts were on the matter?

Nathan said that **The Mighty One** had told him about a man who was very rich, and who had a large number of sheep and cattle. This rich man stole from a poor neighbour, his one and only pet lamb. This lamb was unique, having been raised by the family as a pet, it was precious, loved and even ate and slept with the family. It was not as if the rich man required the lamb for a celebration; he had used the pet lamb to feed a guest, a traveller who had arrived. He asked David what he thought about the man acting in this way, and what sort of punishment must the rich man have? David was furious and said that the wealthy landowner must be punished for his crime, stealing from someone so lowly.

"It is hateful the rich man deserves to die," said David.

The seer turned towards him and said, "David you are that man, you took from another who had less than you; God's judgement is laying at your door! God, says as a shepherd boy, my hand was upon your life, and I anointed you as king over the land. I gave your master's wives to you, and I gave you Israel and Judah. David, you killed Uriah and took his wife for yourself, and despised the Lord, for this reason, your future is going to be harsh. The sword will never depart from your household! It will be plain to all of Israel your indiscretions. And your wives are going to be abused, as calamity comes upon you!"

David mortified that he had been found out, and so publicly, said, "I have done wrong, evil, and in my disobedience sinned against the Lord!"

Nathan answering him said. "**The Mighty One** has pardoned the evil that you have done; you will not die! Even so, this offspring will die through your wickedness, and you have brought shame on your God!"

The seer left, and David was remorseful, grieved about his actions, and humiliated that he had been found out! Embarrassed that in time everyone would get to know all that he'd done. It did not take much for him to realize that all the prophet had said was right. He knew his life was a mess, and he had opened himself up, to an ill-disciplined act of evil. **The Mighty One** had judged him, and the prophetic words were accurate.

As God's elected leader, he was required to live in obedience, and over time he had seen the downfall of those who had attempted to do otherwise. Mortified, that he had broken the bond with his God through disobedience, he understood very well the message given him. Had he not betrayed his calling, and through his behavior, an innocent child was to suffer? The baby was sick, and Bathsheba distraught with worry. He had acted with dishonor, and in his arrogance believed that he could do anything he wanted, without a thought to the consequences. Tears poured from this robust and mighty man, as he recalled the past and the way he had let his God down.

Hadn't he felt **The Mighty One's** blessings over his life, His protection, and kindness, given riches, fame and honor by so many nations. Wilfully, he had discarded all of that and put his desire first. In arrogance, stealing what wasn't his, taking the opportunity to steal another's wife, entirely wilfully, was by anyone's standard wrong. It seemed impossible that he, who was leading others to walk in holiness, allowed himself to throw it all aside, for his selfishness. His thoughts clouded as he remembered: obedience, allegiance, holiness and righteousness, the attributes of a righteous king. He groaned, weeping at the awful truth, he was nothing better than a dog in heat. **The Mighty One's** chosen man, David, was consumed with guilt and in a dark place! Understanding so much, he pleaded with his God for the life of this child and lay in the dust, fasting for the tiny bundle. David's behavior had allowed the enemy of God to take hold causing dire consequences.

Once a person willingly steps away from truth and righteousness, they are a target for the enemy, to cause havoc. David understood this, and yet he was trapped. The child was at the centre of this chaotic involvement, and the enemy will not give ground. God therefore had to allow the situation, because men had free will to make their own choices. Another suffered for his sin, and the enemy had won this battle! It was to be an ongoing reprisal because David had taken advantage of his position and used it for evil intentions.

The Mighty One watched with **The Beautiful One** and **The Breath**. Gazing at David, they grieved at his folly. The shepherd boy catapulted into a place of prominence by God years before. Nurtured, loved and supported by God in so many ways.

When he had walked in obedience, his life was productive and fulfilled. Here was the man whom **The Mighty One** had made a covenant with, given power and opportunities to, who had thrown it all away. Sadly, it had all changed, and his circumstances were now in jeopardy through his wilfulness. Committing adultery with a married woman and killing to hide the sin. All of this had broken the bond between him and his God. It was time for judgement for David as God viewed David's actions of deceit and cunning, unacceptable. He had watched his lustful ways and treatment of Uriah, the soldier, conspiring to have him killed. Standing together **The Mighty One**, **The Breath** and **The Beautiful One** talked about David's future. His disobedience had saddened them, as they loved him. While casting aside the honors they had granted him in such a cavalier way, was appalling.

Despite this, **The Mighty One** was still going to allow the seed for **The Promise of Heaven** to come through David's descendants. His covenant with his God would not be revoked through his disobedience, although there would be penalties through his sinfulness. David was loved and through God's grace, there would be other opportunities to show his allegiance to **The Mighty One.** Plus, the joy of having additional children who would also change history.

Although, sadly too, the future was to have painful repercussions, through the way that he had behaved at this time. David bowed his head. The baby died, and David was bitter in spirit, and accepted that **The Mighty One** had been forced to allow it. So much was his fault! He was a frail leader, weak and had done everything to gratify his desires. He realized with clarity, that the greatness he had achieved was only through his God. Still a weak shepherd on the inside, it was necessary for him to walk closer with God. There was the possibility of a hard climb ahead, but he had done it once, and the over-riding factor was, **The Mighty One** was always with him.

It was a sombre man who joined his troops, appreciating how he had fallen from grace. He had opened a door, and the enemy was waiting. Consequently, in a few years, he would be fighting to hold on to his throne sadly due to his demise into sin. Thankfully he knew with certainty that his relationship with **The Mighty One** was sacrosanct. Confident, that whatever happened, he could trust his God. While in the wings everything was being put in place for **The Promise of Heaven** to arrive in the distant future. Irrespective, David, was always going to be the shepherd boy who had a covenant with God and became a king. Knowing all this, **The Mighty One** looked down at him and smiled. The future was looking good.

Schemes of the Enemy

Satan watched all this with interest. The man, David, was coming through the situation and had gained status once more with **The Mighty One**? What a loser, how was it the Creator was interested in a man with the temperament of David? It mattered not, through his infidelity he had opened up a door, and Satan's minions used it. He laughed with glee…ah yes, the future. David will have children, but his sin will be passed on to his son Amnon, who will be caught up in the same spirit of adultery in the future! Then there was another son, Absalom; in time he will be involved in the more heinous act, murder! David was very misguided if he thought that it had been sorted out with him paying the price for his sin by losing a child. It was not to be! Opening up a door in his life to evil intentions, and flagrant disobedience will have repercussions for the coming generations. Satan laughed; people were so gullible he sneered. It will take a supernatural being to deal with all their sin! Why was **The Mighty One** using weak defiled people like David, another human loser?

The Mighty One

The **Mighty One** smiled to Himself, watching all that was happening in the world. He had terrific plans that all will hear of in time, with **The Promise of Heaven** on the horizon, the Savior of the world. Naturally, God knew that there would be ongoing skirmishes with the evil one through life until the final end. The surprising fact was that consistently down through the ages, the mighty and omnipotent God, continued to use weak men and women, in a loving relationship. Which was why He could smile, because the future beckoned with certainty, as His power was carried throughout the world by people called to be His children. The thread of His will was proceeding, through His nation that was growing as prophets supported His truth down through the ages. Nevertheless, at this time the nation needed protection from leadership that was poor, and He was going to use a man who had integrity to bring them into line. Mordecai was one such man, who would help in this matter and preserve **The Mighty One's** nation and save it from annihilation. Everything in the world was continuing, the enemy was a nuisance, but contained, and once Mordecai was in the court, things could happen on schedule. **The Mighty One** looked down with pleasure; it will not be long.

71

Mordecai and Esther

Mordecai had a visitor, a servant who brought him sad news, which was to affect Mordecai in many ways. A family member had died, and he had been summoned, not to the funeral but on another matter. He sat musing wondering and sighed, it was a curved ball, having to take on a responsibility such as this. Mordecai was a thinker and an honorable man, always being faithful to his Creator. He had been challenged at an early age, to trust in **The Mighty One** and that is how he lived his life, in endless patience waiting to see how he could serve.

Getting up swiftly from his seat, he ordered his servants to pack food for him as he was going on a journey. With Denton his angel by his side, he walked briskly from his home to the palace. He had business there, working for the king as an emissary. After doing his duties, he spoke briefly to an older friend, telling him of his plans for the future. Realizing that he had little time to spare he was soon back home, ready to make the journey after collecting the donkey and provisions with Denton alongside him.

Mordecai was a man highly favoured by **The Mighty One** and Denton knew grand plans were afoot for him. Many miles away, Heaton watched, as Esther wept in sadness, for the way that life had treated her. The angel stood like a sentinel, to support this young girl. He knew that she was an essential person to **The Mighty One** and needed protection. Alone, and forlorn Esther waited to see if her uncle was going to arrive. Seated on the steps, outside the lodgings where she had finally ended up living, she looked vulnerable. The building was once a school, but not now, everything was gone-friends, family, and even the sense of peace security gives. She was a nervous and a worried youngster, who gazed out over the land in sadness. So, many changes in her young life and she wondered what she was going to do. As an orphan, Esther realized that her destiny in life was precarious. Protection, dowries, security, were going to be very limited to someone like herself. Esther had a deep longing to be around her father and mother, memories of the time her father put on his prayer shawl, and the way they had both loved **The Mighty One**. Everything finished, just sad empty memories, such as the stories of the past when she had heard of her ancestors. It was a difficult time, and Esther was frightened, wondering about the house where her uncle lived, what kind of place it was that was going to be her home. Waiting for her uncle to arrive, her mind reeled with questions about the future, *who was going to care for her*, and *where would her destiny be*?

Mordecai's Future

Mordecai had reservations and was concerned. He was a bachelor and enjoyed his freedom. Taking on the responsibility of a child was going to be different. While the thought of the future and trying to marry her off, was also fraught with difficulties! Many troubling thoughts and questions were whirling around in Mordecai's mind. He was also sad about the demise of his family.

Added to which, people and governments were also about to take his attention. Looking skywards, he murmured to himself a quiet thankfulness, on having an advocate! So many different thoughts occupied his mind as he walked; he'd not planned for any of this in his life. It was family, consequently, he must make it work. Although, a busy man, meeting a friend had been useful, talking about his situation, he now had in place, a woman to take care of Esther. Enlisting the aid of an older woman, to come and support his new guest was an essential aspect of his plans. Realising that although he had servants, he required someone to take charge of the young girl, to take care of her and Mary had been recommended by a friend.

Travelling with a donkey as a companion, he went now to pick up his new ward, thinking about so much. It was quite an arduous journey to travel to meet Esther, but at last, he arrived in the area. He saw her from a distance, with just one small parcel of clothes by her side, sitting on the steps. Fragile and young, only about ten years old, with piercing eyes and extraordinary good looks. Mordecai kissed her on the forehead in greeting and took her package and lay it on the donkey. It was quite a trek to get back, so they left immediately, as he wanted to arrive back before the evening. She walked along cheerfully, and Mordecai noticed how quickly she moved. They chatted, with Mordecai making small talk endeavouring to draw her out, so that he could get an idea of his young companion.

Stopping for some refreshments, they then walked for three hours, until the sun started to droop. Suddenly they turned a corner, and Mordecai pointed out to Esther, distant landmarks. Standing for a few minutes, he showed her his home in Shushan, formerly the capital of Elam. It was a delightful place, and Mordecai was an emissary in the court of the Persian King. They soon arrived, as the servants came out to meet them at the gates and rushed around with water for their feet and refreshments. Also arriving on the scene appeared a bright old lady, who greeted Esther with kindness.

Taking her to her quarters to settle her in, Esther bowed to Mordecai, as she left his presence. Mordecai smiled as he called to her as she was going.

"Come and sit down later and we will eat together when we can talk about the future."

Esther nodded and went to her room. Opening a door, she surveyed the quarters where she was to live, beautifully furnished with a balcony over the courtyard. Mary, her companion, had a room next to hers, in this lovely house, which was very organised, tastefully decorated and cared for in every way. Mary showed her around and introduced her to a maid, who was to help Esther too. Esther sat watching on a couch, as Mary instructed the maid for water for Esther to wash in and told her where to store away Esther's scant belongings. Everything was new and relatively daunting for this young girl, who had grown up in more modest surroundings.

It was a beautiful house, and everyone was very kind, but she missed her parents! Esther was sad at losing her parents, having two beloved people, die so quickly, was shocking. So much had happened in her young life through difficult circumstances. The funeral for her mother had been fraught, as everyone was leaving the area, and it had been hard to find a rabbi. At least her uncle had supported the family the previous year, having been summoned by her father, when he became ill. He had arrived with servants and found different people to assist her mother, when her father had died, leaving a servant behind.

When her mother had become very sick, the servant had come back to inform his master Mordecai of the events. Everything was done in good order and with kindness, but it made no difference to Esther grieving for the past. The recollections saddened her, as she got up from her seat, as the maid brought in water, ready for her to wash. As she prepared to eat with her uncle. Dressing, she went down with Mary to meet with her benefactor Mordecai, wondering as to what the future would hold? Later that evening sitting on her bed she reflected on all that her uncle Mordecai had proposed.

After they had eaten, her uncle told her of his thoughts about her living with him. Telling her earnestly, that he was happy that she was under his roof and he was going to treat her as his daughter. It seems he had already enlisted the aid of tutors, to help in her education and a dresser who was going to organise her wardrobe. Mary was going to be her companion and introduce her to other Jewish families, with girls of her age. Esther realized her uncle was thorough and kind and she felt secure, aware that in him she had a protector. Mary also seemed helpful and was very easy to talk to, which was comforting altogether; Esther felt at peace.

Later, Mordecai sat reflecting on his couch about the day, and the new responsibilities that lay before him. Given that he had no idea about young people and that he had little understanding of Esther, he felt things had gone well. Glad that he had gone personally to collect her, although it had been a long journey. Mordecai was keen to get to know her, now that she was living under his roof. As her protector, it was vital for him also to understand her personality. Once they'd met and talked, he thought she was unassuming, in fact charming with a poise that was very mature.

Although, it was not the only thing on Mordecai's mind that evening, his thoughts were dark from conversations he had been a party to recently. Royalty occasionally seemed to lack judgement, and King Ahasuerus described by some, as a sensualist was courting danger. He was enjoying close allegiance with company, not possibly of the best calibre. One of his loyal courtiers had spoken to Mordecai on the quiet, about the kings drinking habits and other forms of debauchery. Added to which many of the people he mixed with, were known antagonists of the Jewish population. Mordecai contemplated that it could be a problem in the future.

As a noted leader, many of the Jews looked to Mordecai for counsel, so he had to consider things in detail and work out what to inform the community! Possibly a waiting game, he decided, no point in jumping to conclusions, let's see what the next couple of years brought! One thing he knew was that King Ahasuerus ruled with no great wisdom, even though he reigned over what was the most significant empire of its time. There was much to consider and the future, well it was far from stable. Mordecai sighed, faith was the answer, and he had that, so he would give it all into the hands of **The Mighty One**, who will bring them through!

Years Later

Mordecai called Esther in to talk with him, and they sat on the balcony watching the sun setting. Esther had developed into a beautiful young woman, mature and happily, with wisdom. Mordecai enjoyed her company loved to hear her sing and enjoyed having her around. She had made friends with other young women of her age and had been most diligent in all of her studies. It was time now to think of a husband for her, and it was for this reason, Mordecai wanted to talk. He was aware of the latest politics and required Esther also to be informed of the events in Susa and have her opinion on them.

It seems there were problems between the King and Queen Vashti, because she refused to appear at a grand banquet. It was a specially extended feast held in Susa for many dignitaries. No one quite knew why she had ignored the King's request, but speculation was rife. A prestigious event attended by people from one hundred twenty-seven provinces of Persia. The kingdom stretched from India to Ethiopia and dignitaries were all represented. The occasion had turned from feasting, into very risqué debauchery, according to gossip, and dancers that were utterly immodest.

The King, incensed at her refusal to attend, had the Queen disposed of, as it was a great embarrassment to the King to have a wife who was disobedient. It was, in fact, unheard of by the people in the land, at this time!

Immediately a scheme was put in place to reinstate the King's authority, and to save his face! The palace wanted to install an obedient wife quickly, and sent out notification all over the land, for virgins to apply.

They all had to go through a vigorous vetting process, which was the reason Mordecai wished to speak with Esther. As an honorable Jew, Mordecai kept to the customs of his people in the way that they lived. At this time in their lives Mordecai reasoned that it was time for his ward Esther, to contemplate marriage. Mordecai held out his hand to Esther and smiled.

"My dear, I am so glad you came into my life; you are beautiful and sincere. Any parents would be delighted at the way you have grown up and become a woman. However, it's time to think about your future, and I have some thoughts that I'd like you to contemplate. In court, they are looking for a beautiful woman to become the King's wife. I know he isn't wholly the man, perhaps I might have chosen for you. Possibly better than some, worse than others, but he is the King, and your position, and what happens to our nation will be secure! Also, as I am involved in the King's service daily, I can watch out for you, and see you regularly. I know life would be different for you, but many of the King's servants are good people, and I believe you could have a good life."

Esther looked at Mordecai, with her beautiful long hair, sweeping eyelashes and vibrant complexion, she was a most attractive woman. "I am not sure what to say, do you think the King will find me to his liking?" said Ether, and smiled.

"I believe he will find you most attractive, what's not to like?" he teased her and laughed.

"Although Esther, remember, there are people in court who hate the Jewish nation, so keep your nationality to yourself, my dear. Whatever the outcome, that way there should be no trouble. Meanwhile, I will put your name forward and see what happens, but.... what am I to do if you leave me?"

It was time for Esther to laugh too, "Well let's see what the King thinks of me before we think of that?"

The Wedding

Mordecai sat at his desk and considered what to do. It had been a fairy tale wedding. Esther ensconced in the Palace, with the King besotted with her, was all so wonderful, ending so much sadness in Ester's life.

It was trouble in the surrounding area, outside of the Palace that concerned Mordecai. Unrest was rearing its head, and in many ways that concerned Mordecai greatly. Fortunately, he had been in the right place to deal with one problem. He had heard of a conspiracy between two of the King's guards, who wanted to assassinate King Ahasuerus. Quickly Mordecai alerted the king's court about the plan, which found the guards guilty of conspiracy and put them to death. No one came to thank Mordecai, but he was glad that on this occasion he had been in a position to protect the King. Regardless, his loyalty, for saving the King had virtually gone unrecognised, although his actions had been noted in royal records. However, Mordecai had other concerns on his mind at this time, as policies that had been drawn up, made him extremely anxious.

An individual leader named Haman had been made a most powerful ruler in the land by the King. It seemed that King Ahasuerus was proud of him and told people that they should bow down to him. People accepted this, except for Mordecai who saw no reason to do so. Whenever Haman came into an area, every official would bow except for Mordecai and his defiance, made Haman extremely irritated. Deciding that he was going to teach Mordecai a lesson, Haman devised a plan to get his own back on him, and on the Jewish nation as well.

As an Agagite, he despised Jews, and now he had power, he was going to influence the King and use it. This man very slyly informed the King that a group of people within his empire would not obey the laws of the land. At the same time, wanting to wield power and kill off Mordecai, Haman got his men to build an extensive scaffolding in readiness to hang his enemy. As these events occurred, one night the King, awake restless, sat reviewing the records of the land. Noticing, that Mordecai's act of bravery, saving him from an assassination plot, had never been rewarded. He summoned Haman and asked him what he should do to honor a man for his service? Haman, misunderstanding entirely got the wrong idea, imagined he was the one for honor and gave the King grand ideas. Naturally, as he thought he was talking about himself, he told the King that the man should be dressed in royal garments and be led through the streets on a splendid horse. King Ahasuerus then told Haman to do this for Mordecai. At this command, Haman was humiliated by the whole experience. Determined to deal with Mordecai and get rid of him once and for all, before he became important, he planned to kill him.

It was at this very time, Mordecai found out what laws Haman had encouraged the King to put in place to kill off, the Jewish nation. Mordecai was distraught when he learned about the plans Haman had contrived for the Jews. Grieved, and overwhelmed with anguish, he put on mourning and went and spoke to the Jews in the area. Mordecai was a brave man, who believed **The Mighty One** had a plan for his people and wanted to protect them. He knew that they needed to look to the God of the past, to find out how this protection could come about. Focused, and understanding this, he realized that they were **The Mighty One's** people, so He would have the answers.

Although, he also understood the reality of the situation; Haman wielded a considerable amount of influence, and a miracle was required to deal with the man! Esther meanwhile in the Palace, heard of the way Mordecai was dressing and summoned him, to tell her why he was in mourning? They talked together, and Mordecai told her of the plans Haman was putting in place, and how their future could change. Esther happy at court wondered if it was necessary for her to do anything, concerned that Mordecai had over exaggerated just a little.

Mordecai explained further details to Esther, about all of the decrees that Haman had put in place over the nation. Informing her that in her position, she was required to use her power, to help save the people. Reminding her, that she was not safe either from the wicked plans devised, as she was Jewish. He told her, "If you remain silent at this time, relief and deliverance for the Jews will arise from another place, but you and your father's family will perish. Furthermore, Esther, who knows but that you have come to the royal palace for such a time as this!"

Esther was bright, and it did not take long for her to realize, after talking at length with Mordecai that this was a crucial period for the nation, especially for the Jews.

The latest politics and Haman's hate for the Jewish nation, made her comprehend clearly, what he had in mind. She recognized that it was not only her position in jeopardy but the future of the nation at stake. If the Hebrew nation was not to be annihilated by these bad laws, Esther must use her influential position, to help. This era was, of course, approximately five hundred years before **The Promise of Heaven** was to arrive. Which was why these two people, Mordecai' and Esther, were part of **The Mighty One's** plan and required to play their part.

Esther decided to act and to understand the principals of seeking a higher power taught by her family; she informed Mordecai that she and her ladies would fast and pray. Encouraging him, to get the Jews in the area to do the same, in preparation for her to go and have an audience with the King. The custom was that the Queen only went to the King when he called her.

As these customs were sacrosanct, it was forbidden to break them, on pain of death, Esther knew she must pray. Fasting and prayer were the only option, and after that, Esther would visit the King and plead for her nation. Not all of her ladies were happy with this scenario, as they had not fasted before and wondered if it was essential. Under Esther's encouragement and guidance, the servants fasted. It was a needful exercise at that time, so they deprived themselves of food and prayed. While in the local area, Mordecai summoned the Jews and got all of them to fast and pray for **The Mighty One's** help.

After a time, Esther, with courage and wisdom, sought her husband the King for his help in this matter. Carefully, she dressed for the occasion, and came to the throne room to meet with the King. The King deep in conversation with Haman, extended his staff toward her. He was curious as to why she had arrived unannounced. Inquiring if she was well. Esther said her reason for disturbing him was her desire to prepare a special banquet. The King was pleased with the answer, although intrigued, especially as Esther invited Haman too, as to what the Queen wanted. Haman went home elated and informed everyone as to his importance. He bragged that the Queen had invited only the King and himself to a special banquet. Feeling overly confident, that his position was secure, Haman decided he was going to get rid of Mordecai who was a thorn in his side.

In the grounds of his magnificent mansion, the shadow of the scaffolding waited, and Haman knew it would be put to good use. Why, the way things were working out, he'd soon get rid of all the hated Jews. Excitedly, he started to prepare for Esther's banquet.

Mordecai, meanwhile, met with Esther and talked about the difficulties that lay ahead, while she explained what she was about to do. Quietly assured, after conferring with Mordecai with his encouragement in everything she was organising, she dressed for the banquet. The time came for the beautiful banquet, and it was sumptuous, nothing had been left out in the preparation of the meal. In the background, a tasteful group played the music that the King liked, as dancers performed to his delight. Esther's dress was alluring, and this beautiful woman endeavoured to use all of her charms to achieve her plan. It was a sumptuous meal with light conversation, as Esther sought to find the right time to bring her petition. After the first day, the King was curious, as to what was the reason for the feast and Esther promised that she would tell him soon. The second day was a banquet of wine, again all beautifully prepared. After a short time, the Queen stood up and bowed in front of him.

"What is your request, Queen Esther? Furthermore, it shall be granted you?" said the King. "I will give you half of the kingdom if that's what you require?"

Then Esther answered and said, "If I have found favor in your sight, my King, and if it pleases you, protect my life, save me from the peril that is coming! I implore you, my King, to hear my petition, for my people and me. I would not have bothered you if we had been sold just as bondmen and women. I would have held my peace, my Lord. Because this is not the case, I am frightened for my future, for my people and me. Uncertain as to what lies ahead! This is my request my King."

Then King Ahasuerus moved from his seat nearer to Esther and frowned.

"Who is this and where is he, that presumes to do this wicked thing?" said the King.

Esther said, "An adversary and an enemy who sits at this

table, wicked Haman, has planned and devised all of this!"

Her words hung in the air, and the room was silent, as the King stared at Haman for a few minutes before rising. He then got up from the table furious and went into the palace gardens. Haman was afraid, as he realized, he had been found out and was terrified. He knew that the King would be planning his demise and recognized the only way for him to survive, was to beg the Queen for mercy.

As Haman stood up, to request his life to Esther, the Queen, he fell upon the couch where Esther was. The King, returning from the Palace gardens and saw all of this, was incandescent with rage.

"Will he even force himself upon the Queen before me in the house and rape her while I am in the Palace?" he shrieked at Haman! The sentence was passed immediately after this action, and they took Haman and hung him on the gallows in the grounds of his house.

As they took him away, Esther fell on her face before the King. She explained in detail about the laws that had been put in place to kill all the Jews. Mordecai was called in to elaborate, how Haman had planned and manipulated laws, to annihilate the whole Jewish nation. Once the King understood, he gave Mordecai the signet ring that Haman had been wearing. The ring was the King's authority for Mordecai, to use as required. Trusting Mordecai with the responsibility, to write new laws to protect the Jewish nation that Haman had planned to annihilate. These were the plans and laws of Haman that Mordecai had to work quickly, to overturn. He had to write and replace the old laws that Haman had devised. In their place he had to bring in new laws that not only superseded them but gave the Jews rights to apprehend those who wanted to kill them. Haman had planned cleverly to rid the world of all the Jews. This wicked plan that was a subtle attack on **The Mighty One,** for this was His nation. Mordecai and Esther had stood boldly against this evil endeavors, **The Mighty One** used them to reveal the wicked Haman's schemes.

Confidently, Mordecai made sure that the new laws went out in all languages throughout the province. Decrees, written down for all the 127 provinces from India to Cush in Africa. Mounted couriers went speedily, to take the proclamation of the King's law for the Jews to protect themselves and to annihilate those who were trying to kill them. It was a fantastic answer to the prayers and fasting, accomplished through **The Mighty One's** protection of His people. It was a great time of celebration but also retribution. In Susa, Jews took up arms against the five hundred men who had planned to kill them. After the battle, there was time to celebrate with joy and feasting. This happened in the same way in many countries. As the Jews everywhere, stood against all who tried to kill them. The nobles and governors helped them because the fear of Mordecai had come upon them. This time in Susa was never to be forgotten, and down the ages, it is celebrated with joy, by the Jewish nation everywhere. Mordecai became a most important part of the King's entourage because he had saved the Jewish nation.

No one forgot the part he played, and he became an impressive figure in the nation. Mordecai was an unassuming man, who helped to save a nation through the care and encouragement of his ward, Esther. This man helped to shape history. A most humble man, who had been obedient in the way he had lived, and never compromised on truth. Given royal approval, he was as important as the King. No longer just a servant in the Palace, he wore a crown and had a high standing in the land. A remarkable man of courage who saved a nation, with Esther, the Queen, ensuring that **The Mighty One's** plans could continue.

All was on track for **The Promise of Heaven** to appear in the future! The Hebrew people were jubilant and celebrated down the centuries how the nation was saved at this time from annihilation. Mordecai and Esther had played their parts, and **The Mighty One's** nation was ready, as future plans became activated. While waiting in the wings, others, such as Jeremiah and Isaiah and Malachi. Men and women ready to serve their God and to herald in **The Promise of Heaven** to worship **The Mighty One**.

Satan

Satan was furious; his plan to get rid of the Jewish nation entirely had all gone wrong. He had put in place a proper scheme, that was going to achieve this, and it had failed, he was angry! He summoned those who had been working for him and questioned them. Enraged, that the plan to demolish the Jewish nation had been unsuccessful, he wanted revenge. Satan screamed and spat, he did not like failure, especially not getting his own way. He was furious, heads were going to roll! Death, destruction and darkness, Satan was out to cause carnage wherever he could.

Jews, he would kill them all, and Mordecai, well he would think of a plan to get rid of this man! Haman had been a great pawn, but he'd got too big for his boots! Having such an opinion of himself, he thought he was indispensable, and it was his plan that the Jewish nation was to be annihilated…stupid, arrogant beings. It was himself, Satan who had devised the plot. Humans, weak and gullible creatures!

He shouted to his minions to get out there and do their job, cause mayhem others were coming! If the upstart, Malachi, thought he was going to be different, he would show him. The nation was in a mess and he, Satan, had accomplished it through the leaders. So, Malachi was not going to make any difference; Satan was going to win. Satan screamed, he would decimate all that got in his way, his voice was heard hurling out obscenities, in his frustration to all around!

Malachi

The Lord looked down and sighed; he had seen the decline of His people, disobedience and sinfulness endemic throughout the land. Unfortunately, all attributed to the leaders, wayward, and decadent behavior. The nation had little leadership, as the priests had strayed from walking the way of Moses, ignoring the truths given them through the law and covenants. Sadly, those priests leading the nation had little passion for their God and lived in arrogance, doing what they pleased.

Watching, seeing the hearts of His people, **The Mighty One** realized no one hungered to hear from Him, as Samuel and others had in the past. The nation was in an apathetic state and needed help to turn back to their God. His plans for His nation were in jeopardy, and **The Mighty One** had to intervene quickly! Speaking with **The Breath** and **The Promise of Heaven** they knew that this was a crisis. Apathy was endemic, especially in those leading the nation. Society was heading in the wrong direction, and the priests were to blame! The future rested on all that was happening now, and although exciting plans were all in place for Elijah to come; the nation needed to get back on course before a disaster occurred. It required a godly man, someone who loved **The Mighty One**, an honorable man to be used in His service, someone who could be a messenger. One individual stood out, a man they could trust, who could carry a message to the people. Malachi loved **The Mighty One**, and he was a prophet who could deliver their message with boldness. He was their man, and **The Breath** went to speak with him to deliver a strong prophecy for the nation's leaders.

Future Happenings

A figure disappearing into the distance was all that the leaders saw of the man whose words had cut them like shards of glass. The leaders, distorted with rage plucked their beards while others held their head in their hands, aghast at the words of the prophet! In the surrounding area, his words seemed to reverberate, echoing predictions that were terrifying in their content.

Commanding words that sent chills down the backs of the listeners! They had not accepted his words, far from it. In a large room near the temple, it was chaos on this day, as the priests voiced their rage in thunderous terms! They were leaders and had gathered to hear a particular word from a noted prophet! None of them expected a rebuke; they were so confident of their abilities; in fact, proud of their achievements, they were aghast! He stood, Malachi the prophet in front of them, in their elegant robes. His words had pronounced judgement on them, stating that **The Mighty One,** had given him the exact words for the leaders of the nation at this time. Furthermore, his lengthy prophetic statement, voicing **The Mighty One's** displeasure, in the lives of the priests, was met with derision and anger. Hearing his words, they realized this was not a little put down by an ineffective priest, a minor criticism; it was a considerable chastisement of gigantic proportion, about their lifestyle and priesthood. His pronouncement on their ungodly actions was scathing and not quietened, on hearing their protests.

His loud dissertation had continued as he strolled around the vast group of dignitaries. Boldly gazing at each one in the face as he walked around, he quite calmly, resolved to deliver all that **The Mighty One** had given him. Sneeringly, the priests tried to ridicule him and asked him whom he thought he was? It did not phase the prophet, as he spoke in a calm and dignified loud voice and said.

"Hear this, you who pretend to be holy!" Pointing his long bony finger, towards them he said. "Look priests at the way you are living **The Mighty One** is appalled! He is who He is, why ignore His power and his greatness?

A son honors a father, and a slave his master. **The Mighty One**, is our father, and he asks every leader, where is My honor? And if I am a master, why do you not fear me? All of the despicable acts you do are seen, especially the way you shamefully despise His name. The cunning ways, and simpering looks, stating, 'How have we disdained your Name?' Ungodly and rebellious ones, who pretend to know **The Mighty One's** heart. He sees your lifestyle and all your actions in leadership!

Understand this, He watches the lousy animals that are given in sacrifice. And observes clearly the way you keep the best for yourself, to make money. Through this action you are cursed for your craftiness; when there is a ram in a flock, and you make a vow, and sacrifice a blemished animal! What does the Law of Moses say? Oh, but you know it well and choose to ignore it! He is a great King, the Lord of Hosts, whose name is to be feared and respected among the nation. He knows what you do, and the disrespect you have for him. How can you be leaders if you live in this way? It is shameful to behave like this and disrespect **The Mighty One.** It is time that you became enlightened and listen to all that he says to you!"

Around him, the priests sneered. "How do you know what **The Mighty One** is or wants!" they spat out at the prophet sneeringly. While a soft murmur was heard in the background, as the prophet now stood on a small platform at the end of the room.

"I will explain to you, even more," said Malachi, staring at the back of this large group. "Understand this: He hears the way you whisper, speaking behind closed doors, when you say, 'He does not perceive or care as to what we do'! How misguided you are, he has seen your unholy ways and listened to your conversations! Just as he used to listen to the Israelites in their tents complaining! Comprehend this, leaders who should be guiding the people, to walk in righteousness. Judgement is coming, and it will start with you, a curse is waiting at the very door of your lives, be watchful!"

At this, many of the priests turned their backs as Malachi continued, raising up his hands as he pointed to all of them.

"He sees all you do, your mumbled discontent, how

shallow your affection is for him. However, you have brought further shame, by embracing the calling of another? How dare you take this upon yourselves and be so arrogant? Understand, ungodly leaders clearly! Levi was the priest anointed in my service says **The Mighty One**, to offer sacrifices; you are interlopers.

He honored me, and my covenant was with him, a covenant of life and peace. He and his descendants honored me and stood in awe of my name, and true instruction was in his mouth, nothing false was found on his lips.

By your actions you corrupt the covenant of the Levites says the Lord! It was their calling alone to minister in the capacity of priests to offer sacrifice. Do you not realize what you have done? You have crossed boundaries, and you do not have the anointing for this sacred task? I will accept no offering from your hands."

Gasps were heard around the room! "Why have you dared to ignore the Law and disregard the words in Deuteronomy, that are plain for all to see? Listen to me, I will recite it to you, to help your memories."

'And now oh Israel what does the Lord your God ask of you? But to fear the Lord your God, to walk in all his ways to love and to serve The Lord your God, with all your heart and with all your soul. And to observe the Lord's commands and decrees that he has given you for your own good.'

A groan was heard from a white-haired man near the back of the room, as the prophet continued. "There have been many warnings of bad leadership from the prophets of old. Ezekiel wrote about this, reminding us that the Lord God is against shepherd's who are not looking after the flock, His people! This godly man understood holiness, something you have all chosen to ignore!"

Again, muttering and loud voices were heard all around as Malachi continued. "Understand your position, arrogant men, who care not how you approach holy things, disregarding the truth, you go your own way! His judgement is waiting at your door!" A few priests turned their backs towards him, and some started to walk away as Malachi continued.

"How dare you treat the laws of Moses with such disdain, **The Mighty One** is angry with you? Listen intently, He sees, the way you live and the contempt that you show in your own relationships, viewing it as deplorable!

It is an example of all that's unholy, embracing divorce in this way, **The Mighty One** hates divorce! Nothing is hidden, He sees and views the way you have discarded the women of your youth, and embraced younger women, as despicable. This example has polluted the people in the land who have adopted this pattern of behavior. It has made ungodliness a way of life for many people, and corruption is rampant.

It is you priests who are to blame, leaders who are walking in the darkness of sin. People are copying your leadership and lifestyle and have not separated themselves from the peoples of other lands. All down the ages, the Law has shown My people how to keep holy says **The Mighty One**, it is my expectation for them. Sadly, your actions have allowed the godly seed to mingle with the peoples of other places, forgetting **The Mighty One's** instructions.

As godly leaders, accepting sons and daughters of other religions is wrong. Listen and understand leaders, through your way of life, you have become unholy, disdained truth and become a stain! Oh, arrogant men! **The Mighty One** stands and watches all that your actions and is angry at the way you treat the people. Do you not comprehend, that the way you continue to disregard the Law of Moses in every area of your lives, is arrogant and wrong. Because you have lived unfaithfully, it has caused many to stumble as they copied your actions. In your arrogance, you lead the people into deception, and they become worse off than before!

Holding your arrogant poise, you put your noses in the air and are indifferent to all that is happening. Priests should preserve knowledge and help people who come for instruction, but your ways have caused people to stumble. It is scandalous!

The Mighty One is faithful, and He will help His people, but you who aspire to lead, He will hold you accountable for your evil ways, judgement will come."

Once again there were mutterings, and some walked away, but this did not deter this prophet, his voice thundered on.

"In due time **The Mighty One** is sending a messenger to bring people to repentance.

The land has become polluted with unholiness, and it is you leaders, who have conceded to this, by your sinfulness. Would a person rob his god? Apparently, you say not, but you have stolen from me says **The Mighty One**, via improper use of tithes and other sacred gifts.

Prosperity will suffer, and a curse will be put upon you because of this. When people are diligent in their tithes, they are blessed. If you test **The Mighty One** in this, you will be surprised, and other nations will see your prosperity and praise you. The ideas you foster, saying that He is not interested and will not bother about people is a lie from Satan. He is a God who gives generously to all people and sees their worth. **The Mighty One** says the ones who honor me will be acknowledged.

Priests live in holy fear, for quite soon the future will arrive dramatically! God's man Elijah, will bring a mighty wave of power and herald in a new era; he will prepare the way for the Messiah. Repentance is the only way, for you and for the people in the future, to receive the promised blessings. Understand, this one-day judgement will be upon all people, the sun will be like an oven, and the wicked will be consumed like straw, leaving no trace. How dare you treat **The Mighty One** with indifference." The priest's voice spoke, inconsolable with rage, as he faced them and shared the prophecy.

However, angry shouting started to bubble up all around, as voices charged with defiance and anger, shouted out to Malachi! Who are you, telling us this, what authority do you have, we look to "Abraham?"

"Hmm!" Malachi looked at them, his small eyes glanced all around him! "Not so!" A large heavyset Pharisee stood up from his seat and shouted out sneeringly, "Who does he think he is, telling us what **The Mighty One** sees and believes?"

The priest moved forward towards him. "The future will show you my words are true; I am the Lord's messenger! This very world will be challenged and changed. Your future and destiny belong to Him, and you should be fearful!"

"You are unbelievable men, where is your reverence? Can it be so difficult to comprehend, that you weary him, when you cover the altar of the Lord with tears, weeping, and sighing? He knows your deeds and will not take anything from your hands. The time of judgement is now. He knows the names of those who defend His honor. They are the ones who will ultimately be safely resurrected. People will be able to tell the difference between the righteous and the evil then! Understand this you ungodly men, as I said, the sun will be like an oven, and the wicked will be consumed like straw, leaving no trace. But the same sun will be a source of healing for the righteous, who will walk over the wicked as if they were ash."

On hearing these last words, many looked distressed and quietly whispered together, acknowledging that it was right, the Lord does hear all things. While a hush went over the whole area and a cry of despair from some God-fearing men, who tore their cloaks, still some others sat and talked in another corner and decided on some action. They were going to make a scroll of remembrance for Him, stating the Lord knows those who fear Him and who value His name highly...The priest looked at this activity, but didn't stop for long and continued.

"Don't you realize that the Lord knows all who fear him, and says, 'You are mine, a treasure. I will have compassion on those, as a man has compassion on his son who serves him.'"

All of you here, who walk in your arrogant way, are men of unholiness; and judgement is falling your way, impossible to escape its reach. No one can abide the day of His coming, and who will stand when he appears, for it is like a fire that refines and like fullers' soap." The prophet stopped, then stepped down from his small podium and lifted up his arms and pointed a finger.

"These are the words given to me for all of you," said the priest, "wake up from your arrogance, realize what you have done and repent. Leaders, you will be judged on the way you have flagrantly disregarded **The Mighty One**, judgement is for all! Elijah is coming, and all the people must be ready!" With that, the prophet turned and walked through the middle of the gathering and was gone! Many of the priests were inconsolable with rage, although some had a more sombre demeanour and went off.

One old man sat with his head in his hands, tears ran down his cheeks, guilty, yes, they were all guilty! If this was what the Almighty thought about them, then judgement was going to be harsh. The priest, Malachi, who was he, it seemed like he had come from out of nowhere? Speaking to them about repentance in such an eloquent way, he was right; of course, they had become self-absorbed? The nation to repentance, well there's a thought!

Then there was the promise, wasn't that from the time of Creation that they were to look for a Messiah? The old man got up, possibly the only thing to do was to make for a quiet seat in the temple. There was only one person whom he'd, nor spoken to for a very long time, who'd have all the answers. Pulling his robe tightly around him, he went off to speak with his God!

Malachi had been used to alert the leaders if they would listen. Down the ages again and again, **The Mighty One** had compassion on people and tried to get their attention when they were being led astray, using different prophets to do so. Soon it was to be the time for a priest called Zechariah, an honorable and humble man to appear. It was another segment of the future that **The Mighty One** had ordained, to herald in **The Promise of Heaven**.

Godly Leadership

All down the ages, problems have arisen when **The Mighty One's** people become arrogant in their strength and leaders of groups turn away from holiness and embrace their own doctrines.

It results in a decline in biblical authority, and away from God's truth. Taking out verses and saying they are no longer current, in fact, old-fashioned, is a dangerous precedent.

It is **The Mighty One's** Word, and those who have turned from Him face judgement. The enemy is cunning, and sowing deception allows evil to be accepted, posing as "God's Word," when it is corrupt doctrine. Leaders have a responsibility to hear God's heart for their people, to weigh up words given in relation to the Bible and to be accountable, which is something that they should expect.

As in Malachi's time, the cloak of leaderships' is not an easy one to wear and trying to please people before God is dangerous. Judgement will happen for all one day, and all who teach, and lead bear a greater responsibility. Although it is not easy to always understand, or possibly agree with **The Mighty One**, but He is God, and one day all will be revealed!

"My feet have closely followed His steps; I have kept His way without turning aside. I have not departed from the commands of His lips; I have treasured the word of His mouth more than my daily bread." (Job 23v 11-12)

Zechariah

The people in Jerusalem were the "apple of the Lord's eye," and **The Mighty One** watched over the city, well aware that **The Promise of Heaven** was imminent. One man who was prominent in **The Mighty One's** thoughts as He watched, was Zechariah. On the day in question, this humble man was about to start his duties in the Temple. Leaving the house, Zechariah said goodbye to his wife and reminded her to ask the neighbours for help if she needed anything. It was his turn to be on duty in the Temple as a priest for a week, and he wanted to be sure Elizabeth was taken care of while he was away. She smiled at him and told him not to worry; the week would go past quickly enough.

He was very conscientious and took his duties seriously, which Elizabeth respected. He belonged to the priestly division of Abijah, a submissive man, humble who realized how important it was to keep spiritually clean and walk in obedience to **The Mighty One**. He had never been raucous, was very quiet, full of humility, while obedient to the truth, disregarding all idol worship. He and Elizabeth had married quite young, she was also a descendant of Aaron, and they lived quietly and peacefully together. Their one sadness was that God had not given them any children. Elizabeth never grumbled about this, just accepted that it was not to be, and was quite sanguine in her approach to everything. As customary, she was up in the morning, brushing the front of the house, with the bread already in the oven, busy as always, as Zechariah prepared to leave for the Temple.

"Be at peace and don't worry, you will do everything right," she said giving him assurances.

Zechariah was a worrier and this week of service as a priest was a great privilege. Meticulous in all he did, he always wanted everything to be perfect for his God. He was going to be staying at the Temple for the whole week, as this was his second duty of the year and he was excited but concerned. "Thank you, what would I do without you, will you be all right for the week?" He asked again, smiling down at her as he hugged her and touched her greying hair. His beard bristled her cheek, and she also noticed he was greying at the temple and smiled back too.

"My dear we are blessed, and our neighbours are good, go in peace," said Elizabeth, "I will be quite content at home."

Zechariah left the house with the sun gently filling the sky and thought how beautiful it was. He was at peace and enjoyed the uphill climb into the city. What a beautiful world he mused, and considered how down the years, **The Mighty One** had taken care of them.

As he stepped into the Temple, he bowed his head, a little ritual he had always done for years. The other priests used to scoff at him, but recognizing he was harmless, they all accepted it as Zechariah's way! He was unquestionably a man of integrity, and they knew they had to do things right, with him around. It was the turn of his division to be on duty today, and later they would take lots, on who was to go into the holy place, and burn incense. The rest of the team would be outside praying.

Soon, all of them arrived and dressed with care, making sure they put on all their priestly attire in the correct order. It was a ritual that had been passed down over the years, Zechariah mused, as he washed, understanding the enormous privilege of worship. Once they gathered and took lots, Zechariah was elected, much to his surprise, as the chosen one. Astounded at this outcome, he wished he had prayed more.

It was a huge responsibility to worship **The Mighty One** in the holy place, a privilege and honor. It took him a while to get his head around it. It was awesome to be selected in this way and an excellent opportunity to serve, although a little frightening. **The Mighty One** was respected, and everyone viewed the inner sanctum in awe, realising that unholiness could undoubtedly be dealt with, as this was no spiritual game!

Everyone knew the ultimate price was death for those who pretended to be righteous but walked in deceit! The other priests put out their hands to Zechariah, recognizing the responsibility that he carried. He nodded to them his thanks, he was not an emotional man but for a few minutes the awesomeness of what he was to undertake, overwhelmed him! These customs, given to Moses for the Jewish people as to how they were to worship their God, were a considerable responsibility. Choosing two priests to help him, he allowed them to attach the sash around his waist with its long cord. The concern was holiness, and the chord gave the priests the capability of pulling the priest out if he died.

Everyone was in awe of approaching the holy place, and to think that anything might occur was overwhelming. Zechariah, the chosen priest, was to take in the incense for worship, but before this occurred, the ashes and new coals had to be taken up and laid. Zechariah had asked two of his oldest friends to help him, and the old men worshipfully agreed. The first priest went in and carefully removed the ashes from the previous day. While the second priest then took his place and reverently carried in the burning coals. It was a privilege and honor to serve **The Mighty One**, and all went reverently and humbly about their task, understanding the significance of all that they were doing! It was finally the time for Zechariah to take his place, to prepare to carry the golden censer to be brought into the holy place with the incense. The priests put their hands on him once again and asked **The Mighty One's** blessing and protection as he took up his position.

He held the golden censer with the incense carefully and walked in to do his task. At a given signal he would spread the incense over the coals for worship to begin. As the burnt offering of incense touched the burning coals a cloud of fragrance arose from the altar, at this, the prayers of the worshippers outside would rise into the presence of God.

It was a beautifully symbolic experience of worship, and Zechariah took up his position, praising God. Zechariah understood the awesomeness of this act and continued to worship his God, in the sweetness of his spirit. He bowed as he stood, entirely in awe of the God of creation power and might, as the incense filled the room. His journey had been a long one, and old age had now come upon him, but he still knew the reality of a God who loved and cared for all.

It was Zechariah's day, a once in a lifetime experience, a privilege that was unique and he was so conscious of the holiness of the place. Lost in praise of **The Mighty One,** he forgot everything else and realized that it was now time to leave. As he started to back out of the sanctuary, he gave one last look at the altar. As he did so, his eyes saw a figure to the right of the platform, a great being, standing quite still, an angel of the Lord. Zechariah felt his whole being freeze, as he turned and faced this incredibly impressive figure. The angel Gabriel spoke and smiled in reassurance to the man standing in awe.

"Do not be frightened Zechariah, **The Mighty One** has answered your prayers and petitions, and you will have a son, whom you will call John." (This is a particular name and meant **The Mighty One** has been gracious.) Zechariah was amazed, at this person, this man and his face turned ashen, at hearing him speak.

Listening to the words of the angel, Zechariah managed to move his feet, which had somehow seemed pinned to the floor.

The angel continued. "He will be no ordinary child, and God's blessing is upon him as he has a special task for him to accomplish! As part of this mission, he must drink no wine nor strong drink." You will have joy and gladness, and many will rejoice over his birth, he will be the forerunner predicted by the Prophet Malachi. Understand Zechariah God can do anything, nothing is impossible for Him!" What is more, the child will be filled with the Holy Spirit, even from his mother's womb. He is going to be a powerful prophet for **The Mighty One**! A voice that heralds in **The Promise of Heaven.**"

At that minute it was just too much for Zechariah, he was overwhelmed. It was all too much to take in…this angel, was this God's word for him? He and Elizabeth were old, how could this be? As he stood there all sorts of fears and anxieties surfaced in this godly man and stuttering, he said. "That sounds ridiculous; we are old!" Zechariah doubted the angel Gabriel's words and said as much. At this Gabriel put up his hand and told Zechariah.

"I am Gabriel; I stand in the throne room in the presence of **The Mighty One**. He sent me to convey this message to you, to bring you this good news, you unbelieving man! As an earthly proof of these heavenly realities, you will be silent and unable to speak, until the day these things come to pass at the proper time."

Zechariah gasped, the conversation had taken only a few minutes, and there was so much to take in!

Outside, the priests waited for Zechariah, and wondered at his delay, in the holy place. Zechariah was frightened, but in awe at the same time, he realized too late he had said too much. Overwhelming he thought, what an incredible experience, why did he have to talk so, he truly believed God could do anything!

Thinking all this through, Zechariah now felt a pull on his sash, the other priests concerned at the time he had been in the sanctuary, wondered if he was alive! As he turned, the angel Gabriel disappeared, and he was on his own.

The man that emerged out of the inner sanctum was very different from the man who had gone in! Zechariah was a man who had always walked **The Mighty One's** way, but he was different. He had an awareness after his experience of a God that was unique and strong; he was challenged and changed. A man who had been humbled, confronted, and who understood more of his weaknesses, developed an even stronger robust faith.

The other priests, now curious knew that something unusual had happened, speculated together as to what he had experienced in the holy place. He made signs to them gesturing to Heaven, the Temple, his mouth and was able to get across the concept that he had seen a vision in the Temple. Everyone was intrigued, curious as to why this old priest had been specifically chosen in this way. Zechariah unable to communicate now, spent time pondering on **The Mighty One's** faithfulness. It was to be some time until everyone learnt of the supernatural encounter, he had experienced.

Of course, Zechariah had become the news item of the Temple, something had happened, and now he could not speak, so speculation was rife!

Once he had completed his weekly priestly service, he was able to go home and share with Elizabeth as best he could. Although helpfully, one of his friends came to the house to share the amount the other priests knew of the scenario. Elizabeth knew her husband was a godly man and although she did not understand completely, trusted him. Whatever had happened in the time he spent in worship at the Temple, she knew with confidence everything was going to work out right. To her amazement, it affected her more than she realized; her life was changing rapidly. In a few months, this barren woman became pregnant; it was a miracle. This was unbelievable; they were both ecstatic, to think that they were going to have a child. All Zacharias could do was to keep praising God; he was so thankful for **The Mighty One's** love for them.

With Elizabeth pregnant, it was the talk of the village, and everyone was curious about this old priest and his wife. What was the mysterious thing that had happened to the old man, so that he could not speak? Everyone wondered and would she be able to carry the baby full term? It was an exciting time, with a mystery and a wonder, everyone around was in awe of these old people. Added to which they had a visit from a family member, which was exceedingly pleasant. Elizabeth was heavy with her baby by the time that their visitor arrived and was delighted to talk.

It was Mary, her cousin, who had come to visit the couple, Elizabeth acted prophetically in greeting Mary. Elizabeth had a prophetic word for her as soon as they met. Elizabeth just knew, that her young cousin was to carry the Messiah, and that she would be "the mother of the Lord." While Elizabeth's baby, still in her womb skipped with joy, on meeting Mary's baby. It was a mystery and miracle that **The Mighty One** had ordained. **The Breath** had touched their babies, with an empowering that was distinct and beautiful.

The news was no surprise to her cousin as she knew prophetically, that she was having a baby, and the two women sat together and talked at length. Elizabeth was thrilled to see her and realized God had supernaturally already had His hand on Mary. She praised God, for all He was doing in her young life! Elizabeth, as an older woman, was able to encourage Mary, and reassure her that the future was in **The Mighty One's** hands. These were exceptional women, who realized that both babies had been spoken about years before they were born. The circumstances, with angels foretelling the births sounds more than intriguing, for some, but unbelievable! It was to a degree a walk of faith, for both women, that for those who did not know the circumstances questionable. Both of these women had a task to do, and they were going to do it, with the Lord's grace. Soon, it was time for Mary to return home, leaving Elizabeth, and although it was a sad parting, both realized that **The Mighty One** had His hand upon their lives.

It was just a few weeks before Elizabeth prepared to give birth and it was a time of preparation, with many giving her gifts. Eventually her time arrived, and she gave birth to a beautiful healthy boy, everyone was amazed. She was the talk of the village. The stigma of barrenness had gone from her, everyone in the village was talking about the family. A miracle had happened to this old couple, and an heir was born in their old age.

When the day came to have the baby circumcised, the people waited for the announcement of the baby's name, which was bound to be Zechariah. It was the tradition that a boy would have his father's name, but because Zechariah could not speak, the people waited to hear what Elizabeth had to say. They were all surprised, for at the time it came to circumcise the baby, Zechariah wrote on a tablet, our baby is to be called John.

As soon as he had written the baby's name, he was able to speak, his tongue operated, and he could praise God! The event was monumental, as Zechariah stood and sang out praise to **The**

Mighty One with a prophecy for his tiny son. It was sensational, the news was soon heard of in the Temple, and everyone was curious and more than surprised, at all this happening to these old people! No one realized that this baby was the forerunner of the Messiah; Elijah, predicted by the prophet Malachi years before.

Except of course **The Mighty One**, who saw the purity in Zechariah's heart and watched all the events that He had planned taking place. While nearby, Heaton watched silently, waiting to see if he could help, as the baby smiled upwardly. This tiny bundle was to herald, **The Promise of Heaven**. It was the start of another adventure, and a significant piece of the puzzle all slotted in, and everyone in Heaven was excited. This baby was going to announce the future Messiah, and all of this was tremendously exciting.

John the Baptist

Early morning came, John and his disciples gathered at the Jordan River waiting to see what the day would bring. He had been away from home a long time now, seeking God's will praying and fasting. Living this way, in the silence of the desert gave him space to reflect. He knew in his spirit that he was a man of destiny, that God had plans for him, in fact for the nation. The enormous challenge was to listen. So many things could invade, and cause disruption. Having a father who was a priest was a challenge too, but John knew that his life, was always going to be different from his father's. Having parents who loved **The Mighty One** was unique, and entirely different from many other families.

At home, when he was growing up, his parents had shared

107

about past encounters with the miraculous, encouraging him. Describing miracles that they had been privileged to be involved in, especially about his father in the Temple and the angel, speaking to him. Hearing about these miraculous events, helped John in his search for truth.

He enjoyed listening to their precious memories of **The Mighty One**. His mother also recalled a visit from her cousin before he was born, a very significant meeting. It had been a fantastic time she said when his aunt had told of a miraculous encounter with an angel.

It was something of an unusual story, but the reality was, that it had happened! Later, his Aunt Mary had married Joseph, and they had disappeared, it had been strange, as no one had seen them for years. Some said that they had gone away to Egypt, returned and were now in Nazareth. It was all to do with politics, or so it seemed, it was to do with old King Herod, who was very cruel. It was a shocking story, when he had sent soldiers to Bethlehem, to kill all the small babies, a dreadful time in history.

This particularly evil thing in the past, killing innocent children, seemed unbelievable, but it had happened. It was all strange, as other peculiar events had occurred in this era, all difficult to understand. In one of the villages, shepherds openly declared that they had seen something odd up on the hills. Added to this, a child, a shepherd's son, had told John that his father had seen angels and a special tiny baby.

The child said his father never forgot about it, often reminding the family, that angels were all about them. It was all weird, but somehow deep down, John knew this was a special time in history. Although how strange, that a smelly shepherd had such a conviction about **The Mighty One** and angels, something he had never seen in the Temple, with the priests.

John was in his thirties, an unusual man, who did not work conventionally. Growing up, John studied the laws of Moses, discussing it at length with his father. He was a thinker and endeavoured to search for truth, realising that everyone was waiting for the deliverer to come, the Messiah. John was unique, he was the man promised by **The Mighty One**, to herald in the Messiah, who would come to free His people. It was true everyone wanted to be free of the Romans and thought that a mighty warrior was needed. Many, in fact, thought that the Messiah would be a great king, who could amass an army so that the tyranny they were under, could be broken.

John's relationship with **The Mighty One** was very different from others, possibly through listening to his parent's faith. It started as a young boy, when he spent time on his own, just thinking and talking to **The Mighty One** for hours. Through these intimate times, he believed that somehow, his God did have a plan to help his nation! Understanding all this was the reality that John had, of a God whom loved all people.

What annoyed him tremendously was the way the priests treated everyone with great disdain. It was unnecessary, using power like that. They were supercilious, thought of themselves so very important, and created a poor example of faith. The fact was, John had little time for hypocrisy. It was everywhere, especially in the temple. It caused the people to have a lax approach towards worship. It was endemic; no one seemed to value their roots, the example of living set out by Moses. They were Abraham's people, but people who had lost their direction. Which was why John ended up in the desert, he felt that he required a way of living, that included growing in his relationship with **The Mighty One** away from the hustle of life. Tranquillity, to worship Him, away from the distractions and hypocrisy all around, was the sense that he had, that this was what he had been called to do. In the peace of the desert, he felt that **The Mighty One** was preparing him for something. It was why he spent time in prayer to find out precisely what it was. Gradually, as time went on, in this nomadic environment, other young men joined him. They saw in John something unusual and unconventional.

Living this way was not easy, searching to know **The Mighty One's** will, took time, nevertheless the solitude made him reflect on life. He did not know what the particular purpose was, for being there in the desert; nevertheless, he had changed, and his desires had altered in so many ways. In this very nomadic environment, he stood, dressed in clothes made of camel hair, with a leather belt around his waist, a man searching for truth. His love for the Almighty One had not changed, and in his heart, he was determined to spend time fasting and praying, waiting for direction. One morning it happened, while praying it came to him, he knew with certainty, what **The Mighty One** wanted him to do.

He had heard quite distinctly from Him about the mission He had from Him. It was not difficult, in fact, it was clear. He was to educate people about the things in their lives they needed to sort out, in fact, sinfulness. **The Mighty One** wanted holiness and required the people to come to a place of contrition, for their misdemeanours, and ask for forgiveness. At present they were jeopardising their relationship, by disregarding their roots in a holy God.

A new era was beginning, and it was preparation time. John sensed that this was an extraordinary time, which could be grasped, or, find oneself receiving **The Mighty One's** judgement, a hard message. To come to a place of humility wasn't easy for people to understand, possibly even self-reflection, examining oneself in the light of a holy God. People were coming to the desert searching, away from the bustle of home life, which helped many reflect, and look at things differently. Many had begun to understand, that to have a relationship with **The Mighty One** they needed to own up to their shortcoming, or sin as it is called and be repentant. It was difficult for others, because repentance, wasn't something most people took on board quickly. Sitting alone in the wilderness, John thought about the patriots of old, who had walked the way of truth and righteousness. They were godly and knew the truth, and they heard **The Mighty One** speaking to them in the prophetic. That had been when prophecy had revealed forthcoming events, declaring that a future messiah, was to come. Pondering over this, he knew that people were still hoping for a deliverer to come, and for many, it seemed that they had been waiting forever!

John wondered about many things, and he felt that there was something on the horizon, imminent; possibly; **The Mighty One** was preparing everyone for an event! Others who watched, proceedings in the desert, and especially the actions of young John were unhappy at what they considered, his meddlesome ways. Unfortunately, in the synagogue in Jerusalem, many were like this and didn't appreciate John's methods. The priests were not friendly to those who went against them, and as a thinker, John posed a threat to them.

It had been apparent to John, for some while, he knew that going against the status quo was asking for trouble, but he knew he was following **The Mighty One**!

Undoubtedly it had occurred to him that they were

powerful people, possibly in time, they might come looking for him, for being radical. It was dangerous to reveal the weaknesses of the temple people (the priests) and all very risky, because they believed that they were the law and must be obeyed. As a young man, and a godly man, his instinct was very cavalier in his approach to everything. Why worry, **The Mighty One's** way and purposes were all that mattered, more significant than them, he mused!

Many had laughed at John in the beginning, at his rough appearance, but after a time they respected him and his band of followers. Some came for advice and help, realising that he was not frightened of the Romans or Herod as many were. John's preaching was profound; it required people to clean up their lives, notwithstanding their status and be obedient to **The Mighty One**. Many came to him for advice and realized that this was a man who was honest in his approach to everyone.

A steady stream of people seemed to trail into the desert, until one day it happened, some very serious visitors arrived.

It was just as John thought that it might happen, Pharisees from the Temple, arrived to check him out; and he was scathing in his comments to them.

"Produce fruit in keeping with repentance. The axe is already at the tree for all who do not produce fruit, in line with repentance," John thundered.

The men went away furious at everything that he had said and reported back to the chief priest on all that they had seen. It was not a coincidence that John was out in the desert, it was all in **The Mighty One's** plan. He was the man trusted by **The Mighty One**, for this big adventure to get the people ready for **The**

Promise of Heaven. He was God's ambassador fulfilling prophecy, to herald in the Lord Jesus Christ, mentioned by Malachi, not that it was something he comprehended himself.

The Heavenly Ones

In Heaven, **The Mighty One** smiled and beckoned to **The Breath**. "He is coming soon, and you must strengthen him, because Jesus starts his life's journey today, and he needs our touch upon him." **The Breath** smiled," What a journey he has had so far, and how wonderful to see him with the people." The two gazed down at the gathering of people who waited for John's disciples to baptize them. **The Mighty One** turned and looked at **The Breath.** "Anointing for service, this is what we must do for **The Beautiful One**. Prepare a full anointing, an anointing that will strengthen him; he has a long and harsh journey to travel, and this will make the difference. The enemy will ever be at his feet to trap him and cause him damage. We must fill him with power for all he has to do!"

The Mighty One smiled again, "John has been so obedient. He is a good man and his followers are sincere. I am sure that many will listen to him. He is a voice in the wilderness, declaring truth, and I believe that soon he will understand about the Messiah. He knows the people of the world must change their views and understand holiness."

The two stood and watched as the people talked to John as he baptized them. Their presence ensured that none of the enemies would put in an appearance. Not even Satan will come near to such mighty beings, but that was of course for later! Gradually in the distance, a figure started to emerge, it had started! **The Mighty One** smiled, **The Beautiful One** was arriving! It was happening, **The Promise of Heaven** was here!

The Chief Priest

Living in Jerusalem was hot and the atmosphere heavy, it did not make the chief priest feel comfortable. He sighed, it seemed everything for those in authority was fraught with difficulty. He contemplated making choices…decisions, he sighed again. While the thought of that young upstart out in the desert caused him to groan yet once more.

The chief priest's light often burnt long into the night as he wrestled with the "John problem." The worry was the people saw in John a kind of wretched compassion. They wanted to confide in him, tell him their problems and make a clean start. In fact, an odd word was often used "repentance." Hmm…humility, what did they know? The real problem was, John was upright and truthful. Some might have said even brazenly harsh. He made the people see that their lives had to be better. Women were singing his praises, stating that when a man was affected by the "John challenge" (as they were calling it), the men went back home better. While the bare fact of the matter was different, he thought.

The people lacked direction, most of them were lazy; they would prefer to get right with **The Mighty One,** (or so they thought,) by being splashed in the river, than coming to see the priests. He was seriously worried. The money given to the Temple was indeed going down. Not so much in the coffers these days.

Another concern troubled him too! It seemed that the people had a kind of "thinking for themselves attitude." If this was not dealt with quickly, it will undermine the authority of the Temple. All of this was very troubling for the high priest. To undermine the Temple's authority was a dangerous way to behave! If the Romans knew his thoughts, he shuddered, anything might happen. They might send more troops from Rome if they had suspicions about people mutinying against recognized authority. It was a bizarre situation!

He sighed, and then there was the devious old devil Herod. Why if he thought that there was any turmoil, anywhere…he smiled to himself, why worry about him? From all the whispers going around, he had taken his brother's wife for himself. What would the pious John make of all of that he pondered? Doubt if he knew about it as yet, it was hot off the press that snippet of news! Still, Herod was a nasty bit of work. Frowning at the problems confronting him, sitting at his desk, he struggled to decide what to do. His thoughts were dark tonight; he had to do something, make a decision and take action! The "John problem" had to be solved; although he had tried and sent some of his more senior colleagues out to the desert to determine what they should do. It was puzzling, nothing like this had happened before. Comforting himself with the knowledge that this problem was new, and in a few weeks, surely, John's popularity will have fizzled out.

All this repentance he muttered to himself, what have they got to feel sorry for in their mediocre lives? They all needed to get to work and let the professionals, his priests manage repentance... that was the real answer! A voice crying in the desert, he had heard of that somewhere, Elijah....oh, what a godless lot they all were!

John's Capture

John was at his lowest ebb; it was airless and bleak in prison. The smell around about was putrid. His eyes, long accustomed to the dark by now, could pick out some of his companions, laying very still in this gruesome place. The numbers had decreased since he arrived in the prison.

Not as many prisoners as there had been, some had been freed, something about a birthday gift. John was glad; this was a miserable place to find oneself languishing. He lay back, his feet shackled and recalled events of the past, leading up to his incarceration. So many had come out to the desert area and listened to his call for repentance. It had been a joy to see people coming all those miles, just to receive. Young and old searching for truth and finding it, in that desolate place.

It had seemed strange to John, to be doing this work, but after seeing his cousin, he understood. It was incredible, that from his family, well the Messiah had come! His cousin was the one that they had been waiting for over the years. Up until his arrival, they had baptized many seeking for God's forgiveness, and he was glad. It seemed, that gradually the population, had come to understand that they had to get right with **The Mighty One**.

It was amazing, as many came, sat and cried, realising their lives were in a total mess and they wanted to "get it right." They knew that they had been giving "lip service" to the ways of The **Mighty One**. Humility and repentance were not an option, John told them; it was a requirement, obedience was the way. It was wonderful how many people had listened and changed. Pensive John lay in this dark place and contemplated all the past events in his life. "The special day" as he called it, which was unforgettable, memories of that time, kept going around in his mind.

The day had started quite normally, with many people arriving, some sitting around just as they had done on many other days. Then, suddenly it happened, "He" turned up in the desert, to everyone's amazement. It was breath-taking, the speed of the events that occurred. However, it also appeared that once Jesus arrived everything went haywire, everything changed. Amazing things happened quickly, and the miraculous occurred. Words seemed unnecessary, redundant once His presence was there; it was all unbelievable.

John was taken aback when "He" arrived; it was just fantastic, this time with his cousin, "the incredible one!" Sitting, musing in the dark of the dungeon, with vermin trailing over his tired feet, he remembered every detail of that time. It had started out well, "the special day" that changed everything! Regularly, he had seen people come to be touched and baptized in the Jordan for repentance. His disciples encouraged the people and people were coming to talk, and things were going well. Suddenly on this day, it all changed, "He" was there! John's heart missed a beat as he thought of the occasion.

He suddenly saw him, walking up the path to meet him, his cousin Jesus. It was like a lightning bolt had come down and touched the world. Suddenly everything was alive! John had seen him, known him.... but not known him! Again, it had been so long, and John could not be sure that they had ever met, but somehow John knew who he was. It was not so much seeing him as to what happened next!

Into John's spirit came a mighty anointing that was so

extreme, it nearly took his breath away. He felt a blast of pure joy lifting him to a place that he had never dreamt existed. Understanding, in a moment, that this was a pivotal time in history, that all of Heaven and eternity waited with bated breath.

Once he had seen him, John stepped forward and greeted his cousin with a hug, asking him why he had come?

Jesus smiled at him and said, " I must be baptized too, to fulfil everything, as my Father requires."

John stood, listened to his cousin and replied. "I am not worthy to do this thing; I should be coming to you!" Jesus smiled at him.

"John it is a requirement."

Taking Jesus by the hand, John led him into the water of the Jordan and baptized him. It was an incredible moment; John knew he'd never forget. The heavens opened, and a voice cried out, and a dove descended. It was as if all eternity was poised at the anointing and moved with joy.

John was transfixed, everyone stood motionless; it was a moment of jubilation that overwhelmed everything. A wave of excitement seemed to hover over the Earth; it was as if it was the start of a revelation…that was going to go on…and on! Something wonderful had occurred. John's eye became wet, as he recalled the magnitude of the moment. It had happened quickly, over in a flash, but it had happened, and John knew it was a significant moment in history.

No, he did not understand it all, but it was **The Mighty One**, who had touched John! After that, Jesus disappeared, said goodbye and John saw him just once more. However, in John's heart something beautiful had occurred, he knew that God was doing something extraordinary and it was happening through Jesus!

John's disciples wanted to know about all that had happened, and suddenly out of John's mouth, it came!

"He is the lamb of God who takes away the sin of the world!" They did not quite understand all of this, but they knew that this had been a significant time and watched all that John did and copied him. They realized this was the Lord's man, the one that they had been waiting for and they were in awe! Some of them left John to search for Jesus.

After that, well more people came and not surprisingly so did others, who thought it was time to get rid of this noise in the desert! Early one morning, the soldiers came to lock John up in prison, and they did it before the crowds arrived. The priests had wanted to do this for a long time, and now it was a reality. They took him away quickly, and rushed him through town, to Herod's palace. They were fed up with him bleating on about themselves and causing unrest as they told Herod. They were convincing, and Herod himself wanted him silenced; he had said too much, for too long!

John ended up now in a dungeon where he had been for some time, waiting and waiting! At times he became frustrated, wondering at the events that had occurred. Most days he mused about all that had gone on, and what it had meant? Recalling the fantastic day when his cousin had arrived was etched into his mind. The event had resonated again and again in his mind and he pondered on so much, but today he questioned himself in this dreadful place.

Was he possibly the one that everyone was waiting for John

wondered? The prophetic words he had uttered were terrific. However, was He "The Messiah?" All these thoughts reverberated in his mind, and feeling low, he wanted some answers. He could not help himself; he needed to know for sure if Jesus was the one? After contemplating this over and over in his mind, he sent a message out secretly, asking the question. "Jesus, are you the one, that we had been waiting for all this time?" After a time, a reply came to him, a note from his disciples, telling him what Jesus was doing. When he heard what they had to say, John was thrilled. The miraculous was happening, the lame walked, the blind given their sight. It was tremendous, astounding! Jesus was the One they had been waiting for; prophecy fulfilled, the redeemer of the people had come to Earth!

Strange that he had come in that way, and beautiful. John's heart was at peace; he felt happy, at the thought of the Messiah, the Savior of the people coming to Earth. He had arrived in his lifetime, that was why the people needed to repent! He had come. The Messiah had arrived...prophesy revealed, excellent! Although being here in Herod's prison, wasn't a great place to celebrate. John knew that Herod was angry with him, as he had explicitly preached about his lifestyle. Highlighting Herod's relationship with his sister in law, stating it was wrong. Although, John still clung on to the hope that he would be freed, like the others? He sat with his hands together; he was at peace, and it was a good time to contemplate on **The Mighty One**, on how He had led him always, and to give Him thanks.

"Holy one I worship you with reverence and awe; thank you that I have seen the Redeemer of your people. I may go to you in peace now when the call comes: for prophecy has been revealed, in the world, the Messiah has come!"

He thought of his father and the angel all those years ago, how amazing, but that had been then, and now, he had seen something even more remarkable. **The Promise of Heaven** had come to Earth; the Messiah had touched his life, prophecy in the making, it was breath-taking! John lay quietly, even here in this dreadful place he could feel **The Mighty One's** joy. The air was putrid in the dungeons, and other prisoners lay all around him groaning, but he was at peace. Away from the dungeon things were happening in the Palace.

The guards had been talking about the banquet and the many people who had arrived to attend the celebration, which was lavish. It was to be a massive ceremony with many dignitaries attending, and plenty of entertainment. Music, dancers and someone had mentioned a dance of seven veils. John knew that Herod was always pursuing immoral opportunities and had done so all his life. Above the dungeon, a commotion, soldiers voices, seemed to get closer and closer. Footsteps outside the dungeon and chains rattled, as the cell door creaked open, what was about to occur? It was a group of guards, and they were calling out for him. He had been summoned to come forward. It would seem that he was not going to be freed. Walking next to the guards, he knew this was not going to be a good ending, but he was at peace. As he lay his head upon the block, the sword felt cold to his head. **The Mighty One** had a strange way of leading His children he thought!

The Angels

Meanwhile thirty years ago before John's death, events that were startling occurred. **The Mighty One's** plans were being activated. A tiny wonder that was to change history was about to enter the world. It was a unique and unimaginable event, which was why the angels had been summoned to meet together. They were ready to celebrate. "Come, Denton, we have to gather together, **The Mighty One** praise Him has called everyone. It's time to go!"

"Heaton this was planned, **The Beautiful One** has arrived, and we are going to greet His arrival; how amazing He is!"

"Yes, the time for **The Promise of Heaven** is now, let us go and greet him!" As the brother angels flew off to join the multitudes assembling, the excitement in Heaven was overwhelming. It was an event like no other, and all of the heavens knew that this was the start of a significant time in history. It was a celebration of joy, and possibly intrigue as all of the Heaven wondered where this adventure was to end. Ecstatic with praise, the angels were happy at the wonder in front of them!

The Hillside

The shepherds were resting, curled up on the hillside above Bethlehem, with the sheep around them nestled safe and secure. Galleon was watching; it was his responsibility tonight to be on guard to ensure the sheep had protection from the wolves prowling the hills. He blinked, somehow it seemed brighter, for although it was late in the season, the night was beautiful.

The area seemed to be bathed in an aura of light which appeared to bring peace and tranquillity all around the hillside. Galleon pulled his shawl around him, musing at the way he had become a shepherd. Remembering how the kids around him had derided him. Sheepshank and worse names had been thrown his way so often, shouted out crudely in the village, complaining too that he smelt. Galleon did not care his father had been a shepherd before he became ill and died, so he was proud to look after his mother and sisters in this way.

Sitting here, watching the flock, he thought he had the best job ever, how he loved the peace and security of the hills. Suddenly he was disturbed, something was happening! Startled by a sound, his heartbeat faster, as the sky grew even lighter and he thought he heard noises in the distance. Music, he thought, but he knew it could not be!

Suddenly he got to his feet; it was music! He could hear singing, it was so very gentle, his thoughts had conjured up an image, but he knew that it could not be…he was standing on a hillside; it was not possible!

He nudged Josiah fast asleep on the ground, in the ribs to wake him. "Jos can you hear something?" he whispered in his ear. Josiah sat up and then shook the others. They sat up bleary-eyed, afraid of the unknown as the sky was illuminated, lit up as voices pierced the air.

"It is a beautiful sound, and it seems to be getting louder," said Galleon. Gradually a crescendo of beautiful sound emanated everywhere echoing around them. As slowly and with such sweetness, angelic hosts filled the hillside and the whole sky. The heavenly beings brought a rapturous sound that was pure and sweet, a sound that swept around them, a beautiful oratory of praise that covered the countryside. It was the sound of Heaven, a sweetness that was like none other, a mist of joy, which crescendoed into a colourful expression of "love."

The music was angelic. A breath-taking mesmerising sound that wafted through the atmosphere transfixing the shepherds. They had never heard or seen the likes of this, and they stood transfixed. Standing, bathed in the splendour of the heavenly mellifluous sounds, reverberating all around them, the shepherds were mesmerised.

The angels were rejoicing, praising and giving thanks, singing, their joy echoed across the valley. There were thousands, resplendent, magnificent beings, lifting their arms as their voices echoed across the countryside with praise. The sheep lay still, peering out watching the fantastic spectacle around them with their protectors. It was as if the animals recognized that this was a piece of Heaven, arrived to invade Earth. They viewed it all silently watching with humility, as the picture unfolded.

The angelic voices elevated around them into a beautiful crescendo of harmony, lifting the spirits of the shepherds, who now knelt in rapture. The light surrounding the angel's presence lit up the sky. It was a surreal scene, an incredible rapturous performance from angelic hosts that sang with joy, which rebounded around the hillside.

The presence of thousands of heavenly hosts was like a prism of colours that sparkled, with an effervescent beauty unequalled. As an array of beautiful aura darted and danced around it was fantastic; this was the force of Heaven in rapturous praise, that seemed to go on and on and on. The sound was sensational and echoed over the hillside a beautiful melody that went on and on.

Suddenly, a most beautiful being gradually descended

before them. Standing before the shepherds now, this heavenly glistening individual, conveyed a strength that was almost tangible as he spoke.

"Do not be afraid; I bring you good news of great joy for all the people. Today in the town of David a Savior has been born; He is Christ the Lord. Today this will be a sign: You will find a babe wrapped in cloths and lying in a manger."

As the angel spoke, a vast chorus of other beings joined him and lifted their voices in a crescendo of praise that filled the sky. The shepherd could hear their words echoing all around them.

"Glory to God in the highest and on Earth peace to men on whom his favour rests." As they watched the sky adorned with divine beauty, the wave of sound that echoed around like a wave of joy, gradually disappeared as softly as it had arrived. The company of heavenly host had left the hillside, their praises drifting away just as gently as they had come. Swiftly the shepherds roused themselves, hugged each other and danced a kind of faltering jig in their happiness.

"We must go and tell everyone!" they said to each other. "Wait," said Galleon. "First we must go and worship the baby in the manger, as they told us to do."

"How amazing a Savior has been born for us, he must be the Messiah that was prophesied about down the ages; which is why the angels came to tell us the good news!" said Josiah. Making sure the sheep were safe, one of them stayed behind while the others hurried off.

The shepherds were excited and left the hillside enthusiastically, a talkative group, intent on finding the baby that the angels came to declare. It seems the men felt they were on a mission, ready to tell everyone their news.

Locally people despised them, although they could not fault the tireless way the men worked far away from their families. The continuous routine of walking the hills and living under the sky was the shepherd's way. The reality was that they always smelt of sheep and although they were happy, honest men, had few aspirations to do or be anything other than a shepherd.

To think that God had seen them as unique people, enough to declare His plan to them, heralding in the Messiah how amazing was that? The shepherds elated, hurried along, as they knew that they had a long walk into the village. On arrival, they looked about wondering just where they would find this significant baby.

"Look at the star, its shining right over the place we are making for, the manger, I know where that is," Josiah announced and led the troop onto the outskirts of the village to a cave adjacent to an Inn.

As they approached the area in the quietness of the night, they could hear the sound of animals quietly in the background. Creeping through the back area of an Inn they saw a lantern glowing through a stable door.

"Come on let's go in," said Josiah as they pushed open the door, unprepared for the scene in front of them. They were there inside, just like the angels had said, the baby and the mother. All of them instinctively bowed as they came in; they were overwhelmed by the scene. Soon they were kneeling and bowing, as they came in front of the mother holding a tiny wee baby in her arms. The men knew that this was the Messiah that the angels had spoken about and they were speechless. These were rough men, and they realized this was a particular moment in their lives. A young man stood next to the woman and talked to the shepherds.

"Hello, I am Joseph, and this is my wife Mary, how did you know we were here?"

Galleon looked up and said, "It was the angels, they came to see us up in the hills singing, they were terrific, we guard the sheep, and there were thousands of these angels, thousands! They told us we had to come down here and search to find the Messiah. This is just an incredible moment, a baby here? It is so lovely, so extraordinary, and we are so happy to be here."

Taking a breath, and looking about he continued, "So we brought you a little present".

At this, he nudged Josiah, who had a small lamb under his arm, which he put down in front of the mother. The mother Mary looked up and smiled and said, "Thank you for your kindness."

Pointing to the baby, she said, "This is Jesus, and he has just arrived, so it is wonderful that you have come to see him."

The shepherds moved closer to see the baby, as the cattle lowed quietly in the corner on the straw. It was warm inside the stable, and the lantern gave out a pleasant glow, framing the child asleep so peacefully.

Watching On

The angels, Denton and Heaton, stood outside and watched everything that was happening, while a mighty angel stood inside observing **The Beautiful One's** journey. "He looks so vulnerable, as a tiny baby," said Heaton.

"I am so glad that **The Mighty One** has some powerful angels around to keep away 'Blackened' and his thugs."

"Yes, I agree," said Denton.

"It does seem very strange that **The 'Beautiful One'** would opt to come to Earth, unprotected like this. He looks so vulnerable, and to be born as flesh, an awesome act for God's Son, everything will be different for Him, living this way."

Denton nodded, and Heaton said, "I know that **The Mighty One** praise Him has a plan. He always knows best, but the future will be very different for **The Beautiful One**. However, the three of them will have talked about everything, they always do. So, we must be prepared to be ready in any way he needs us in the world.

The Shepherd's Rejoice

The shepherds crept out of the stable, as they went, Galleon bent down and touched Mary on the arm.

"Thank you for letting us come here and see baby Jesus. He is going to be such a special man! I will never forget this moment!" He said and went out.

Outside the sky was lit up with one extraordinary bright star, which seemed to shed light on the whole area, illuminating it and framing it in a golden aura.

Heaton and Denton watched the shepherds go back up into the hills, their voices gradually getting fainter as they moved further away. The mighty angel stood in the same position motionless, near to the tiny bundle in the crib, as Joseph sat by his wife quietly speaking. The couple knew that this was a precious time and both curious as to what to expect next. Later, Mary sat and reflected, recollecting the visit from Gabriel months before, telling her she was to have a baby. It had all seemed strange at that time, added to which her meeting with Elizabeth who was about to have her miracle baby. It was for sure all so unusual, and what of the future, where was it all going to end, she wondered, gazing at her beautiful baby?

Requirements Fulfilled

Sitting here in the manger holding her precious baby, Mary knew that this was an extraordinary time. Baby Jesus was unique. She marvelled at everything and guessed that there was more to come! How strange that the shepherds had arrived telling them about angels in the sky singing, what was that all about she wondered? So much had happened, and now this beautiful baby was part of their lives, and she wondered about going home. Nevertheless, Bethlehem was quite lovely she thought, maybe Joseph could work for a while here, it was at least away from the stigma at home. People had whispered when she had walked past at home, embarrassing her; of course, they did not know the truth of all that had happened. She sighed, and furthermore they most probably wouldn't have believed any of it, she thought!

She settled the baby Jesus into the crib and went to talk with Joseph who was feeding the donkey. "Joseph I was wondering, we have to get Jesus circumcised, and go to the Temple in time, but do you think that we might find somewhere to live around here?" Joseph looked up; "Strange you should have mentioned about living around here Mary; I thought that myself. I will talk to a few people and find out our options." He smiled at her, "I am not at all keen on becoming the local celebrities, so we will move out from here quickly, those shepherds were so enthusiastic. I am not sure whom they would tell about Jesus?"

Mary laughed at him, "I agree, I cannot imagine anything worse! I will pack up our belongings, while you talk to the locals, and then we can go."

Joseph left later on and went off into the neighbourhood to find people to talk to and to consider what they could do. Mary organised the baby and put together their meagre belongings. Soon Joseph returned with some exciting news. It seems as if he'd met someone who lived about fifteen miles away. The exciting part of the news was that where this man lived there were three empty homes, a family had left on mass for Jerusalem. "Mary, this sounds as if we could set up home there, and I most probably could find work, what do you think?"

Mary agreed, and they set off, with Mary sitting on the donkey with the baby, excited about all that lay ahead of them. Weeks later, installed into their new home things were going well. Joseph had some work doing a little business in carpentry and Jesus had been circumcised. Time was going quickly, and it was nearly forty days since baby Jesus was born. It was now the time for the couple to make their way to the Temple in Jerusalem, for Mary's purification ritual, after childbirth.

Setting off one morning, they eventually arrived at the Temple, which was not as busy as it was at festival times. It was meaningful to bring the baby Jesus, and to bring their gift of thanksgiving for His birth. After speaking to the duty priest, he sent them on to Simeon who had come into the Temple that day prompted by the Holy Spirit. Simeon was a wise elder, steeped in the ways of God and knew the Laws of Moses.

The Mighty One loved him for his obedience and had spoken to this godly man a great deal. He had told Simeon that one day he would see the Messiah, and although Simeon did not quite know how this was to happen, he trusted God. When he saw Mary and Joseph somehow his spirit quickened, and he was full of joy, he knew with certainty that this was the day.

Joyfully he took the tiny child into his arms, he knew that this was the Messiah and started to praise God, saying:

"Sovereign Lord, as you have promised, you may now dismiss your servant in peace. For my eyes have seen your salvation, which you have prepared in the sight of all people, a light for a revelation to the Gentiles and glory to your people Israel."

Mary and Joseph marvelled at what was said. This godly man then prophesied over them all, telling them that this baby had a destiny that was huge. Many will love Him, but many would hate Him. This child was incredibly unique, not just a leader He was going to reveal the truth in all situations. Because of this, His life was holy, hidden in God. He was the Redeemer that all of Israel had been waiting for, the Messiah, **The Promise of Heaven**.

Turning to Mary, he continued by telling her that in the future, she would find anguish, in all that was going to unfold in this child's life. The couple amazed by his words thanked him and started to leave the Temple when an old lady called out to them. She was an aged woman, a prophetess, Anna, the daughter of Phanuel of the tribe of Asher.

Anna was a woman revered by all in the Temple and spoken about in hushed tones; she was different, holy somehow, and never left the Temple, worshipping night and day. Having such an intimate relationship with **The Mighty One**, she knew that something was about to happen, as He had already spoken to her about the coming of the Messiah.

On seeing the trio, she immediately knew and came alongside them, and prophesied over the baby, giving **The Mighty One** thanks. This prophetess was ecstatic. Her face beamed and her spirit soared as she realized that this tiny One was the future Messiah. Giving thanks to **The Mighty One**, for allowing her to see **The Promise of Heaven,** she talked with the parents and gazed down at the future Messiah. Here was the One they'd all been waiting for all these years, The Messiah!

Mary and Joseph were embarrassed by the flurry of activity in the Temple concerning their baby. The publicity was terrific, but they knew after hearing the prophetic words, they needed to keep a low profile. The family were quiet on their way back home; they had a lot to think about, considering the words prophesied by Anna and Simeon. On their return, they sat down and talked, happy although a little overwhelmed by all that had happened, and to a degree, wondering what all this meant for the future. Life was tranquil here, pleasant, both of them were contented, while Joseph was busy working. Not having any answers, they got on with just living and caring for each other, watching Jesus grow, and like many other young couples, enjoyed family life.

Time went by, and Jesus was nearly two years old by now, and one evening a strange thing happened. Impromptu, the couple had visitors call, important men that had come from different countries to visit them, wealthy visitors. These noisy impressive dignitaries arrived at their humble home, with many servants. They arrived with much pomp and ceremony, leaving their entourage outside while they came into see Mary and Joseph.

The couple wondered what the neighbours thought; it was bizarre, this humble couple, having wealthy Magi visiting them. The four men were gracious and told the couple that they had been following a phenomenon in the sky, that brought them into the area, to find their home. They had been on a mission; they said to come and worship a king, seeking him for quite some time. In fact, they had started out months ago.

It seems that when they had arrived, they had gone looking for this king in Jerusalem, at Herod's palace as they thought he would be there! When they arrived at the Palace, they asked Herod what he knew about this particular baby. He was not helpful, dismissive in fact, and they were about to continue their journey, intent on locating this mighty child until Herod stopped them.

It seems that he had found out from local temple people, that there had been a sort of prophecy given about Bethlehem years before. Once Herod had informed them of all of this, the Magi left Jerusalem to search Bethlehem, to investigate. It seems, that central to their search had been the star that they still followed, which had brought them right here, to the small house of Joseph and Mary. The couple were overwhelmed by their visit and listened intently to all they had to say.

It was then that Mary and Joseph introduced them to Jesus and showed them their little son. On seeing the child, they bowed low in homage and worship, then spoke together in languages that the couple did not understand while bowing low again. They then took out gifts for Him. It was all unbelievable, in many ways,

133

having visitors like this, who also had servants and gave out lavish gifts.

Mary and Joseph were taken aback, surprised, the gifts were ornate and beautiful, unique and surprising…gifts of gold, frankincense and myrrh. Bowing down again to the tiny baby, they worshipped the child and told Mary and Joseph how important His life was to the whole world.

Their excitement was palatable; they spoke in whispers telling Joseph and Mary that the future was going to be difficult and they must be careful because Jesus was to become such an extraordinary man. The little one smiled at them, good-natured and happy, Mary nursed him tightly wondering about the gifts and the men.

For Mary and Joseph, the whole visit was extreme, and after a short while, the men bowed and said goodbye. It was not a quiet send-off, with so many servants; it was quite spectacular, and the camels and horses were noisy on the cobblers. It was a fantastic visit, quite a spectacular event and Joseph and Mary were speechless. The Magi were smart, old men seeped in wisdom, who had come on an errand to see a mighty child that was to challenge the world.

Travelling back to their far countries, they were ecstatic, as they had found the King! Moreover, they chose to ignore Herod's plea to come back and tell him where the King was. They could smell cunning, but also, they had a dream that warned them to take a different route and to avoid this evil king.

Escape

After this visit, Joseph and Mary talked about what they should do. They were a little aghast at being thought particularly unusual, but it was pretty apparent, few people had significant dignitaries call on them from the East. They decided to leave it a while and see if many people mentioned it.

However, this was not to be, as that same night in a dream, an angel appeared to Joseph. He told him to get up and to get away immediately, to take his family to Egypt as they needed to escape, as danger was all around them. Herod was going to search for the child and kill him, and that they were to travel to Egypt and wait until **The Mighty One** told them to return.

He woke Mary, and they quickly packed their things, understanding that this was serious, and they needed to get away quickly. Because they sensed the danger, they had no alternative, but to escape, they started out for Egypt immediately. Travelling at night was a considerable risk, entailing a perilous journey, but there was no option.

The couple had left promptly, taking their precious child, and managed to travel a distance from Bethlehem before the sun came up. Running away, the Magi, and now this warning dream from an angel, about Herod seeking to kill their little boy. Perturbed, they had a considerable amount of questions in their minds, of all that they had encountered. Nevertheless, they were secure in the knowledge, that a higher being was watching over them. Traveling took some time, until they eventually arrived in Egypt; and although they were exhausted, they knew they were safe.

Once they arrived there was a lot to do, first they had to find a home and then build a life here, far from family and friends. They both understood it was necessary and for Joseph, an advantage, having an occupation that was adaptable.

While Mary took care of Jesus, Joseph started a business in wood, as a carpenter. Content that they were safe, far enough away from Herod's authority and with a deep trust in God, they often chatted about events, and the future. Not sure what lay ahead of them and their little one, but firm in the conviction it was always going to be eventful. Hidden away in a cupboard, lay the gold frankincense and myrrh, often a puzzle to both Mary and Joseph's mind, what did it all mean? Although confident in their future, that they'd eventually return home, they required patience. All of which was passing rapidly, and the little boy Jesus was growing up, surrounded by a happy family. **The Mighty One** looked down with pleasure, what a delight to see the story unfolding in this way, just as He had planned. **The Promise of Heaven** was well on the way, and He smiled at **The Breath**; the timing for everything was just right!

Some time passed, and one day **The Mighty One** spoke to Joseph in a dream, telling him that Herod was dead, and it was safe to return to their own country. Relieved that they were able to go back home, the couple were excited about the future. Once they had decided to go, they packed and said goodbye to friends. Conscious they need to return incognito, they decided to return to avoid Bethlehem. Because of this, they decided to go to a district in Galilee, into a town called Nazareth, familiar to both of them.

Herod, the Killer

The background of King Herod was impressive, a Roman citizen, born in 73 BC a man who was both of Jewish and Arabic descendants. He was a schemer who took advantage of the Roman political unrest to claw his way to the top. A powerful man, manipulative and in many ways a tyrant, bully and murderer. He strengthened Israel's position in the ancient world by increasing its commerce and turning it into a trading hub for Arabia and the East. Throughout his life, he was industrious. His massive building program included theatres, amphitheatres, ports, markets, and temples. Because of this he enforced massive taxes on the Jewish citizens to pay for it, who hated him.

The Senate in Rome nominated him King of Judaea and equipped him with an army. He became the unchallenged ruler of Judaea, a position he was to maintain for thirty-two years. Manipulative, he kept order in Israel by using secret police and tyrannical rule. Working well with the Roman conquerors, he knew how to get things done and was a skilled politician. By cunning, he won favour with those in power, granted a Tetrarch of Galilee and Perea by the Roman Emperor Augustus Caesar. A strategist, he constructed the city of Sepphoris and launched an ambitious building program, both in Jerusalem and the spectacular port city of Caesarea. He had many wives and children, always at the centre of political and family intrigues in his later years. He would definitely ensure his sons, would be as ruthless as he, seeped in blood!

To further solidify his power, he divorced his first wife, Doris, and married Mariamne. A brutal man who eventually killed his father-in-law, several of his ten wives, and two of his sons. He ignored the laws of **The Mighty One** and chose the favour of Rome over his people. Sitting quite disconcerted now, on the balcony looking out on the sweeping hills, he was angry.

He had a concern that someone was after his throne. Considering himself an influential leader, he harboured regrets at finding himself with all his responsibilities, even the comfort of the Palace had not given him the satisfaction and peace he craved.

He was mad, insane, and very determined to put down anyone who would usurp his power. A man whose very hands were seeped in blood, cunning and manipulative he was not going to allow anyone to steal his throne!

At present, he sat seething after entertaining some Magi, wealthy wise men who had called at his palace, looking for a king? They had not returned! Demanding local scholars to attend him while they were there, he sent a soldier to find someone who knew about local customs. Later that day, they arrived, and he asked the men if there was any information written down regarding a young king to be born.

As always, conniving and crafty he told them he was interested in local news, and ways to support the community! Were they aware of any historical facts that fitted all this, anything that could help? He planned to deal with this situation quickly and listened intently to anything they had to say.

The Pharisees, pontificated to a degree, about a foretelling, something that had been written hundreds of years ago, about Bethlehem. He had informed the ancient old men, the Magi, and sent them on their way, making sure they would come back and inform him of any king they found! It was all peculiar, a decidedly odd happening. While they were there, Herod was quite congenial, so he would bide his time and strike when he knew all! At least they were informed as to what the local prophecy had to say, so he would see what would happen. Although, the men seemed to be in a hurry and desired to continue their journey quickly, to find their destination. They obviously had influence, with a large entourage and had travelled a distance from the far east.

Herod was not interested in any of that; his great concern was that they were looking for a king. To begin with, when they arrived, he had not given them much attention; it was as they started to speak about a star, they had seen that he had listened well. Then they had babbled on about searching for a king, that was when he had become very attentive! Herod was a canny leader, and on hearing the word "king," his hackles were up.

As an influential leader, he was confident, but it was a time in the province when unrest was rearing its ugly head, in every area. Herod realized it was something he had to deal with, but to hear this news, from these "odd people," of a king, was a shock. As a cruel and thorough leader, he knew precisely how to silence the people from their mutterings. A few executions will always do the trick! It was one way of keeping the people in order, dispatch them, and be seen to deal swiftly with the thugs; who cared if they were guilty or not?

An angry and scheming man, that was Herod, although currently in his mind there was a dilemma. Uppermost in his thoughts was the wise men he had entertained. He had given them hospitality, asking them to come back when they had found the king! The problem was he had not heard back from them and time was marching on! How long should he wait, what should he do? Where were these old fogies and why hadn't they come straight back once they had found the king; it had been weeks now, and he had heard nothing from them? Annoyed with himself for not sending a soldier with them, he contemplated as to his next move? He paced the room, gulped down some wine and shouted to one of his servants.

His feet hurt, and he was angry, his servant ran to his side and bowed. The Magi had said it was a baby, why hadn't he thought of this sooner! He summoned his best horsemen, a cavalry group that would do his will and never count the cost. Fifty of these men will be able to put out all the opposition he decided, then gave orders. His soldiers made a great deal of noise as they galloped out of Herod's palace. It was dark and silent, as they rode on to Bethlehem to do Herod's will. It was a big task, and they rode quickly, keen to accomplish their master's bidding. On this night, exactly what they wanted to accomplish was a rather dark deed! The officer gave the command on arrival.... all babies under two, are to be put to death!

Satan's Cohorts

Satan and some of his cohorts had taken up residence in King Herod's court; it suited many of them. It was a dark and evil environment to encourage more evil. Herod especially a willing subject, hooked on pornography and with a sexual desire that was never satisfied, he was happy to act out any thought of evil put into his mind. They knew that **The Mighty One** had plans for this area, which was why Herod's court was useful.

Satan had told them all to be watchful, not to make any more mistakes. Somehow it seemed they had missed killing a baby, and he had been outraged when he found out. A problematic leader, was he going to be satisfied with what was happening now? They smirked together, after hearing Herod's plans it confirmed that their leader was going to be pleased with this outcome, just the sort of ugly evil deed he planned.

Yosef

In Bethlehem, a young family sat around a small table; the oil light flickered showing a crib with a small child in it. The woman sat holding a basket as she talked with her husband.

"We are a little way from people in the village, although I know you like it husband up in the hills, when Yosef gets older it may be difficult, we may need to move closer?" Her husband grunted and then said, "Well maybe, we can think about it...wait, what is that noise down the valley, soldiers? What are they doing around here, this time of night?"

He went outside to look. Way down in the valley he could see horses, soldiers and swords flashing in the moonlight interspersed with screams. Going swiftly back to their house, he cried.

"Run woman, I don't know what's happening, but take the baby to the hills!" The woman grabbed her shawl. Scooping the child up into her arms, she ran up into the hillside fearful, to find safe hiding. Looking for an area where she might find shelter took some while.

Her husband meanwhile grabbed a club, went in the

opposite direction, towards the village, to help his neighbours. Lights and screaming rent the night as soldiers went from house to house brandishing their swords.

On this evening, wicked things were happening in Bethlehem. Villagers awoken from their slumbers were dazed as soldiers went from house to house killing. Turmoil was everywhere, as a child's lifeless body was thrown to the ground, slaughtered by the soldiers. In another dwelling a woman lay dead, clutching her baby's lifeless body in the doorway.

In the street, a man was hacked to death as he tried to protect his family. Screams of pain rent the air as the community tried to intervene, and stop the soldiers, killing. Yosef's father, running down the hillside was appalled at the devastation in front of him, as he neared the village.

With the piece of wood still in his hand, he moved to the houses in front of him. A soldier saw him approaching, noting the club in the man's hand and full of his own importance, rode swiftly over.

Lifting up his sword he took one mighty blow at the man and killed him instantly. Observing the way, the man had come into the village, the soldier looked up the hillside, in that direction. Recognizing that there may be families up in this area, he started riding up towards habitation, looking for any family that could be in hiding in the hills!

Yosef's mother ran; she knew that something was terrifyingly wrong, hearing the screams from the village. Needing to escape and intent on protecting her baby, she ran further up the hillside as far as she could. Reaching a line of small trees, she raced to them, to find safety for her baby. Familiar with the area, she knew that there were some caves nearby that she had seen when grazing the goats.

She hurried until she came to the place where they had been, a rocky area strewn with caves. It was an area half hidden by small trees, within the rocky hillside. It had little caves hidden all around, but what she required was a place out of harm's way. A little cave high up that would be safe from danger. Quickly looking around, the woman noticed a recess high above, which would be difficult to reach.

Deciding that was what she required, she started to climb. Clambering up towards the small recess was painful, with the baby in her arms, and the sharp rocks around cutting into her feet.

After a couple of attempts, she managed to achieve the climb! Scrambling close to the crevice, and leaning over rocks, she put her hand inside, to see if there was enough space for a baby. Her hand scratched at the floor of the area, not big, but big enough she thought. Wrapping her shawl around Yosef, she pushed him neatly inside. Thank goodness she had fed him, and he was such a gentle little boy.

Climbing down she turned and heard a sound; a horseman was riding up the hillside.

She started to run in the opposite direction to the place she had hidden her baby. The soldier saw the woman and shouted at her. "Do you have children?" The woman continued to run as the soldier drew level with her. "Answer me"! He commanded, and as no reply was forthcoming, he used his sword and cut her down!

Herod's Palace

The soldiers arrived back, and their commander went in to see Herod. "All accomplished?" he asked. The commander smiled, "We accomplished everything successfully, and with few witnesses, as you asked, unfortunately, a few extra casualties as some parents held out and it was worse for them Sire."

"Good, good no one will be too concerned about a little place like that, and you got rid of all the problems, excellent. Away with you now, tomorrow is nearly upon us, and good riddance on the work of today, you have done well!"

Shimon

Shimon, a young woodsman, was up on the hillside above Bethlehem. Taking out his tools he started to attack his first tree. The sun was coming up over the hills; it was going to be a hot day.

All around him goats were grazing, and he wondered why some of them had not been milked by this time in the day. Everywhere was very silent he thought, even the birds didn't seem to be in this area much.

His recalled that his young wife had told him that a day ago, soldiers had ridden in and made some killings. It was her cousin who'd heard about it.

Anyway, it was of no concern, he was starting out in business, and he needed to hurry and get delivering the timber. Suddenly, he heard a whimpering, and there it was again, a sort of weak baby cry. He looked about him, was he imagining things? There was no one around, very quiet everywhere and then once again it started, a baby's cry. Putting his tools down he moved towards some rocks; it had been in this area he had heard the sound. He stood perplexed; maybe he hadn't heard anything? Having a new wife put all sorts of pressures on his life.

No, there it was again…a whimper and it came from up there, a few rocks away, a short distance, it was faint, but he had located the sound. It was a tiny cave, a little recess, on the rock face, and Shimon climbed to reach it. Stretching his arm, he put his hand into the hole; inside there was something wet and alive in there! He withdrew his arm, holding a bundle, well, well, well, a baby! The child was weak, hungry biting his fist and red from crying, and Shimon lay him on a flat stone and went to catch a goat. He didn't know much about children; although, his wife was pregnant, he certainly knew about hunger.

After finding a goat, he collected the milk in a small pouch that he carried. Lifting the child gently into his arms, he fed it with some milk. Finding a baby, a hungry baby at that, who would have thought?

Someone had hidden the child away, possibly to do with the nightmare the other night, he wondered? The baby drank, apparently, he'd not been fed for a long time consuming the milk quickly. He smiled at the bundle, glad that he had rescued the child, but whose was he?

Once he had finished his work, he went back down to the valley. Arriving in the village, he talked to an old friend, who told him about the events of the past days. Pondering as to what he should do, as the baby was an inconvenience, but he was also loathed to give him away. He'd already realized that a boy child was a valuable property for the future, especially for a woodsman. Nevertheless, it was not an option to take him home with him, as his young wife was pregnant. So, he decided to enlist the aid of an old couple who lived on their own in the village. Talking it over with them, he inquired if they would be willing to look after the child for him. The couple agreed to do so for a fee, mentioning that they had known the family and the baby was called Yosef.

It seems that the mother had required a little help after he was born, and they had been on hand. After events of the other night, it seemed that possibly the parents were killed. So, Shimon gave them money to look after the boy and said from time to time he would pop in to see how the baby fared. He also told them if an emergency arose, how to find him. Not realising that in a few years, five years in all, Yosef would be living with him when an outbreak of cholera struck the village. The pair were undoubtedly destined for a life of service together.

Evil rejoiced

The hordes of hell were beside themselves with glee; their master would be so proud of the seeds they had sown. Evil was going to dominate once more! Evil was triumphing! Satan was happy, and he laughed. It had been quite a good evening he decided; his cohorts had done well!

"A voice, weeping in Ramah, that won't be silent!"

The Gospel of Matthew records the event in this manner:

"Then Herod, when he saw that the wise men deceived him,

was exceedingly angry; and he sent forth and put to death all the male children who were in Bethlehem and all its districts, from two years old and under, according to the time which he had determined from the wise men.

Then was fulfilled what was spoken by Jeremiah the prophet, saying: "a voice was heard in Ramah, lamentation, weeping, and great mourning, Rachel weeping for her children, refusing to be comforted because they are no more."

The enemy of man laughed; he had achieved a good result through King Herod. Evil had won this battle, and they were going to win more in the future, gullible people who thought that they made decisions, how stupid they were?

Puppets, that's all people were, feed them temptation of any kind and they were hooked, and they thought that they had caused the devastation. Satan sneered, he was determined to win, and the next prize was really big!

The Crucifixion

The angels had been poised, watching the scene below them for a long time. It had started in an olive grove, with **The Beautiful One** on His knees talking to **The Mighty One**. It seemed to be a scene of agony and pain, a kind of wrestling with a question that wouldn't go away. The angels didn't understand the reason for the pain and anguish, or the conversation that went on between these beings. **The Breath** joined the pair and seemed to anoint **The Beautiful One** at this time giving him strength. All of Heaven had watched the daily communing of the Trinity, which was always quite upbeat. Today it was strewn with all kinds of sadness that was concerning, and the angels realized it was all to do with **The Promise of Heaven** and His lifestyle.

Under the trees, **The Beautiful One** in agony of spirit, knelt on the ground speaking to His Father. It seemed as if His whole demeanour was broken, racked with pain as He wrestled with something. His brow was damp with bloody sweat, which trailed down His arms as He rubbed His eyes. He was in deep sorrow almost torture, kneeling in humility, His words came in whispers.

His friends asleep quite nearby were oblivious to all of this. He had challenged them earlier, rousing them to pray, urging them, as this was a vital time for Him. They had nodded, although, in reality, it hadn't made a lot of difference, as they soon became comfortable and slept once again.

He knelt once more **The Beautiful One,** the Son of God, or as we know Him, **The Promise of Heaven.** Recognized in all of Heaven as **The Beautiful One**, He knelt communicating with His family. It was such a strange scene to see **The Beautiful One** waiting in this way. The angels, Denton and Heaton, watched with interest, so much was happening they didn't understand. The attitude of the two powerful beings in Heaven, listening to His voice, seemed restrained, strangely compassionate and sorrowful. It was as if they knew something deep and painful was about to happen. **The Breath** gently put out His hands and breathed a stream of power over **The Beautiful One**.

Sorrow was written over His face, and the angels wondered what it was all about, this deep sorrow. A powerful angel waited silently by the side of **The Beautiful One** in case he called out. All felt the intense pain that was coming from this man, in agony of spirit. Keeling half hidden by the olive trees, He agonised in thoughts and prayer.

"Father if it is possible, take this cup from me, but not my will but yours!" **The Beautiful One** whispered, with grief etched on His face. **The Mighty One** reached down again, near **The Beautiful One** and lightly touched His shoulder.

In the distance, noises, perceptible in the night air, something was happening that sounded ominous. It started to come closer, feet could be heard marching and then excited voices. Jesus went over to the disciples and woke them. "Wake up My friends; My time has come, be brave!" In a few seconds, a mob burst into sight, brandishing all sorts of weapons, threateningly antagonistic. All of them were decidedly out for a fight, and right at the head of them was the disciple, Judas. He moved toward Jesus, **The Beautiful One**, and put a kiss on His cheek. Jesus looked at him, "You greet me with a kiss Judas?" and moved forward towards the mob, "Why do you come with weapons, I have none? You could have arrested me in the Temple at any time."

The men grabbed **The Beautiful One**, and the disciples angered, started to retaliate and fight. Peter tried to step in front of Jesus to protect Him and reached out assaulted a man by cutting off His right ear. It was Malchus that Peter had attacked, one of the servants of the High Priest, Caiaphas.

The Beautiful One turned to His friends and told them that this wasn't the way to do things. He then lay His hand upon Malchus and healed him. The disciples' fearful now, ran in all directions, to escape being captured by the mob and left Jesus on His own.

Quietly, **The Beautiful One** allowed Himself to be taken away by this group of marauders. The angels were aghast, watching the whole scene with despair, concerned as to how it was to end. They trusted **The Mighty One** but were appalled at the abuse inflicted upon **The Beautiful One**. Conscious that He was in a vulnerable position, they wondered as to what destiny awaited Him? Aware that one word from **The Mighty One** and the whole force of Heaven would come to rescue Him. But it was not to be!

It was a night of horror and darkness that the angels viewed, silently. Observing all that was happening, they agonised as **The Beautiful One** was led away. Beaten, mocked, while his skin was torn from Him, as soldiers cheered, and dressed Him as a king, mocking Him, they then pushed a crown of thorns on His head.

Aghast at everything, the heavenly beings watched as priests used their powers to mock and taunt **The Beautiful One** with false witnesses accusing Him. It was a harrowing sight and the angels were horrified. The sight of evil in so many guises, being used against Him appalled them. Stunned, they viewed the priests rushing Him across the city to the Roman governor to stand on trial. The humiliation which He endured, shocked them. Obediently a powerful angel, waited, still by His side, unseen from human eyes, ready to support Him if He cried out!

The immense power and hatred as the crowd shrieked abuse, yelling for His death was evil. It was as if an unseen force allowed the people to forget all of the miracles He had done and seek His demise. The two angels viewed it all with deep sorrow, as the pronouncement was given to put Him to death. Later as **The Beautiful One** took the dreadful walk out of Jerusalem, they were there watching His agony. The way He struggled with the weight of the wood on His back, as people screamed abuse at Him.

Another young man was eventually instructed to carry it; the whole sight was unforgettable!

The angels were experienced, witnessing so much down the ages, but this was appalling. They wondered as to what was to happen next, why had it been allowed? Knowing as they did **The Mighty One's** power, they didn't understand why **The Beautiful One** had to experience all of this.

Although, as Denton reminded Heaton, **The Mighty One** always has a plan; He knows what to do; it will work out right! Their duty was clear and with the angel, Michael, they stood in the valley of death as a scene of horror was enacted out in front of them! A stake in the ground, soldiers, swords and the vile abuse of words, until death, reared its head, this was a dark place to be, for anyone.

Quickly, the soldiers thrust **The Beautiful One** to the ground. Then the sound of a mallet crashing down on His body was heard, which was agonising to watch.

Thick brutal nails were thrushed cruelly through His feet and hands as the mallet hammered Him to the wood, although not a bone was broken, as prophesy had declared. Abused, with blood pouring down over His body on to the ground, lay the Savior of the world, **The Promise of Heaven**. The angels watched the agonising scene in horror, at the depth of pain inflicted upon this mighty powerful man, **The Beautiful One**; who could have summoned angels to take Him away from here!

It was a scene of silent agony, the suffering of colossal depth, on a man innocent and holy. Nails protruded through His feet and hands, it was a scene incredible and terrifying seeing **The Beautiful One** hanging there on that wood. The sinless One, who had all power, of his free will, silently giving up His life, such a terrifying picture of sacrifice that was agonising to watch.

All of the supernatural watched the events, and the angels in Heaven waited, hoping that He would call out for help, they were ready to go...and do anything! Then they heard His cry. "My God, my God, why have you forsaken me?" at this, His head dropped down, as He cried out.

"Father into your hands I commend My spirit!"

Later a soldier wanting to know if He was dead, stabbed His side, where blood and water flowed out from Him! Lightening lit the sky, as thunder rent the heavens and over the world a grief that seemed to bring its own silence.

It was the sin of the whole world that coursed down on this man, hanging so still on the cross. This was a victory, that none had anticipated! The arena of the world was to be touched by the death of this sinless one, a revolution of holiness, which reached down to free the Earth, through His sacrifice. His precious holy blood still flowed, coursed down, as His supernatural power, that death could not hold back, swept over the world. It was a time like no other, as a revelation of hope was revealed for all humanity, and the power of the enemy was finally broken. Consequently, as His body broken, lay still, hanging now in death, **The Mighty One** shook the Earth! Graves awoke, bringing out their inhabitants. Frightening for many as the dead came to life. It was an occasion of astonishing magnitude and depth causing the atmosphere to reel from its strength. Heaton spoke in an unbelievable tone, so contrary to his usual buoyant self and whispered.

"It's finished, over, how could this be? His breath has gone, His face, I can't see it. Denton fly nearer!"

"Come away, Heaton this is no place for us, we are not powerful enough, but Michael watches on."

"Yes, he will always be in place, he is not like us, he will always be ready to do **The Mighty One**'s 'praise him', commands," said Heaton.

"But, **The Beautiful One**, the Christ, gave up His life, it wasn't taken from Him; He gave it all up. Why he could have saved Himself, called for an angelic brigade, but He gave it up, that is amazing!" said Denton. "He came in human form, never sinned and gave His life for all," said Heaton.

The angels, Denton and Heaton, were travelling to Heaven for a new assignment, but they were deep in conversation.

The Mighty One praise Him, has allowed this to be so He will have a plan," said Heaton.

I know, but I never thought '**The 'Beautiful One'** would give up, I felt so sure He would call us to help Him," said Denton.

"For sure, if He had done so, there were millions of us ready to fly to His aid," said Heaton.

The angels flew on, both musing about the events and the way things were going to work out, quite soon they were passing the Temple area.

"Do you remember, right back in the beginning, the garden and the promise?

The Mighty One 'praise Him' stated, that His heel would bruise the serpents head?" said Denton breaking the silence.

"Yes, but I never understood it, this must be how it was going to finish, but I never thought it would end like this!"

"All I know is **The Mighty One**, 'praise Him', always has a plan, just like the other times, He always has a plan!" said Heaton.

The angels were flying over the city and could see something spectacular was happening in the Temple. Many priests were hurrying along all in the same direction, making their way to the building.

"What is happening there, all those priests rushing to the Temple?" said Denton?

"I'm not sure, but on this day, anything could happen," replied Heaton.

Neither of the angels spoke, understanding nothing happens without the knowledge of **The Mighty One**. They also realized that this was a sacred time in history when anything could occur.

Further along, on their journey to Heaven, they encountered other strange things. Tombs had opened as an earthquake touched the city. People in grave clothes came alive, as the powerful supernatural blood of '**The Beautiful One** ' reached down and freed them. The world was in turmoil, and the angels flew back, wondering about so much, although they had few answers.

In Heaven, silence seemed to be everywhere as the angels stood transfixed looking to the Throne. **The Mighty One** sat motionless, separated from **The Beautiful One**. It was a time of grief and pain that was excruciating, watching on. Around the Throne in Heaven, the seraphim's encircled it, giving praise to **The Mighty One** and all the created beings, did the same. It wasn't a script rehearsed; it was a definite time when all creation waited with bated breath, watching to see events unfold. **The Beautiful One,** beaten and scourged, with such agonising pain that reached Heaven, leaving all creatures transfixed by His agony.

It escalated into a time of anguish, as **The Beautiful One** was nailed to the cross, and **The Mighty One** reached down to Him. It was as a triune Godhead the three existed, and as one felt the pain, it also engulfed the others. It was as if **The Mighty One** Himself was nailed to the cross, as **The Beautiful One** had said, 'the Father and I are One!'

It was a battle only **The Beautiful One** could achieve. Born into the world, he had embraced flesh and declared His uniqueness with **The Mighty One**. His intention and aim had always been to free people from sin, and to accomplish this, He gave up His life, as a sacrifice. He had won, through His own sinless perfection, and claimed victory over Satan, now disarmed. **The Promise of Heaven** had won the victory, and the enemy's rights were broken over the world.

Exposed, hanging on the cross with the weight of the sin of the whole world descending onto His shoulders. He had accomplished all. It was a tremendous task, but He did it! He gave up His sinless perfect life for others and paid the price for their sin. The Lamb of God, the Savior of the world.

The Mighty One aware of all, realized that the final part of the plan for **The Promise of Heaven** was being enacted, victory was won at Calvary, although the enemy had to realize this fact!

The Enemy Surrounds

All of Heaven watched, as "Blackened" descended, surrounded by his pack of supernatural angels, ready for wickedness. Straight to the cross they came, poised ready to strike...laughing, shouting to his cohorts to see the demise of **'The Beautiful One.'** Gradually the air was punctuated with screams of delight as Blackened, confident that he had won the battle, punched the air with taunts.

Unheard of by human understanding, a mob of evil rejoiced. Confidently a vast, dark evil horde flew around the area in jubilation, "We have won, " cried Wap, flapping his gruesome arm at the cross, as his tortuous features opened up revealing a cavernous mouth. Sneering, he spat out at the solitary figure hanging so still. Satan's hordes were all around, dark animated and demonic, excited, thinking it was victory.

Evil, punctuating the atmosphere with profanities, deaf to the humans watching, roared with deep cavernous laughter. It echoed, on and on, straight from the pit of hell, yells of mirth!

"We have won," screamed Blackened.

"The battle is ours, and the world is ours, we are the victors!" he shrieked again, as the cackle from voices of dark beings, amassed around him. The angel Michael stood waiting, as the hordes of dark beings encircled the cross, and spat in his direction. They dared not touch him but flew nearby. He never moved, just stood and waited, this magnificent warring angel, intent on doing His Master's bidding, never flinched. The repercussions of all that was happening, were not understood, as yet by the spirit world of darkness, or for that matter all of Heaven, that was for later!

The angels also watched, and viewed the scene with horror, as hordes of evil, always in pursuit of **The Beautiful One**, flew into action. Leaping, shouting, they performed a triumphant march of darkness over all. The heavens transfixed, saw the evil and was aghast. Looking on with bated breath, the heavenly community wondered what was to happen next? The act of a sinless Savior, given for the love of humanity, such love that was far-reaching and beautiful, planned in Heaven. Hung on a wooden gibbet, some called a cross, who would have imagined that such a thing could happen?

Not understood by the enemy, who underestimated the power and planning of **The Mighty One**. Who built a bridge from Heaven to Earth. Designed through **The Promise of Heaven**, **The Beautiful One** the Lord Jesus Christ. The power of sin had been broken! This stupendous act of love, witnessed by the silent world of the supernatural, was a sacrificial death of salvation. Put to death on an old broken tree, this incredible man, the Savior of the world, had outsmarted the enemy of all. Not realized as yet, by the enemy who was defeated, that his rights to keep people in death was forever finished. This was a war that had been won on the cross, a gift given with such humility and love, that it was undoubtedly breath-taking. This gesture of love to all was going to be a shock to the forces of darkness, once they realized what had happened!

Just a Broken Man and a Tree

So many events happened before the crucifixion, and on a small farm early one morning the Romans were calling to get things ready! It was a noisy deputation that clattered up to Shimon's farm on business, an incident that was to change the life of one man. It was the clanging of steel that woke Yosef out of his slumbers. The dawn wasn't even up, and in the courtyard, he could hear the sound of voices and horses. Suddenly, there was a noise, and he listened as his name was shouted out. He moved from his straw bed towards the courtyard wondering at the commotion.

"Yosef, you lazy son of a dog why aren't you up and working?" It was Shimon his owner glowering at him over a doorway. Standing nearby was a Roman officer resplendent in his uniform with guards, who were also scowling.

Without a glance in Yosef's direction, he spoke to Shimon in a thick heavy Italian accent. "Do not be late with the supplies, it is a busy day, and all will have to be in place in good order, don't forget, everything in place! On arrival, I will be at the gatehouse, so come and find me at once. Once you finish and all is completed to my satisfaction, I will pay you. Everything must be correct, all deliveries on time. Mistakes will not be tolerated, by order of the commander, we have important people around, so see that you arrive early, is that all clear?"

Not waiting for a reply. The officer turned, mounted up and went off with his two companions in the direction of Jerusalem. Yosef stood and watched; he was about thirty-three-years-old, dirty from living outside as he slept in an outhouse near to the cows. Shimon owned him, and he worked on the fields, or wherever his master wanted him to work. He was an orphan left in a cave when Herod had sent troops to kill off the babies. It seems his mother had hidden him and then was killed; no one knew quite what had happened. Shimon, a young man at that time, was working as a woodsman when he had heard him crying and rescued him. Afterwards, a family had taken him temporarily and looked after him as a baby for Shimon. Finding him in this way when his parents had died, had been a gift to Shimon, it meant he now belonged to him. Unfortunately, when he was about five-years-old, an outbreak of cholera was catastrophic. The guardians had died from the disease, leaving him destitute, and Shimon collected him and brought him back here to live. His wife was not pleased and made it quite clear he was not living in the house, and that he must live out with the animals. It had been disastrous for a small child, but he had adapted to his circumstances over the years. Sadly, life's harshness did not change for Yosef, as everyone shunned him calling him names, thinking that there was a jink on him with all this bad luck! He was a servant, the lowest of the low, given food on the understanding he worked.

For years now Yosef had worked like this, although not easy, he had never known a different lifestyle. Moreover, Shimon's household was not a happy one, and Yosef often heard shouting, although he was outside with the animals. It was a sad situation as Shimon's children were jealous of any attention given to Yosef and had made their father keep "the dirt" as they called him, virtually away from the family

As a servant, Yosef was a good worker, but always silent around people, often seeming to have a better rapport with animals. That was not a surprise, as he had spent more time with animals, than with people. No-one wanted a loser and having no family, wasn't just a disadvantage it made a person vulnerable. As a servant he was owned by Shimon, so he had no rights, and must do whatever his master asked of him!

Today Shimon stood out in the yard, shouting out orders to him, to get the donkey and get out to work, they needed to fell a tree. It seemed the Romans needed more wood for their work, and they had come out to order it from Shimon.

Yosef went and harnessed the donkey, and Shimon handed

him a small axe, reminding him to bring it straight back as it was valuable. The young man started out towards the pathway that led to the woods that had the sort of tree required. It was necessary to find the right size of tree to cut down, as the Romans were no fools, and it must be a certain size to take to the city. In this area, it was silent, peaceful and refreshing especially as it was the early part of the day. With the sun not yet up, he continued to search for the right tree and trudged up the hill to get to the other side of the wood. In a short amount of time, he reached the area he wanted, as the sun gradually began to make an appearance on the horizon.

Yosef patted the donkey by his side. "Not so far now old friend, we are nearly there!" Climbing down the other side of the hill, the team neared the trees that Yosef wanted to locate. The area was not a wood as such, more a cluster of trees. Although as he got closer, it sounded as if some birds had got there before him. Yosef heard them singing as they approached; he liked hearing the birds sing, it reminded him of the past. Once upon a time, his mother had sung like that, soft and sweetly he thought, although he wasn't completely sure he remembered.

Amongst the trees now, he gazed around for a tree that was the size he required. The Roman had made it clear what they wanted, stating it was a special event. He wandered around the area for quite some time, to make his final choice. Tucked away in a clearing, he found just what he was looking for, a straight tree that had a beautiful bark and it seemed as if this could be the one, as it was not too large. He checked again around him, to see if he had selected the best possible tree and set his axe to work. The tree was not too large, so it was quite easy to fell, and seemed to be the right size for what Shimon said the Romans required. The whole thing did not take too long, and Yosef was pleased with his work.

He then trimmed off all the branches and leaves to his satisfaction, to make it easier to transport. Sitting down on it for a few minutes to get his breath back, he rubbed his hands up and down the side of it feeling the bark. Curious as to what the Romans wanted it for, but also extremely hungry; he must keep going he thought and return quickly.

Shimon although brusk, might leave dates on the table for him by the time he got back so that he could eat. It was not an easy task getting the tree tied up, enabling it to be pulled by his donkey, but at last, he had done it, and they were on their way. It was a scramble up the hillside, and Yosef had to help pull the load up, so that by the time he descended to the other side, he was sweating. The sun was waking up now, and he could feel a little of its warmth on his back, as they came in sight of the yard. Once the load was in the courtyard, Shimon met him, coming out of the house. Motioning Yosef to come over and talk to him, he walked to the barn.

"Eat!" Shimon said pointing to the dates. "Get some of that grime off, we go to the city right now!" and walked into the house. Yosef stuffed some dates in his mouth and went to the water trough, dipping his face in the cold water, he rubbed himself. With the back of his hand, he wiped his face and looked down at his legs with the streaks of muck on them. Using a pitcher, he washed his legs and arms hoping that his boss would accept his appearance. Shimon came out of the barn and shouted to one of his lads about various chores. Coming close to Yosef, he pointed to the well and a pitcher of water.

"Your head man, use the water on your head!" he said and with that lifted up a pitcher of water and poured it quickly over Yosef's head. "I will not have the Romans think all of us sleep in a pig sty!" He said with a grin, as Yosef tussled his wet hair.

"Load it up securely." He said pointing to the cart in the yard. Soon the tree was loaded safely, the donkey secured, and the two men set out towards Jerusalem.

Yosef was curious; first he never had been to Jerusalem as no one had ever taken him there. Shimon and possibly the family did not want a "dirt hand" as they called him, travelling with them. Yosef a rough man, with no schooling, was barely able to read or write. He was a nobody, and no one cared, and why should they care about a nobody? Times were hard; it was enough for people to pay their taxes and survive!

Many years ago, an old woman had taken pity on him, and tried to teach him some necessary skills. It was a kind act, but it was not consistent, and as he'd always slept rough, no one bothered about helping him further. Which meant that he had no schooling or social skills, except for writing his name; this was all that Yosef could do.

Shimon owned a small family farmstead and used his boys for working in the fields. Although with Passover and the Romans all around, he was always apprehensive and more so at this time. At present, he did not want his boys being noticed too much by the Romans, as they had a habit of taking what wasn't theirs, and healthy young men were always useful to them.

Shimon knew the journey was going to be quite tedious, he sighed, a long trip, although the pay was the incentive. It was quite a climb up the hills pulling the cart. Suddenly, rounding a corner, a fantastic sight met their eyes. Down in the valley, Jerusalem lay, and there in the centre was the Temple, gleaming, breath-taking. Yosef was excited; this was wonderful, and he could not wait to see what happened in the city.

They stopped after a time in a field, gazing at the view again, to give the donkey a short rest and then continued downwards. It took time to travel, but once they were near, Shimon asked someone for directions. It was noisy with dust everywhere, as many soldiers marched along the road. Officers on horseback kicked up debris, making it even worse. It was also hot, making this whole journey a confusing melee of people and animals. Yosef overwhelmed with the noise, travellers and the entire scene, was surprised at everything. People had come in from everywhere to celebrate the Passover. Jerusalem was a fantastic sight of noise and bustle. Arriving on the outskirts of the city, the two men made their way to the area they needed to be at, which was a little quieter. This area was busy with soldiers, continually moving around shouting orders. After another long walk, they arrived at their destination. Leaving Yosef by the roadside, Shimon went to ask for directions from the officer in charge at the gatehouse.

Yosef thirsty, wanted a drink, but he knew that he must wait with the load until his boss came back, and told him what to do. He spoke to the donkey and patted his neck. "Not too long to go old friend and you will get a drink!" He whispered as the donkey nuzzled up to Yosef.

Shimon came back relatively soon, but it was not good news, they still had to wait for the officer to send someone down to them, to show them where to put the timber. It had been a long walk, so Yosef sat down and waited with Shimon on some rocks nearby. The area was some way out from the city, with a lot of large boulders around, leading to a couple of long pathways. Away in the distance, they could see a sizeable area, which had high substantial wooden steaks erected. There were soldiers around

163

about everywhere, but not as many as they had seen earlier.

After a while Yosef wandered further in, to see what was on the other side and then going behind a rock, relieved himself. After looking around, he sauntered back to Shimon, to see what was happening. As he returned, an unusual looking soldier came to Shimon and beckoned him, at the same time shouting commands to other soldiers nearby.

"Take it through to the area down there!" he said, pointing to the load. The two men turned the load around and started in the direction that they had been directed to take the load. It did not travel easy as the area was rough and rocky. In fact, the officer shouted to some soldiers to assist them. Meekly the soldiers supported them, by pulling the tree along the track to the area that Yosef had seen earlier.

The two men followed with the officer, who indicated a spot where Shimon was to unload. "Here!" he shouted. "Put it in here and start digging the hole!" he pointed to Yosef. The two manhandled the tree from off from the cart and dragged it to the place the officer indicated. Two holes were already apparent in the same area, newly dug out. It seemed that the hole that they had to make, was to go between the two others. The officer shouted again.

"Dig the hole there, deep enough and get it right!" The ground was hard, dry and unyielding to the implements. It took an age to try and get a semblance of a hole, with the two men working together. Yosef was surprised; he'd never known Shimon to work with him in this way, apparently getting paid was the incentive he thought. It was a hard job and took time as the ground was hard and dry, but gradually they managed to break through and make a semblance of a hole. At the same time, soldiers came by pushing two criminals along; one sounded a foreigner, who shouted obscenities at the soldiers. The soldiers were angry, and not averse to punching the men and cursing them.

Soon the two men were laid on the ground, on wooden steaks, either side of where Yosef and Shimon are digging. Everything soon became apparent, as to why they were here. Yosef understood clearly as to what the tree was to be used for now and shuddered. Looking over at the men nailed to the steaks in the ground was a big distraction. While by this time the two victims let out spine-chilling screams. It became a disturbance that neither of the men appreciated, and Yosef heard Shimon swear under his breath, something about the Romans. It indeed wasn't the easiest way to earn a living, pretty dirty money, gained at others expense!

After a few hours, the job was nearing completion. Above them, the two men strung up, kept up a torrent of continued moaning and swearing. Shimon, trying to ignore the obvious distraction, walked over to the tree to check the size of its slim trunk. He measured the depth of the hole required, as it had to be entirely correct to get paid. Finding it was all in order, they manhandled it next to the other crosses. Once they had done this, they waited for direction from the soldiers or the officer in charge. By now Yosef was very thirsty, and he knew that they needed to water the donkey.

He asked Shimon if he knew where they could find water. Shimon told Yosef to take the donkey down to where the road forked. The soldiers tethered other animals there, and it was near to the water trough. Yosef took the donkey and wandered down the track to get water and gazed into the distance.

Far away, he could see a significant commotion, coming

down in his direction. A crowd coming from the city of Jerusalem, more trouble he thought. It was a massive crowd that seemed to be getting closer, a considerable heaving mass of people coming towards where he stood. Yosef started to hurry; he did not want to have anything to do with the Romans.

Eventually, he reached the area where the animals were, and found the trough that the donkey could have a drink from, which was quite near to the guard post. He also looked around for water for himself, a pitcher or anything. Seeing nothing available, he bent down and scooped up a handful of water from the animal's trough and put it to his lips. He was not proud of drinking in this way. The liquid felt fantastic after being so thirsty. Living rough over the years had taught him to make the most of every opportunity. He had been so parched, consequently any liquid would have been a welcome relief.

When he eventually lifted up his head from the trough, the group of people grew much closer, while the noise of their shouting was disturbing. Fairly soon, they came around the last corner into full view. There were soldiers and a crowd of noisy people shouting and yelling. At the head of the group was a big man carrying a large crossbar of wood. Right behind him, came a tall man struggling to walk. The man's clothing was streaked with blood, and he had blood all over His face too.

The crowd was quite dense pushing each other to get a good view of the prisoner, as they gradually drew closer and closer to Yosef. He could see that the man with blood on His face also had a crown of dark thorns, pushed down on His head, and every time he moved blood ran down his face. It was Him they were jeering!

166

Quite quickly, the man appeared, just a short distance away with the crowd still berating him. As He walked closer to Yosef, the noise became tremendously loud and Yosef thought how tired and in pain He looked. Suddenly, He was there next to Yosef, with the mob just a short way behind Him. It was all very close to where the trough stood, in fact, right past where Yosef was standing! All of a sudden, the man fell, as His feet gave way from under Him. It happened quickly, extremely close to where Yosef was. As He lay on the ground, Yosef bent down into the animal trough, and swiftly scooped up some water and put it on the brow of the bloodied man lying under his feet.

The man got up and with His eyes on Yosef whispered His thanks, so quietly no one could hear. The soldiers shouted at Yosef to get away from Him, and the whole crowd shouted obscenities! Quickly the crowd continued on to where Yosef had left Shimon, the area where they had been working. Realising that his donkey had enough to drink, Yosef followed behind the massive crowd, at a distance, to return to Shimon. With so many questions in his mind…*Who was this man with such a sereneness about Him, and what was the crowd doing with Him?* His mind was confused, and he just wanted to get away from this place?

Yosef took the donkey and stood behind the crowd of people watching from a distance, at the scene in front of them. He could see Shimon, the soldiers and the bloodied prisoner. They were all grouped around the area that he had been working, and it was not a pleasant scene!

On arrival, the large man carrying part of the cross lay it down on the ground and walked away. The soldiers meanwhile manhandled the prisoner, roughly pushing Him to the ground, on to the wooden beam. The people, driven a way back from the scene by the guards, stood watching from a distance. Some were from the Temple, who were also standing surveying the scene. Yosef only guessed that they were people from the Temple, because of their clothes. At one time, some had come to Shimon's place, demanding he pay the Temple taxes. Although Yosef was not at all sure as to what happened, Shimon was not keen on paying lip service to anyone. But Yosef knew what the Temple people looked like, pious self-serving men, with a miserable demeanour.

As he moved forward through the people, he tied up the donkey to some rocks, and made his way to the side of Shimon, only to find that he was fuming! It seemed that a little Roman soldier had come to him and told him in no uncertain terms, that his services were not required! That an officer in charge, would go over and talk to him when he had time! Shimon was even more furious by now, with the work finished he expected to be paid for his services immediately. Around about them the crowd started to move away from the area, walking back towards Jerusalem. It seemed that their enthusiasm had died down, happy no doubt that they had seen the prisoner get what they thought he deserved!

Around about a group of women were to one side of the clearing watching, some sitting on boulders nearby weeping. In the area, the air was still, silent and uncomfortable with no breeze to give relief. All eyes were on the soldier's movements, as they manhandled the prisoner. He lay silent, as they hammered strong long nails into his feet. Hearing the resounding thud, at every strike of the mallet made Yosef shudder.

They had used the tree that Yosef had cut down; his heart felt grieved, why did he have to be a part in all of this? It was unreal that a human being would have so much pain inflicted on him and yet stay so silent!

The prisoner's body was now attached to the wood, as a steady stream of blood poured down. Incredibly the man still uttered not a word. In the background, weeping could be heard, from the women who were watching as the soldiers spread His arms, while another soldier hammered nails straight through His hands. The sound of the mallet once more crashing down on the wood, was terrifying in the stillness. Sobs and gasps heard distinctly all about, but not a sound from the man on the cross. Leaving Him on the ground, with blood pouring out from His wounds until the area became crimson, the soldiers prepared to lift the cross up. Yosef felt sure that this man was innocent, although he knew nothing about Him; he had seen it in His eyes. It was a dreadful barbaric scene, that affected Yosef with a great deal of sadness. Who was this man that everyone had followed, goading Him with obscenities? He did not have any answers and was intrigued and sad. Something inside this big burly man they called "the dirt" felt pity for this man who seemed helpless. What had He done to deserve such pain and hate and who was He?

All of a sudden, an officer called to the men and gave them a sign that they nailed to the top of the cross. The soldiers also shouted to another comrade, to come and help with the erecting of the cross. Gradually the three men managed to lift the cross into the hole that Yosef and Shimon had made. Yosef wished that they had never dug the hole, he did not want any part in this killing, to his mind; it seemed that somehow, he had also contributed to this man being hung on the cross. *Why had they made such an excellent job of the hole, why hadn't....*so many questions from a man who was nothing and knew nothing? The cross had been lifted up and was now in the centre of the other two men, hanging on crosses. Yosef knew that they were thieves because he had heard the soldiers discussing them at the waterhole. He gazed up at the sign

169

above the head of the man on the cross, unusually for him, he asked Shimon what it said.

"This is Jesus the King of the Jews." Yosef, confused thought if he was a king, why kill a king? He heard one of the Temple people shouting at the officer. "Get that sign down; it is not correct! The Roman looked down at him superciliously and said. "What I have written I have written," and walked off. The women around were crying, and there were a couple of young men with them, watching the proceedings. Yosef stood looking up at the man Jesus; He was unique somehow, different. Yosef could not say what it was that made Him that way. All he knew, was that he wanted to help this man, although he understood that it was too late, he could do nothing.

The soldiers sat together, sitting by the side of the prisoners gambling, speaking in a thick Italian accent. Yosef could just make out their conversation and listened intently to all that was said!

"He said he was God or something, and that he could build the temple in three days, what a load of rubbish," said one.

"Yes, you are right but letting Barabbas the murder go, surprising!"

" Obviously he was disliked by the Temple dignitaries, and they were determined to hunt him down," said another.

"However, I want His tunic, so let's play lots for it. It's a nice piece of material, although its bloodied, I'd like it!" The two soldiers started to gamble.

Yosef stood, watching and listening to all of this, while Shimon had gone to try and get his money. Around about, insults were being shouted out to the man on the cross, "King Jesus", from

SMILE, then spread your wings and FLY!

Hi Dick,

Enclose the book, maybe some parts 8, 16, 8 and segments from the following pages — However,

I recognise that it is very long, so no problem if you find it is just to much for the service!

Every blessing

H.

some of the Temple people who were watching nearby. Yosef looked up at Him, hanging bloodied on the cross, who was He and what had He done to be hanging there?

Shimon eventually came back and angrily hitched up the donkey, holding the donkey's head, he snarled at Yosef. "You have to wait here and dig the next holes; I've got my money but only on the understanding that I leave you here to work. The Romans are expecting more prisoners and will inform you where they require more holes. Once the work is completed, finished, leave here, come back, or find another place to live; I care not!" Shimon bellowed over his shoulder as he walked back to the donkey and cart!

At the same time, the men on each side of King Jesus began swearing and calling out, although Yosef did not hear what they said. Distracted, he turned and watched Shimon walk off, bewildered. He was on his own that was for sure, and he knew no-one was going to help him, the "dirt." Being alone was something that Yosef accepted, and being owned by Shimon, but this was quite different! Why, he had lived and worked for Shimon for such a long time now, he had believed that was where he belonged, as a servant. What was he going to do now, and where was he to go? His mind was in a turmoil, as he looked up at the cross again.

It was not right, why should this man, the King die like this? He looked at His feet so bloodied and swollen, and realized that this man, King Jesus, must be in great pain.

Suddenly, he turned and walked away from the scene, back to where he had been before, near to the soldiers where the water trough was situated. He eventually reached the water trough area where animals were tethered, next to the guard post. He bent down into the water trough and taking off his dirty outer shirt, he lay it in the water and filled it. He carried it back to the crucifixion area and deliberately walked to the cross, where the man "King Jesus" was hanging. He lay his dirty wet shirt on the bloodied feet and wiped them. The man looked down and again, and Yosef saw His eyes. It was an amazing experience; they seemed to bore right through Yosef, the "dirt", with such tender love. Yosef then did something so peculiar for Him, he bent low, and wiped the feet again and kissed them. As he did so, he felt a massive blow to his temple, as a soldier brought the flat side of his sword over his head.

"Get away from the prisoner," he barked gazing down at Yosef on the ground. Yosef got up from the ground and grabbed up his shirt that was now at his feet. He felt blood trickle down his face, and, although shaken by the blow from the sword, it was not that, which had made an impact on him. It was the moment when he'd touched the bloodied feet of the man "King Jesus," it had been a fantastic encounter. The experience had challenged and changed him. Yosef the one they called the "dirt", knew that this was no ordinary man hanging silently on the cross. In an instant, as he had touched Him, something had happened to Yosef, which had never happened before in his whole life.

If he'd been able to articulate and put the experience into words, he would have said it was a fantastic encounter with love. The incredible love of a Savior had reached down inside him and touched him to the core. All he knew, was that he had a purpose, he was not on his own anymore and that this man loved him.

He could not speak about it; this dirty defiled man, but he had received a miracle of happiness that had washed over him. Yosef was healed from so much, the brokenness that had been part of his life was gone. The King of the Jews had touched the "dirt" and cleansed him of past humilities and pain. Something had happened inside him that was so firm and resolute he would never be the same again! He was a child of the future; he now belonged! He had a purpose, and he was not just a slave!

"I am your man!" he tried to mouth, articulating the words to the man hanging so still. "I will always believe in you," he tried to say, as tears fell swiftly from his eyes. Yosef, this poor man watched the scene around him with sadness, and yet with joy. His face was awash with tears. Here was a King all right. A royal King, and to Yosef, he had also become now, his Savior!

Quietly viewing this sat Denton and Heaton, wondering silently what **The Mighty One** had planned. While Yosef sat motionless recognizing that for once in his sad life, he had a purpose. He knew that whoever he met, he would tell them about a Savior who loved them too. It was a story that would never end!

Burial

His body hung still and cold as the wind whipped up grit and dirt around about, in the darkness. Sobbing, from bystanders, filled the air. While the noise of shields, swords and voices sounded too, as the distinct voice of a Centurion was heard above it all as he gazed up at the cross. In an emotional voice, he said," Yes, definitely something special, about that man!" The reply from Joseph of Arimathea standing next to him wasn't audible, as the men stood silently waiting.

Nicodemus next to him nodded, they had come to take down **The Beautiful One's** body from the cross. The Centurion meanwhile had come over to give them his help, watching events, he had spoken out as **The Beautiful One** died, loudly declaring.

"That this was truly the Son of God,"

Like many who had encountered **The Beautiful One**, the Centurion realized that he had been in the presence of a man of quality, unique, a man never to be forgotten! The word holiness was not a word in a soldier's vocabulary, but the Centurion's face showed it all, as he bowed his head to the cross.

Joseph and Nicodemus waited to accomplish a daunting task, as the three men started to work together, to lift the body down. They had a ladder, and gently the two men with the Centurion started to free **The Beautiful One's** body from the cross. Nicodemus climbed up the ladder as the men lifted the limp body of the Savior, and freed it from the nails and cord, which had kept it in its place.

Seeing the torn flesh and the gentle face of this man who had done so much good, made it difficult for the men not to show their emotion. It was a delicate job, and they did it with such love. Gently they freed His feet from the tortuous nails, as blood dripped on them to the ground. Then taking his hands into their hands, they pulled out the nails driven deep within the centre of them. After this, they lifted their precious friend and Savior down, from the place of abuse.

His head was still bleeding where the crown of thorns had been, and some dark needles still hung from his precious head. A scruffy individual who had been labouring, also gave his help, in lifting the body to the ground.

His mother at the foot of the cross ministered to him. As gently and lovingly, they laid his head on to her lap, she received it, seated on the earth, and with her back to the cross, she attended to his broken body. She loved him in death, as she had loved him in life and wiped his face, with tears that streamed down. Lovingly, she pulled out the thorns from his head and kissed every gash.

Joseph and Nicodemus also ministered to his body, so that all was done, in accordance with temple law. They laid him on the coat of Joseph and anointed him with a mixture of myrrh and aloes. Nicodemus had purposely brought them, before wrapping him in a linen shroud.

As a respected, wealthy man, Joseph a follower of Jesus had access to Pilate and had asked for **The Beautiful One's** body so that he could attend to His burial.

He had been permitted to remove Jesus' body from the cross and bury it. Although Pilate, surprised at the request, not so much that Joseph of Arimathea was making it, but perplexed at the speed of death. Jesus had died after such a short time on the cross; sometimes people hung there for days before they died.

The men were studious in the way they accomplished everything, finally wrapping him in linen, they took him away to his tomb to be buried. They were intent on doing everything correctly, with love and dignity and to eventually lay him in the tomb. It was all completed, to ensure his burial was carefully esteemed, with all honor, they tended to Him. Once they had laid him in the tomb, they gazed down with tears on their cheeks, hesitating, reluctant to leave.

Finally touching his head, they said goodbye.

They looked back, nothing more to do, for all intent and purposes this was the end of the matter! In all of their minds lurked the one question, why?

He was a mighty man, a miracle worker, holy, and they knew he'd said so much, that they repeated.

"I am the way the truth and the light.... no man comes to the Father but through me."

Which was worrying, if he couldn't stand against the powers all around, how could they? Killed, crucified and it was the end of the story, what were they to do now?

Outside the tomb, women stood weeping, as soldiers put a large stone in place, it was the end; nothing mattered anymore, their world had come crashing down!

Around the disciples, in the supernatural, the enemy danced with glee. Joyful that they had managed to kill off, the one person who had made them fearful. The one destructive force that might have desecrated their darkness, they were ecstatic! The enemy of holiness was partying, and his hordes believed they had accomplished a great feat, the Savior's death! They believed that they had won the day, they were ready now to conqueror all!

The Hidden Scene

The Beautiful One lay in the tomb, cut off from His loving friends! The grave was also full of dark evil beings, all trying to cause chaos, ecstatic that they had the victory.

This evil mob surrounded him and tried to crush him in any way they could, to inflict their powers. These were the hordes of hell on a mission to repress his remains. Dark specimens of evil, all around, trying to eradicate His very being, if that could have been possible.

While suddenly a commanding voice shrieked orders. The voice evil and awesome screeched powerful words straight from the pit of hell.

"Out you stupid ones, He has won! He has no stain on him, the sinless one; we cannot hold him!"

A dark mass arose up and shouted in response, "He has taken on their sin, it has made Him one of us!"

Satan came forward, punched the others and grabbed some small minions around the throat.

"Get out you stupid imbeciles you cannot fight his power; he has accomplished all. His death won a victory. His spirit has already gone to Heaven!

We were mistaken and played into his hands; his power is mighty we cannot hold him. His sinless perfection broke every chain that we wrapped over him; no darkness can compete with such force.

The Mighty One laid the world's sin on him, but it could not stop him, he was holy and has won the battle!" He paused and then spat out.

"Yes, there will be more battles, and we will get even, but we need a different strategy now to make a difference."

Once again, he spat an ugly venom over the area. "Evil will prevail, I will win; out of here you imbeciles, the atmosphere is too clean for us, escape and start working!" The extraordinary ugly beings began to move out until the dark tomb was left silent.

The Tomb

The Beautiful One lay quite still, as another being, entered the tomb. It was **The Breath** holding out his hand.

Silently **The Beautiful One** took it, arose and went forth out of the tomb. As he moved from the grave, he left his grave clothes where he lay and his face covering. Immediately he was robbed as **The Beautiful One** and went out with **The Breath.**

It was to the far reaches of hell that he was destined, to do **The Mighty One's** will. His work was almost completed, except for one final mission to accomplish legalities in the basin of hell.

The Mighty One had promised at the beginning of creation that the enemy's power, would be broken. His promise, in the beginning, was fulfilled now, through **The Beautiful One**. It was in the place of darkness, where the lost ones waited, that the Messiah had to go.

He had won the battle, so he went to fulfil the requirement so that all should know and see his victory.

At the time of Noah, when the waters filled the earth, many had no opportunity to reach out to **The Mighty One**. The mission for **The Beautiful One** was to preach and declare his message as Messiah to those in chains.

That is how He stood, radiant in the dark cloistered place and routed the enemy and set captives free. He spoke pure words of truth and light bringing a sense of purity and wholeness to suffering souls. As the overcoming victor, He trampled the enemy's chains and led out many, who had been locked away in that dark place.

Those who had been diligent in life, and kept themselves holy, had patiently waited over time to hear this message. At this time, His loving nail-torn hands, touched the chains of many incarcerated by the devil, to free them. Many bowed in praise and thanksgiving for the victory over hell and death.

The Beautiful One carried the message of truth and love, to those waiting in the depths. To those who had loved and followed the covenant of the Lord. This beautiful Savior preached to them, as he toured the dark folds of the earth, declaring truth.

The darkness recognized him now as the mighty victor and could not challenge him. As the overcoming one, The Lamb of God, who holds the keys to death and hell, all of the hordes of evil had to make way for him, and that is what they did!

Once he had accomplished all he was called to do, he returned to earth. Walking away from the tomb, he smiled at the angel still standing guard at the door. The angel bowed as he walked past to this overcoming King. He was the sinless one who had died for all, and His power was ferocious. Outside, even the sunlight seemed to smile down at the figure that walked through the graveyard. It was time to go to His father and yet there was still a little unfinished business here. His dear ones, he must see them and reassure them that he was alive, that was his first thought.

His Friends

Night had hidden them, as they tried to wipe out the memories of the past atrocities, while the day of Shabbat had lingered on, as they sat talking. At last, the morning had eventually

179

appeared to rear its head as Jesus friends sat huddled together.

They had spent a long time, voicing their thoughts continuously for hours. Comforting each other, in any way they could to ease the pain in their hearts. They were confused, frightened, and kept repeating events continually.

Why were they asleep when the soldiers came? Why didn't they deal with Judas a long time ago, most of them had found him hard and calculating? What about all those false witnesses, who were they?

The Lord killed, but what about the miracles, the things he'd said, it just didn't make sense? Question after question kept them all wondering, whispering and crying. If only they had all done more, fought, for their friend? Yes, they should have given the soldiers what for. They tried to recall his words, why hadn't they listened more?

The only person who did not utter a word was Peter. During the night, Mary, the mother of James and Mary Magdalene, had sat sighing for hours, whispering, drenched in tears, forgetting their duties in the house.

The thought of the cross and their friend dying in such a dreadful way had inflicted such grief on them; they were virtually all inconsolable. The hours had been long, a time of profound sadness like no other!

They were all in shock, the death of their mentor and friend had come as a complete surprise, as they'd thought him invincible. Another underlying anxiety was causing them fear, thinking that the authorities, might come looking for them? It was indeed a possibility.

Frightened unsettled, wondering what the future had in store they talked in whispers and after lengthy discussion, they decided it was time to separate and go back to their roots, to the one thing they knew all about, fishing.

Peter was the most heartbroken, nearly inconsolable. Realising that the one man he had trusted, and thought was supernatural, had died. The shame of the way he had behaved in the situation compounded everything.

He was in despair, having lied about knowing his friend, the dearest person to him, at a time when he needed him the most! All night long, when he sat silently pondering over everything he grieved, and at other times, he kept repeating, the same words, over and over........

"How could I, lie, pretend I did not know him?" The others had told him firmly; they were all to blame....... hadn't they all run away when the soldiers had come to the Gethsemane, but it had made little difference to Peter?

Gradually as the light of day started over the horizon, the women put on their shawls. They had decided in the night, to make their way to the tomb as soon as it got light and take spices.

The men had made a face when they'd told them, grunting something to the effect that it was pointless.

Slipping out quietly the three women left the safety of their home, wrapped in their shawls they walked to the place of death. Walking together, none of the women spoke, intent on their thoughts.

Tear-stained sombre faces said a great deal about the group making their way to the graveside. With the sun just making an entrance they hurried to the place where he lay.

Not wanting to speak to anyone they had left the house quickly, to avoided looks and useless chatter with neighbours. An amazing man, how could this happen; to think that they had watched his crucifixion, so many thoughts crowded into their minds?

Mary was the first to break the silence as they walked together, "We have forgotten something, we cannot do anything when we get there because the soldiers put that huge boulder across the grave!"

"Well we are almost there, so let us see if anyone is around to help us," said the other Mary." The women pulled their shawls closer to them; the morning air was crisp on their faces. Although it was the sadness of their errand that was making them feel dejected and cold.

"The nails in his feet and hands!" Mary blurted out. "How could they have done that to the Lord, he never did anything wrong?" "Such pain, what a death, dreadful!" said Mary Magdalene. The women had slowed their pace as they talked, as if reluctant to face the burial ground. Gradually they began the steep climb to the allotted area where the tombs were.

"After coming into Jerusalem, with people cheering him and waving palm branches. It just seems inconceivable, that they then allowed him to be crucified!" said Mary Magdalene, standing to catch her breath. That villain Barabbas set free, and to kill the Lord, what were the leaders thinking?"

Breathing heavily after the long walk she continued, "My mind keeps going over everything, he said, why did it happen?"

They continued where the pathway forked and climbed even higher to graves on the far side. Jesus' grave was in the most beautiful area, given by Joseph of Arimathea one of his disciples. Joseph was wealthy and owned a large plot; he had anointed the Lord and overseen the burial, giving his tomb for him.

On turning the bend nearing the area they were making for, two guards rushed past them, wide-eyed with fear. The men did not stop on meeting the women. They ran past muttering that there had been an earthquake, the stone had rolled away, and a 'being' was there.

"That was strange, they looked frightened," said Mary," Did you make out what they were saying?"

The other women shook their heads as they quickened their pace. They all wondered quite what they would encounter. Rounding the corner, the women came to the clearing and saw a fantastic sight. The angel Gabriel was standing next to the tomb leaning on a huge boulder. He was the first thing their eyes noticed as they came out into the open. Although they did not know who he was, they realized he was different, unique, but an angel, this was possibly lost on them.

The whole area seemed so very different today, and surprising, the huge stone put there by the soldiers, had been rolled to one side and no longer hid the tomb. The women hurried to the grave, ignoring the angel in their concern to see the Lord.

Stepping into the tomb to see the body, it appeared to be empty apart from the grave clothes; and the women were mortified an empty tomb, where was the body of Jesus, who had stolen it?

The angel spoke as they stepped outside. "Do not be afraid, I know you are looking for Jesus who was crucified. He is not here he has risen, just as he told you he would. Go quickly and tell the disciples. He is raised from the dead and is going ahead of you into Galilee. There you will see him. Go, for now, I have told you!"

The women motionless for a few seconds listened and clutched each other in a hug. When they turned around the angel had vanished, and they were alone.

Once they had seen that the tomb was empty, the words of the 'being' gradually resonated with them. A message, that was all they needed! The substance of all that they had heard lifted them off their feet, and each kept repeating the significant word, He has risen! Ecstatic they hugged each other again, and hurried off, down the path back from where they had come from relieved; he was alive! Happy and filled with joy they could not wait to return and tell the disciples what they had seen. Unbelievable; the Lord was alive! It was beyond comprehension; they had spoken to an angel. What was that all about, and this breath-taking news? Their excitement bubbled up into laughter as they hurried down to tell the others their news.

Suddenly they rounded a corner and saw Him. They knew, but doubted it was.......it was so unbelievable; that he was alive and there in front of them. Jesus held out His hands.

"Greetings," he said. They came to Him, clasped his feet and worshipped Him. Jesus said to them. "Do not be afraid. Go, back and tell the brothers and Peter, to go to Galilee, tell them, this is where we will meet."

The women were overcome with emotion and couldn't speak; the Lord was here they were speechless. As soon as they moved, He vanished.

Left standing on the pathway with boulders and sunshine

all around them they stood, utterly motionless, looking at each other in a kind of trance. Alive, why, it was terrific news. Words dropped from their lips. "How wonderful, what a miracle, Jesus is alive, it is amazing!" their words came tumbling out all mixed up together!

The women now hurried on; they could not wait to tell the disciples the astounding news. The Lord is alive, and furthermore, He said to go to Galilee, and He would meet them there, they were overjoyed with the news!

"He has risen. He is alive," they cried running into the house, shouting. "He is alive; he lives, he lives, brothers he lives!" The world took on a different hue, and the women danced with joy. He was whom He said He was, the Messiah!

Heaven and the Promise Revealed

The heavens were alive with an air of expectation, as the two angels Denton and Heaton arrived in the heavenly sphere. They had been on assignment when they were summoned to attend this gathering and were mystified. It had been a dark time since the earthly happenings. The event had crushed so many in Heaven when **The Beautiful One** had been broken and killed. It had caused even the elements to lie still and menacing over all the Earth. Therefore, this new development was a surprise, and they wondered as to what **The Mighty One** was going to say and do? Although the two angels knew that **The Mighty One** always had an answer, they were curious...

"Heaton, **The Mighty One,** praise Him, has called for an

assembly, so we must go into the heavenly city," said Denton.

"I wonder what could be this important, after seeing **The Beautiful One** so broken, nothing seems so crucial now? "

"Well we never get called back from assignment unless it is vital, so this must be pretty big stuff?" murmured Heaton.

"I suppose we may find out what happened to **The Beautiful One**, I cannot believe that we had to leave Him!" Denton replied and then exclaimed, "Why look, everyone is approaching, and I can see significant people joining them. Everyone is coming for this announcement from **The Mighty One**; it must be big!"

"Oh yes, I see Elijah, Moses, Ezekiel and others all moving this way too, this must certainly, be a big announcement," Heaton replied.

A vast assembly of wondrous proportion was gathering in Heaven as **The Mighty One** came and took the central place. **The Breath** stood next to Him, while the cherubim and seraphim encircled and surrounded them. Michael, the mighty warring angel, stood behind the two of them. Gradually, a cloud of perfume arose that was intoxicating, announcing the presence of the Lamb of God, the Lord Jesus Christ, **The Beautiful One**. The gold gleamed on the floor of Heaven, as all around lifted up their hands. It was a scene never to be forgotten, an exhilarating time of triumph that lit up all of the heavens. A rapturous joy, that was so beautiful it could not be explained. The shouts of triumph and praise were tremendous. As music echoed around and lifted the scene into a level of joyful praise, never experienced. The angel's voices reverberated to a tone that was wondrous in its harmony. Louder and louder the sound echoed a rapturous accord that was beautiful and wonderous in its depth.

Here was a party like no other, as **The Beautiful One** arrived, His presence was electric. Everywhere was bathed in an extraordinary splendour, as the person of **The Beautiful One**, the Lamb of God took a pivotal place. The angels bowed in reverence and awe, as **The Mighty One** held out His hand to the most wonderful of beings, the Son of God. **"The Beautiful One"** as He is known in Heaven had arrived. He had experienced pain and death and won the victory over Hell and the grave; this was **The Promise of Heaven** in its fulfilment. The Lamb of God has turned the advance of evil over the Earth and won. **The Mighty One's** plan had become a reality. His prophetic words at the time of Creation had become a certainty. **"The Beautiful One"** had done it, won the victory, and all of Heaven was rejoicing! The keys of death and Hell were now in the hands of the mighty and wondrous Savior, the Lamb of God, **The Beautiful One**. The chain of evil severed, people everywhere could appropriate the love of a Savior, and accept His gift of salvation. It was a rapturous party of joy in Heaven, for the victory accomplished, won at the cross. The pain and anguish of death had vanished, the grave could not hold the beautiful sinless, Son of God!

He stood radiant, still with the scars that spoke of sacrifice visible on His body. His presence formidable in stature, **The Darling of Heaven,** the Anointed One the victor. The Son of God who had defeated Lucifer, stood visible, awe-inspiring as lightening shards reverberated around his person. While all around, thousands upon thousands of angels lit up the sky, in an incredible presence of praise, lifted higher and higher.

Hands raised in jubilation awe and worship. While heads bowed to the victor, for all that was accomplished as the streets of gold glistened with light, in this most triumphant of scenes. Heaven radiated with joy at this victory, that echoed on and on, defiant and beautiful, heralding a future of promise. **The Promise of Heaven** was a reality, **The Darling of Heaven** had won the battle at the cross as **The Mighty One** had planned! The enemy would still be defiant, so the battle was not finished, but the hold over the Earth had been won, now, in victory. Accordingly, all of Heaven rejoiced!

Although, Satan was not going to relinquish his hold over mankind easily. He will continually try to infiltrate and infect the world with misery until the end comes. A cheat and a despot endeavouring to court people through evil intentions, will one day face judgement.

The Lord Jesus, **"The Beautiful One"**, had won the spiritual battle, but now it was a war that **The Breath**, the Holy Spirit would mastermind. His job was ongoing to empower people, to understand the significance of the sinless Son of God's gift. At the cross, **The Promise of Heaven** had yielded His life for all people. The Savior of the world had won the victory, to give a unique gift for all mankind!

On acceptance of this gift by faith, a supernatural spiritual exchange happens. The glory of salvation, powerful, and life-changing sweeps over, as the darkness of sin is swept out. It was not the end of the matter with evil, unfortunately; there would be battles, but the victory was secure.

A mighty struggle, with sinfulness, was to continue in every place as the enemy was not going to give up. Continually trying to woo the world into evil, as wickedness tries to take over. Unfortunately, it is apparent that in the struggle for righteousness, all will have a choice, and yes, the battle was going to be harsh, and all of Heaven was going to be affected. Although, the winner has already been announced, His name was The Lord Jesus, **The Beautiful One**, **The Promise of Heaven**.

The Mighty One gazed over the joyful multitudes in radiant praise for **The Promise of Heaven** and smiled. It was a remarkable time of joy, although He realized that there was going to be a cost for many in Heaven in the future, because of evil.

Feeling sad, as He loved His heavenly family, He knew that many would lose their lives in the ensuing battle that was to come. The enemy of creation was behind all of this, and the wickedness of sin the barrier.

Standing watching too, over all the Earth, He saw the children of **The Promise of Heaven**, praising Him. The people of the Church, who loved their savior were also going to feel the thrust of evil all around them. No one could escape the darkness bearing down. Soon His disciples will be scattered and eventually killed, but the Word will go forward, and holiness will win. The cost of following a Savior was hefty, but He smiled as He had a plan that was imminent, to support, sanctify and empower the Church. **The Breath** was going to arrive and perfume so much of the Earth with the wind of Heaven.

It was to be an exciting and amazing time, when an army of believing people will stand up for righteousness. A Church of people will be born, empowered to fight the battle of the cross. A people of destiny who will be significant, and route out the enemy. He walked back to the group, that stood and worshipped **The Beautiful One**, and smiled.

His overcoming Son had done it, duped the enemy and won

the victory in every way. It was just the beginning. His actions had changed so much. In the future, He was to have the title the Ancient of days. It was He who would unlock the books at the end of the age, after winning the right to conquer death and Hell. The beautiful angel of deceit, Satan, will be vanquished eventually locked away for a season when peace could once more prevail over all the Earth. **The Mighty One** was content; all was deliberately planned; righteousness would always win the day. He laughed, as this was an adventure that He had planned since creation, exciting because the victory had already been won! **The Promise of Heaven** had become a reality! Although there was more to come, and the Heavens waited with anticipation, to see what was to occur in Jerusalem?

Awaiting the Breath

Heaven was full of excitement with so much happening around them in the supernatural. The party for **The Beautiful One** had been significant, and the anticipation for the future was everywhere. **The Breath** was on the move, and the three powerful beings had been in deep conversation after **The Beautiful One** had arrived back. The angels knew the signs! It was time for an event that would resonate throughout eternity. The extraordinary power of **The Breath** was to descend to Earth. He was to fragrance the world with His supernatural presence. It was excitement, awe and enthusiastic joy that radiated in the heavenly sphere. His presence had been felt throughout the ages, as He anointed men and women for service.

Possibly this was something else, an extraordinary occasion

when all around the world, His presence was going to be felt, changing the atmosphere! It was to be an outpouring of His presence in the universe, that was to be awe-inspiring. An anointing that was to change faith into a dimension of power and love for the children of **The Beautiful One**. A continual supernatural encounter with Heaven, here on Earth, for all who hungered for it! Once this happens, they are transformed, enriched and cleared of the dross that so many have embraced in their lives. The angels were ecstatic, at the way **The Mighty One's** plans were being activated and the changes that were happening. They observed everything with joy, waiting to see the might of Heaven invade Earth in such a vibrant way!

The Breath

After the crucifixion, the disciple's met with **The Beautiful One**, the Lord Jesus and they were euphoric. Finding He was alive was a fantastic experience, and to know that He had risen from the dead; and that the grave could not hold Him, was virtually unbelievable, although entirely accurate. Eventually, it had been time for Him to return for the last time to Heaven, and they had seen Him rise and go away.

It was a most significant and beautiful time, but His last words were. "To wait in Jerusalem for the Holy Spirit to come." It was overwhelming in some ways, and they were excited but in awe of everything, wondering what was going to happen next? There had been so many tremendous experiences with the Lord, all indelibly marked on their memories, and they knew that they could trust Him implicitly, but all of them were curious. The Holy Spirit, what was this and how were they going to find Him, or was He going to look for them? Many questions surfaced in their minds; however, He had said go into Jerusalem, and that is where the disciples gathered, wondering about the future. Albeit, their curiosity, had been turned around in their minds, and now they had slight anxiety and questioned as to how will they know for sure when He arrives?

Once the Lord, **The Beautiful One** had come to them after the crucifixion they had been elated. It had been overwhelming, glorious because when they had seen Him on the cross, they had thought that His life was over. Meeting him later they understood a little more of what it was all about; He had overcome death…He was a victor, a winner, the Messiah!

They had talked to him and had a meal together, although they did not quite understand it all entirely yet. It was undoubtedly breath-taking, and they were all astounded that the Lord had risen from the dead. Meeting Him on the side of the Lake Galilee was fabulous. It was all nearly unbelievable, so much had happened that had taken their breath away. The culmination of all of this was to see the Lord taken up to Heaven. It had been amazing, hearing Him say goodbye, rise up in the sky and vanish; and they had seen it happen. They were taken aback, overwhelmed.

At the time of His leaving, He had given them instructions. He told them to go and wait in Jerusalem, and obediently, they had done just that. The angel had confirmed it at the same time. The quandary was that they had been waiting for some time now, and they were nervous and more than a little confused, as to precisely what it was, they were waiting for in Jerusalem? Their minds were full of questions, *what was it that they had to do?* Money was beginning to get low, and because it had been some time since they had waited, many had become disillusioned and gone off. Peter was concerned, had they got it right?

It had already been some time since they'd had the conversation with the Lord, and doubts had crept in. Some disciples had questioned what they were all doing and had decided to return to work. It seemed that a lot had happened in a relatively short space of time, and emotions had been all over the place. The pain, grief and guilt of the crucifixion transformed to a place of wonderment when they'd met the Lord. Although their families had scoffed at some of them, why bother their looks had said, even though words had not been uttered! One friend had announced; "Your occupation is a fisherman, why run after someone who is already dead? None of them had answered the accusations thrown at them. Instead, they had clung together and avoided people.

Meeting **The Beautiful One** at the lakeside when He had cooked for them was magical. Even Thomas, who had doubted at first that He had risen from the dead; had been humbled and believed and called Him "God." All of that was some while ago, and here in Jerusalem, it was another matter.

Waiting and anxiety had made all of them a little fraught, understandably they sometimes got under each other's feet. However, they tried to be consistent in prayer, obediently watched to see what was going to happen. Nevertheless, the real quandary was waiting! It was the waiting that had been frustrating; inactivity was making them all restless, what was it that they had to wait for, in this place?

Today Peter had gone out to the Temple and came in to find the others in a melancholy frame of mind. It was so busy and noisy in Jerusalem that he felt homesick for the quiet of the lakeside, himself. Many people were milling around outside, it was festival time, and crowds had come into the city to celebrate.

"What is your thinking Peter?" asked John breaking the silence as they sat up on the roof on their own.

"I know that the Lord said to wait, but some of the brothers are disappointed it's taken so long, wondering as to just what is going to happen." Peter looked up and smiled.

"I am not sure about anything anymore, John, but what I know and believe is this, if the Lord said to wait, that is what we must do. He will show us when and until then, we must be patient," said, Peter.

"Let us pray and ask Him to support us," said John. "I believe like you, that He will come, but we must help and encourage the others so that they are confident too!"

The two men knelt down and prayed for help and guidance and then went to bed. The early morning sun was coming up in the sky over Jerusalem, as Peter stood on the rooftop, looking upwards.

It was a beautiful day, and the sun gleamed on the Temple roof as he contemplated what to do. They had seen the Lord return to Heaven and had obediently come to Jerusalem as He'd asked them to and waited. Although, at this moment he wondered if it was here that they were supposed to be? Chiding himself, he smiled, the Lord knew everything. He would find them wherever they were! Maybe it was today that they would meet up with the Holy Spirit.

Then precisely what was exactly meant by meeting up with the Holy Spirit? Question after question went through Peter's mind. Watching the city, he pondered on the past, as he gazed over

Jerusalem. The cross, the empty tomb, walking with the Lord along the shore. What was it, He had said to Peter, "Feed my sheep." *What exactly did that mean, and could He do it?* Questions and thoughts went around Peter's mind, as he sat there watching the sun breaking through on a new day. Shortly, he was joined by other disciples. They had eaten little but prayed together, waiting for the Lord's direction. Maybe today the Holy Spirit was to arrive? It was nine o'clock in the morning, as they gathered together quietly talking.

Suddenly, it happened…He arrived **The Breath**, the Holy Spirit, moved upon them and touched them all. His closeness was tremendous, soft but firm as He filled them and brought change. As the anointing fell, the disciples felt His love and sweetness, while tongues of fire caressed their heads anointing them until they were immovable with joy! He was changing them from the inside out, breathing into them, a spiritual awareness that was meaningful. A cleansing occurred as past pains were swept away to bring healing of a spiritual depth that was astounding. It was a compelling touch of the supernatural power of Heaven, healing and filling them with spiritual might and strength.

They were changed, consecrated through the power of **The Breath**, that was strong and engaging. It was as if they were immersed in a fountain of pure joy and wonder. The splendour of the King, brushed over them, breaking into their lives with a presence that was revealing. They praised God, as the flames of healing, wholeness, and purity poured upon them, as a Heavenly language poured out from their tongues. Their words uttered an expression of praise and adoration to **The Mighty One**, with words wholly unfamiliar to them, but beautiful, that now coursed down from their lips. They radiated God's presence, and everyone around them heard their exclamations and were astounded. The disciples danced and laughed and used this new heavenly language with joy.

The street, now busy with people heard and saw the commotion. The disciple's inhibitions had vanished, as they became immersed in a joy that was overwhelming and glorious. Laughing, dancing with an anointing that was so vibrant and glorious, they were never going to be the same again.

All this was the evidence of **The Breath's** beautiful presence of power, strength, wisdom, and discernment. It was an experience that these uncouth fishermen had never known. Gifts of the beautiful Holy Spirit tumbled from them, empowering them for ministry. The flame of healing danced on their heads, as they received an anointing that was spectacular.

These men dry from the hurt and pain of the world, felt a love that wrung from them, all the pain of the past. The streets packed with people saw something of Heaven invade Earth. People laughed and pointed at these holy men, who now danced in the streets, embraced by the love of God. Some thought the men had been drinking, but it was only nine o'clock in the morning. Amazed at the eloquence of these ragged men, they wondered how they could be heard so fluently, in so many different languages. While a glow of fire seemed to be on their heads, people astonished realized from their clothes, these were uneducated fishermen, who had now become eloquent speakers.

It was the dross of life that was dismantled and cleansed from them until they became vessels of truth. The sadness of losing their Lord, plus the exasperation of waiting had been stripped away, in the certainty of their ongoing relationship with Christ! Life's difficulties and trivialities forgotten, these men now empowered had changed, they were bold adversaries for their Lord.

Seekers of the "Way" as they would be called one day; understood the difference between religion and relationship. Realising with certainty that God had come and clasped them to Him. **The Breath** had arrived on the Earth for all peoples, on belief in **The Promise of Heaven**.

Here was the early Church in action, the start of its journey. Heaven had come to Earth! The miracle had happened. The body of Christ was being equipped by **The Breath**, for the task at hand, and **The Mighty One** looked down with joy. Peter the uncouth and feeble fisherman, radiant with strength and joy, stood and preached to the crowd. He accomplished this with an anointing of holy boldness that was supernatural in its strength. Miracles happened as people became convinced through listening to his preaching.

The reality had happened, the Lord Jesus Christ was the One they had been waiting for, "The Messiah!" The significance of the empty cross and tomb was accepted; He had risen from the dead! The world would never be quite the same again, because of this certainty!

Peter fearlessly stood apart and spoke eloquently of the words uttered by the prophet Joel years before. This dirty, uncouth fisherman, who had disowned the Lord, standing on the streets of Jerusalem declared the truth. Revealing to all, the prophetic, the reality of a Savior, Who gave His life for all. What a transformation for this man Peter! Miraculously, **The Breath** of God's anointing, engaging and sincere, had made a huge announcement to the world through these weak disciples! The Church was born, and it was to go on and on claiming the wonder, of a Beautiful Savior who had died for all…

"The prophet Joel said …'that in the last days, he will pour out his spirit on all people. Your sons and daughters will prophesy, your young men will see visions your old men will dream dreams. Even on my servant's men and women I will pour out my spirit and they will prophesy'" …this was happening!'

Strategies of the Enemy

Satan was beside himself, shrieking at his minions, as to why they did not get the disciples out of Jerusalem. He had told his key people that they were to be vigilant, not to allow **The Breath** to arrive! Life was going to be very difficult now, the empowering of His people, he hissed, was a travesty!

Here was the enemy that he had feared most; he must not allow the world to know that this power and holiness were real! **The Breath**, as they call Him, had arrived. The men in Jerusalem were now the untouchables, it was a catastrophe, and Satan howled with rage! Reaching out, he assaulted those nearest to him, mouthing the word "calamity", and other things! Breathing out heavily, something putrid, he said through clenched teeth; "Well more like, a minor irritation, but we can win!" Again, he breathed out a distinct odour of something unclean that arose all around him.

"Hmm listen carefully, I am going to give some of you explicit instruction as to where to work, and I want no slip-ups; the job must be achieved, with excellent results. This is war!"

"Systematic purges on all fronts, that is the way to get them, it will take centuries, but we keep at it. The job has to be deliberate and smart! Do not leave any calling cards, and we are going to be as smarmy as we can, but so evil, no one will believe that it is not the reality of life." Composing himself even more from the initial shock, he gave a deep throaty chuckle and continued.

"Nice on top and wickedly sinful underneath. Do not let any of them win, this is a dirty war, and we know how to fight dirty." On hearing all this, there was a chorus of cackling that was straight from the pit of Hell as he continued.

"Hmm, yes, discredit Him, that will affect it all, no one must know that this," His voice was a mere whisper, "That the Holy Spirit stuff is real! That should get many of them, the 'so-called churches' in the future, avoiding any thoughts of," His voice lowered again, "**The Breath** arriving!"

Let's further irritate the Romans, get them to throw the Christians to the lions, to avoid them becoming important, make people hate them."

The mob around him cackled with glee as their dark, throaty voices conveyed their enjoyment of the moment.

"Take up strategic points in countries and hold your position of power, do not give way! In the future, plan the dark ages well and make religion old and tired!"

Glaring at all around him, he continued. "It is your job, to make sure that way off in the future everyone believes that this ministry is over the top, no need to have any of this in the Church! Get many straight-laced people to believe, that it is all sensationalism, claptrap and hugely embarrassing. Make it look as if it is not current, in the past outdated. So, people will believe it is not important to be empowered!"

He breathed another offensive odour, and mused, yes, that was the way; things were not so bad after all.

"No one will believe the happenings in Jerusalem were real, gullible Church, yes discredit it all!"

He shrieked again at the massive army in front of him. "Strategy, I must have a strategy and cunning! When 'do-gooders' come and try and evangelise," Satan continued, "make the Church respectable accepted by society, sanitised. Religiosity, stilted, all crap trap, yes feed them that, and we've got them, and as for this Jerusalem stuff, a thing of the past! Once it is shown, as old outdated nonsense, no one will want anything to do with it."

He shuddered if they knew...well, he Satan, would be finished! Satan glared, musing about the events; he had watched and studied the strategy; it must be the imbeciles he had allowed to conduct the final scenarios which meant that **The Breath** had arrived.

Angry with a powerful desire for revenge, he considered his next move; he was going to win and achieve power. In time, wipe Christianity out from the world, make it so unfashionable, *oh yes, all good, reasonable ideas,* he thought. Going over everything he had said he thought his plans were good, a framework for evil in the future.

Hmm, yes, yes, Satan's mind was thinking about so much, a lot to plan, but there were all sorts of ways to win, and he would think of them all. He frowned, the trouble was, there was power in **The Breath**, challenging to cope with; they would have to be careful with Him, he was a force to be recognized! Filling people with the gifts of the Holy Spirit, imparting holiness. All of this was problematic for Satan because he knew that they worked! Oh well, he must become more subtle, more conniving!

His additional plan to set up different realms, with powerful evil masters who would be so influential that even the might of Michael, the warring angel, would be pushed back, would achieve everything.

He was going to show all of Heaven and Earth, that he, Satan was a force to be recognized! Of course, victory had been achieved at the cross. But these stupid humans could be duped; they would not want to follow a God who expected holiness! Just so long as they did not understand the ramifications of it all, especially the blood of Christ, his eyes grew dark, what a thought!

The idea, once they knew, he cringed, they must never get to know! He would ensure he was always one step ahead, that was the answer. Everything respectable in churches, lots of regalia, eventually books on how to do good, everyone will believe that this was holy power. Yes, that is the way to do it! Make sure the wrong people became leaders, unsavoury acts, building a world of weak government. His thoughts then turned once more to strategy; promoting religion in all its forms, an ideal way, no power just a lot of words, hot air great!

Also, religious power struggles, then they would fight and kill each other, brilliant! War, hate violence, that is the way to do it he thought, seeds of unrest. He called his troops together; they were going to win whatever, so now was the time to make individual evil plans to fight the might of God!

Strongholds, stupendous, this was the time, when the different realms and powers would become a reality, in the supernatural world. His eye glinted, evil must win, he mused, it was going to take years. Hmm…a drop of poison in a sea of righteousness, he could do it! **The Mighty One's** plans, to build a world for them, how misjudged! Weak, ineffectual beings, oh yes, he could deceive them! He was going to win, and evil was going to take over the world!

Behind the Scene Year's Later

Many centuries on, the two angels Denton and Heaton had been summoned to join a training assignment.

A senior approached them stating, "I need your assistance, come with me, the high angel started to fly off, and the two angels followed him. "At this time, I am going to give you more intensive training," said the angel.

"Over centuries you have been escorting and helping different people, and there is an extra dimension that I want you to understand. Being a part of the heavenly throng, I am sure you are aware that enlightenment comes in different stages? So, this training session is required to educate and teach you about something that not all eyes can perceive.

Supernatural powers are everywhere, and human beings have a spiritual dimension, that is sometimes dismissed, because it is not perceived. During our time together, you will understand this better, as I will show you the supernatural side of people's lives. Watch and take note."

By this time, they had flown far into the world, arriving at a nation in a large busy area where many people were buying and selling. Before them, a community of people of all personalities and gender stretched out. Some were shopping, others were at restaurants and some were standing about talking. The angels stood in the street watching all that was occurring.

It was a busy society with everyone pre-occupied with their lives, going about their daily chores. What was strange to the angels, as they looked at this time, was that many of the people were not on their own. It wasn't as if they had other people around them, it was a phenomenon of a different kind that seemed to be attached to them. Watching with interest, the angels noticed things that they had never seen before, about individuals. It was not about their bodies, or about their dress or manners, because they were all diverse within a variety of cultures. It was something that their eyes had not been open to before, although they had been around people for centuries. The people were actually not alone; there was another dimension attached to all individuals, an assortment of religious parties.

Countless people had a spiritual being adjoined to them, that was indeed not of Heaven. It seemed strange, but the people moved around with this attachment, that was supernatural in its context, hidden but a part of them. When the individual moved, so did the appendage with them. Denton and Heaton watched with interest as many spirits pushed and squirmed their way on buses and trains all attached to the people. Unseen by the human eye, these spiritual forces were there causing problems, encouraging people in behavior traits. The people were unaware of any of this, that they had connected up to spiritual forces, by their choices and lifestyles of unholiness.

It was an education for the angels watching, as the personalities of the evil beings, gave a dark spiritual awareness to the characters of the people. To a degree, it was a puzzling supernatural sight, as many people carried around the influences of wickedness. It was as if they had stepped into something unclean, that had then taken hold of them.

All around, the influence of the demonic was apparent in the personalities of people in their actions, and behavior. They also viewed some individuals, in the throes of wickedness, stealing lying and some involved in violence. In each case the spiritual dimension enticed people with thoughts of evil to try and get them to act in offensive, hateful ways.

It made the angels realize that the enemy was not slow in influencing societies and the world in any way he could. All around about, they could see a spiritual dimension of darkness hidden from the naked eye. It was a sign of the enemy's desire for power, trying to use the people of the world to achieve his aims.

After watching for a while, the angel leading them beckoned them on, and they flew out into a country area. They arrived at quiet and desolate place that was the ruins of a temple, below them was a mass of large stones that at one time had been erected for sacrifice.

It was a place that was abandoned. An altar had once stood there decades ago, had been used to sacrifice dark matter. Evil deeds had been accomplished in this place and languishing on large sacrificial stones were the evilest of beings. Moreover, the whole area had been given over to the enemy. While a small plaque erected, stated the use of the altar for sacrifice, was very evident.

The angels stood a short way off, watching as a car motored towards the place with two people in it. After slowing down, it eventually stopped, and the people got out. They glanced at the sign and walked over to where the stones of the altar were and sat down.

"So many humans are naive, and never think about spiritual consequences," said the angel in charge. The young couple sat and talked on the rocks trying to resolve an issue, thinking that they were alone. The evil spirits cosied up to them, and suddenly the couple started to quarrel. The dark beings around them encouraged the two to disagree. It seemed as if the unseen group threw them evil thoughts. It was an excellent opportunity for the dark ones around them to encourage the two in their arguments, which became nearly violent.

Suddenly the man said, "I'm sorry, maybe this is not the best place to resolve our problems!" and pointed to the sign.

The woman laughed, "You don't really believe all that mumbo jumbo, do you? Oh, come on then, let's go home and talk, that might be better!"

The two returned to their car and motored off.

"It is evident that when a place has been used for evil purposes, unless the area is cleaned up and claimed back through **The Mighty One**, evil spirits can remain," continued the angel.

Not waiting to see any more, the angels flew on and came to a large housing estate, where loud music and extraordinary excesses were allowed. It was a way of life that influenced many into things that were impure. The people in these communities had police cars on street corners, as the society was rife with gang wars and unrest.

It was a place where they could see hate, violence and murder attached to many young people, where the enemy had taken control.

The supernatural powers of darkness were attached to so

many through pornography, drugs and uncleanness, which was everywhere, even on very young people. All around was the evidence of the enemy, in doorways and on houses, where spirits of darkness sat surrounded by their owners. Along the street, places of worship had doors barred, long since given up wanting to be around the area.

Except for one man, who owned a shop in the locality, who had a different view on life and who was not frightened to voice his thoughts. In his shop the atmosphere was tranquil, and around the outside, they could see angels. They heard his voice as they flew down speaking to a young man.

"There was ever only one man who cared," he said. "Look at this," he handed a young man a tiny cross and smiled at him. "When you are frightened and don't know what to do, take out this cross and say. "Jesus, I know you are the Savior of the world, please save me."

The shopkeeper was a Christian, who loved the people here and helped them, and was known by **The Mighty One** as a man who followed Him. He was the light in the community to show people the love of a Savior, and this is what he did every day. The angels did not linger in this area, but flew on further, and came to a housing estate with a large church in the middle of the community.

The church seemed to be popular with a number of people going in. While in the car park, a lot of people were just arriving as the angels flew down. Some were part of the congregation and were starting to gather together for a service, and others seemed to be visitors, as they hesitated as to where they should sit.

The angels flew down and went into the church, which had many people already seated, listening to a speaker. As they walked in the presence of holiness from **The Breath,** filtered down and was felt everywhere. It was beautiful, a relatively hidden aura, that gave an expectancy in the atmosphere. **The Breath** of holy anointing around the place of peace, changed people as they allowed it to. In the area near the front of the church, near to where **The Breath** was anointing, angels stood all around Him watching the events.

As soon as His beautiful person came into contact with folk, strange things happened. People started praising and worshipped and falling in repentance for the things they had done. As they did so, the dross in their lives vanished. Other things were happening, as the spirits of darkness encountered the light of the Holy Spirit, **The Breath**. Nasty spirits of sinfulness, folk had brought in with them, rushed from their sides, out of the church away from people.

The dark of sin could not stay when the light of His presence exposed it, as all around, echoed praise, for **The Promise of Heaven**, thanking Him for giving up His life for all. The encounter also brought other aspects of His presence, as astounding giftings were received from **The Breath**, as people came in the humility of spirit.

The Breath anointed, and gifts of the Holy Spirit were received for service in the body of Christ, such as healing, deliverance and words of knowledge. Evangelists, prophets, teachers and all kinds of ministry gifts were also received from **The Breath**, the Holy Spirit. It was a significant scene of worship at the front of the church in repentance and praise, as people received these gifts for service, in all forms.

Once **The Breath** anointed them, they were changed and received. Joy was apparent in abundance, as others received discernment and wisdom. It was a beautiful scene, and the leader's voice was then heard speaking from the front.

"Listen up people; we are not serving a God of wood, He is **The Mighty One**, and tells us that we are to seek to see a change in our lives. To allow **The Promise of Heaven** to be our Savior and to thank Him for dying for our wrongdoing!

The Bible, God's handbook tells us what to expect.

"My preaching is not to be just wise and persuasive words, but a demonstration of the Holy Spirit. So, your faith might not rest on men's wisdom but God's power! The anointing for living and preaching must come from **The Mighty One**, this is how it's to be people." People responded, walked forward as he spoke and knelt at the front of the church in repentance and praise, it was a lovely accumulation of people that were giving praise and worship to **The Mighty One**.

It seems that the church was made up of various groups, and as the angels moved around to see what was happening elsewhere, they noticed other things.

In the adjacent church hall, there were folk coming in, sitting talking, and surrounding them, other supernatural powers. It was all very similar, to the people in the towns, somehow.

Looking closer the two angels could see everything that these folks trailed around with them. Hate, jealousy, envy, gossip and other spirits clung to them, vying for a space in the lives of each of them. While near the back of the church, people sat in their seats and watched the service, also surrounded by a vast array of "beings."

As they watched, a man's voice was heard speaking to

someone in authority nearby.

"I have decided to join your congregation; do I have to fill in a form?" the man said. A leader's voice was heard, quietly thanking him and encouraging the man, who was called Joe to join, stating there was no paperwork required. What wasn't seen by everyone, was the spirits of darkness that were attached to the man Joe. He was carrying a considerable number of resentful, spine-chilling spirits, along with a spirit of division and uncleanness on his shoulders. Once accepted into membership, he is then introduced all around this area of the church and recognized as a member.

Nearby a large lady, a very pious woman sitting next to him was asked if she would like to join and be a member too. The man in authority smiled at her. Apparently, she was a believer he thought and gushed as he welcomed her. This woman had a spirit of religiosity, but other spirits also danced around her as she trailed them in. Carried on her shoulders was a spirit of religion, legalism and manipulation. This woman was full of pride in who she was, and the dark spirits adored her. Looking at the person who had been speaking to them, the angels saw he was also carrying baggage. Denton and Heaton were directed to one side by the angel who had brought them to this place.

"No doubt some of the things you have seen have surprised you, especially the various supernatural beings around people."

"Although, it will be apparent to you, as part of the heavenly support unit, the huge amount of heavenly beings, assisting many in the world I am sure you will have seen the numerous heavenly beings departing or arriving from Heaven, to provide help to people, just like yourselves. Angels have been working down the ages, to accomplish **The Mighty One's** will, just as you both do, on assignments. The angelic force from Heaven, contend with the enemy around the world in this way. **The Mighty One's** desire that all His children will be taken care of, and this is one of the ways we accomplish this. In fact, His words written down for them state many things, such as this."

The Mighty One, said, "...Call to me and I will answer you and I will tell you great and unsearchable things you do not know!"

"Today angels, I have shown you different things, entirely new to you both, to make you aware of another spiritual dimension around people. Because you have been on assignment for a long time in the world helping and supporting people, it is needful for you to be more informed. It is vital to understand the supernatural things that are happening in the world, and the attack on people. The enemy is smart, and it is vital that you remember this, and support personalities where possible, as he tries to infiltrate everyplace, especially churches.

Unfortunately, where people move from one church group to another, dissatisfied, they trail the same problems from place-to-place, without allowing **The Breath** to minister cleansing. This is problematic to fellowships and causes some churches to have many difficulties. Support and engage with godly leaders as much as you can, helping them through these battles. Society is fighting a war that they are unaware of and can only win through **The Promise of Heaven**. His blood protects, cleanses and empowers, it was given at Calvary, and all who call out to Him are protected.

Thankfully **The Breath** is empowering the Church and that is magnificent, which is why we are to assist wherever we can, in all ways. It is apparent that some areas and homes are infested with evil, and regions of the Earth have been given over to spiritual darkness.

This is not a problem when people give over their lives to **The Promise of Heaven**, which is why encouraging the Church in evangelism is vital.

In this church, the enemy has crept in because people do not use discernment or wisdom or ask **The Mighty One** to show them the way! Once people are anointed and seek **The Breath**, evil runs away! Sadly, the world has become permeated with evil, as people have used their free will detrimentally, to do evil. Murder, rape and other things are out of control, everywhere.

The enemy's ego has been encouraged through witchcraft, black arts, pornography and other dark matter. Society believes it is in control, and they are not, the enemy has them doing his will. Through these things, they allow more of the enemy of holiness, full range in their lives to manipulate them.

As we see around all parts of society, the enemy is working. All damaged by the blight of darkness trying to stand against **The Mighty One**. Wars have also left an indelible mark on some areas with spirits of evil encamped around nations, bringing hate, murder, rape and incest. Children can also be influenced too, through their families, as darkness can travel through generations.

Real freedom and protection are only assured through the gift that **The Promise of Heaven** brings. The blood of **The Beautiful One** brings cleansing and gives deliverance to all who have submitted their lives to Him in free will. Once the gift is accepted, change happens immediately, because He is the victor!

Angels, this has been a training time, and I have brought you to these different areas to help you understand the full extent of the opposition. Your responsibility is to help people escape from the clutches of the evil one, as much as you can.

Some of the supernatural powers have been evident on our journey, but your eyes must see much more. Darkness becomes apparent when you look through the eyes of holiness. Although you have both worked hard for the Lord, there is much to learn. Towns, cities, and nations are blighted by the enemy, all hidden from human eyes, but it is real and occupies so much of this world. Once people make a choice and decide to stand against holiness, righteousness and truth, the enemy has an open door and can infect people.

Motives that are pure but unprotected, can be influenced by the evil one. All of which you have seen, as we visited the different areas on our journey here. **The Beautiful One** came as **The Promise of Heaven** and gave up His life to protect the world from evil, so that all can escape by trusting in Him.

The protection is there for all who invite **The Promise of Heaven** to be their Savior. The battle is ongoing, but the victor is **The Mighty One**, He reigns supreme and has won. Consider all that you have seen and recognize time is getting short before the enemy tries to assert his authority for the final battle, be watchful!"

The angels went back to the assignments they been detailed, with a greater desire than ever to help this needy world.

The Church of Today

Denton and Heaton waited as the leader spoke to the people. The church was full, and it was a 2035 AD, a problematic year for the world where change and power were increasing in the hands of dubious leaders. Around the globe, the church was subtly persecuted, side-lined by most in power, as people looked for alternative things to worship. Disturbing times, as thousands of people moved around the globe to find safety. Anarchy was everywhere as world events caused unrest. Wars were constant, everywhere disenchanted people took the law into their own hands. It was a world that was unhappy, where earthquakes seemed to voice their discontent, and people lived in fear of the future.

Tonight, a group had amassed together to hear from their leader. He stood quietly looking over the people and then spoke. He was an older man, full of wisdom, concerned for his people.

"Today friends, I want to share and speak to you about the things the Lord has told me about. Mostly about the future and the difficulties we may encounter. What is vital to stress is that we are not on our own, we have each other and a most powerful adversary in our God. The God we worship is **The Mighty One**, powerful, and the Victor over all, whatever the battle we face.

Tonight, I am going to speak in a very forthright way, as He has challenged me with prophetic words for the future. Having led you for a long time, we have all experienced transition as a church family. At times, sadly we have seen the church marginalised, people leave, and sickness beset us. One day judgement will come for us all, and as your leader, I will be judged. Consequently, I must ensure that the church is ready for the future in whatever way is necessary.

The facts we are to remember, is that we are victors through the powerful blood of **The Beautiful One;** but it is going to be a rocky ride, and we must be strong.

Consequently, we must prepare and pray for all that we will have to face. Unfortunately, with a heavy heart, I have to tell you, the past has been easy, compared to what is to come!

Prophecy tells us that we will be subject to even more challenges in the future. The Lord has confirmed this to me powerfully, which is why I must convey this to you tonight. We have an advocate in our God, and He will take care of us. He has expectations of us, on how we live. We are called to be holy, which is not an option. No compromise, because once we do, cracks will appear in our walk with God.

I understand that in today's world the word holiness seems a strange word. But living this way changes the atmosphere around us, and that is the way we are to live. Perilous times await us all, and at this time, sadly many will abandon their faith. Deception is everywhere, and it will touch our lives. There will be wolves in sheep's clothing, ready to entice people away from the truth. The question today is this.... are you going to be one of the millions who will succumb? It very easy to shout no, when amongst the family of God, but when faced with persecution or temptation skilfully presented, who will be the first to be taken in by subterfuge? We can read so much in the Bible to help us, and in the book of Isaiah, it says this:

"So, justice is driven back, and righteousness stands at a distance; truth has stumbled in the streets, honesty cannot enter."

Truth is nowhere to be found, and whoever shuns evil becomes prey. It is old-fashioned language, but a good description, indicating some of the ways the future is shaping up, so we must be aware of the part we have to play. Remember the future belongs to **The Mighty One**, as does the present. Live with confidence that

He will be alongside us in all we do. We are the Church and need to continue in all that we have started, studying the Bible and building each other up, as we have done over the years' friends. This is relevant to families, especially, to nurture each other, to ensure that we build a strong army of believers confident of their faith.

Hopefully all you know that the Bible is **The Mighty One's** roadmap for us all, the manual for life's adventure. Read it avidly; it is the key to support us through difficulties in our lives. It informs us of **The Mighty One's** expectation for us on living and helps us to draw close to Him. It also reminds us not to bury the talents we have been given. Which, tonight I urge you to consider, as so very necessary. Many here have been anointed by **The Breath** the Holy Spirit, for service. It is clearly encouraging, as the Lord has shown you so much. However, some have stood deliberating, and tonight dear ones, I must help you to see a little of **The Mighty One's** expectation for all of us because time is getting short.

Our spiritual journey must be centred in using the gifts of the Holy Spirit, as we have seen over the years, **The Breath of God** is vital, and our food for survival, in public and private worship. It is most significant, I mentioned this at the beginning of my talk, and many here understand the relevance, but many are just onlookers, I urge you to start participating!

A graphic story that Jesus told reminds us that at a wedding, some bridesmaids ran out of oil (the Holy Spirit) waiting for the bridegroom to come. These bridesmaids lost out, all very significant for us, the Church. We need to be anointed by The **Breath**, the Holy Spirit. Please understand, that the Lord Jesus is coming back, and we are required to be ready, full of the Holy

215

Spirit. Yes, we are blessed as a people, on the winning side, on an exciting and awesome adventure, with everything we require to succeed, but we must participate.

As Christians we are in a unique position, as the Lord Jesus Christ is our Savior. We do not know when He will return, but everything points to being very soon. We are to ready, diligent in all we do and remember we are part of the more extensive Church family. The Lord has shown me that it is urgent that we are prepared, ready for service.

As a part of the Church around the world, there are millions of us scattered everyplace. Some isolated, possibly tiny groups, where two or three people together, all make up the Church. Of course, in the future, we may too, become like this, isolated and have to accommodate ourselves in different ways. We are not our own, and our destiny is to walk declaring this, although we may be asked to pay the ultimate price!

In the outset, the First Church also met with persecution, remember the way many were sacrificed to the lions? Just keep in mind that **The Beautiful One** is more powerful, than any circumstances that might try to overwhelm us! Above all, live under the beautiful anointing of **The Breath.** It seems that some consider this ministry too emotional, be warned, the Holy Spirit is a gift to the Church. When you do not seek His infilling and indwelling, you are discarding God's gift to the Church! It is the lifeline for the Church and judgement on those who ignore this empowering.

It is not enough to know about **The Breath** but be filled with His power. This is the only way to live as a Christian, and how the Church was born as the disciple's waited in Jerusalem.

Through the years you have been taught well and know the Scriptures, so apply this knowledge in your life. Yes, behind the scenes the enemy works and has done since Eternity. However, our support and assurance are in the triune God we worship, who never sleeps. **The Promise of Heaven** has come, ultimately, it is up to us to live empowered by the Holy Spirit as the Church, evangelising, declaring to this needy world His truth. This does not mean people, being busy, and building a platform of good works as often happens in the church!

When the Lord Jesus, **The Beautiful One** walked the Earth, He never did anything unless He consulted with **The Mighty One**. It was a lesson He taught His friends, the disciples to adopt. Which is why the way of faith, must be in the dynamic of the relationship between Earth and Heaven. **The Breath** of God must be inherently part of all of that. Therefore, prayer is the bedrock of our faith, the food for survival as a Church. It was the way that the staged assaults on the Lord, were defused and handled by Him, and vital for our survival. Power will govern, and it is up to the player to ensure that the right power has the right of way.

We have a mission, to cry before the throne of grace, for the people of the world. It was a battle that commenced in the Garden of Eden, contending for the world, and is still ongoing. Obedience and disobedience reap its rewards! It is easy to blame establishments and leaders, when things go wrong. But evil continues, and Christians can combat this by understanding the power of prayer. Obviously, we must also allow the Holy Spirit, to transform us, so that we live acknowledging **the Mighty One** in our lives constantly. Living daily, mindful of God's values at the center of our lives, must be our aim, through prayer and repentance. Prayer is the answer; which is why we are encouraged to seek and

217

pray. The Bible points this out quite graphically. Because we fight against principalities and powers in the heavenly realm, we never dreamt were real.

Let your kingdom come.........Lead us not into temptation......... "Love the Lord your God with all your heart, with all your soul and with all your strength and with all your mind, and your neighbour as yourself."

"These are all scriptures we know, but the application is up to ourselves, to be diligent and loyal. We are the Church, not a building, however ornate and welcoming it is. Unfortunately, the time of unspeakable evil will arrive soon enough, so we must be ready to be accosted by the enemy and be immovable! Continually declaring to the needy world, the love of a Savior. Remember, we are the Church family, not an isolated group, we are the body of Christ. While around the world, many elements of the Church are also declaring their faith, in various ways. Korea, Syria and the United Kingdom are examples of this.

Today, I propose to communicate some of their stories to you, their stories, to encourage you all as the Church. These are examples that we can remember when times get tough. Recognize many face a battle continually in the world today, but the Church continues to support communities. Many may describe it as the hidden Church too. In the future, we may become the hidden Church, so we must make preparation with great wisdom about all that is happening. It may come as a surprise to hear the way they function, but this is the way many have adapted as the Church!

Brothers and sisters consider all I am telling you to tonight because persecution is everyplace, and it will become apparent more and more. However, we are overcomers and can stand in His strength because our God is **The Mighty One** the Victor over all.

The Hidden Church

The speaker moved nearer to the people, and Denton watched as the man spoke with passion.

"Dear people, much of what I have discussed tonight is vital for the people of God, to develop and grow. Because gradually we may find that the Church is fragmented, as has happened in many placed throughout the world. However, it is still working and growing and sharing the love of Christ. So often we are unaware of the way people live, and in North Korea they are unique, hurting people, although surviving, living for the same principals as all of us. It is essential that we realize church can be applied in many different ways and in North Korea, they function as the hidden Church. Christians there face persecution, but the Church still functions, although different to what we call the church, it is still "church."

In one of the prison camps in North Korea, much is happening that will astound us. The Lord has touched many in different circumstances and tonight I want to disclose the life of one of these people. The regime in this nation is harsh, often people who have nothing, forced into prison, on a word from a neighbour, or something similar. Listen to this young man's story, and how he found faith in evil circumstances, through the Church, and be encouraged! Silently, he lay a prisoner, a ragged bundle of rags, hidden behind broken fencing. Surrounding the accommodation they called "huts." His breath, coming in short bursts he lay, hunched, skeletal, with sunken cheeks, and dark eyes half closed, still. His wispy grey hair hung in small clumps over his head, surrounded by large bald patches. Clutched in a filthy hand, he held something tightly.

His face was contorted in terror, as he tried to crawl further into his hiding place under the building if that was possible. Opening his mouth to reveal black teeth, he started to gnaw on a tiny square of wax in his hand. In his weak state, his breath came jerky, and he had difficulty swallowing. Endeavouring to consume the wax he persevered, then lay still, as a tear ran down his cheek. Suddenly racked in sobs, whispered words fell from his mouth. His deep Korean voice hardly perceptible was distraught. Desperation, desolation, how, could this broken man be helped?

Living in an interminable harsh environment, with fatalities daily, scant food, continually working dawn to dusk, Hye-Jin was defeated. In two years, his teeth were rotting, falling out just like his hair. It was the regime of terror in the nation that ensured people knew who had the power and respected its hold on society. Some while back, Hye-Jin's father was hustled away one night because of a little infringement and imprisoned. Just before this, he had tried to explain to his son the Christian story. Hye-Jin had shrugged it off, frightened of anything, not of the state. He did not want to be accused of being involved in a Christian organisation and taken away.

Although the state, relentless, never left anything, and years later, they had taken him. His crime, a wilful father, youngsters had to pay for a father's misdeeds it seems. Once imprisoned, he had searched for his father, but could find nothing. Traumatised by so much, he lay and tried to remember the word repeated by his father? Those words had special meaning, and suddenly it came to him -

he remembered." Jesus" that was it. His father had said that He was a mighty God, powerful and that He had died for everyone. At that Hye-Jin shuddered, even thoughts like that were treasonable!

In North Korea, it was inconceivable that any person was given more significance in any way, than the enormous statues, the ancestors or Gods, the people had to bow down to everyday. According to the regime, this must never happen on pain of death? His father had shown him something, he remembered. Hye-Jin searched for two tiny fragments of wood in the Earth, recollecting, it was a cross.

Gazing at the slivers of wood in his hand, he moved them into the shape of a cross, recollecting his father's words and considered them. He was to bow down and worship this Jesus! Quietly he contemplated all of this…if Jesus was a God, He had power. If He had power, could He help Hye-Jin, or would He want to help him? Why would He want to help, unless, to show His power? His father had used a significant word, not one, Koreans ever used. He said…" Jesus was love," what was that?

Suddenly, his stomach convulsed and Hye-Jin knew he had not long, he had seen it with others. Days of watery soup and many without anything, the body closed down until it gave up. He felt defeated, wretched, he knew chewing on a piece of candle wax wasn't going to help; this was the end!

He looked at the two tiny pieces of wood in his hand, if this Jesus was real, where was He? Certainly, He was not amongst this degrading community? However, wherever He was, He might be able to hear…if Hye-Jin spoke His name. In a harsh deep guttural voice, racked in pain Hye -Jin spoke out His name, "Jesus." Looking at the cross, He repeated it, "Jesus." Then with a boldness that just came over Him, Hye- Jin said, "I believe you are a God, higher than any of those around me, and you have love, I need that love and your help."

As this wasted, broken man cried out in his desperation, a shaft of sunlight broke through. He lay still, as its rays reached down and touched him, God's love was there. **The Breath** of God washed over him to minister peace and love; he was not alone.

They found his body eventually, and the guards threw him over the fence, there was no need to exert themselves with a grave. Dead prisoners were tiresome...another problem to deal with, no one would know!

In a comatose state, confused, Hye-Jin awoke on a cot, startled by an old man.

"Get better son, sleep; you are safe now!" Later, Hye-Jin awoke to find a piece of bread and a small cup of warm tea waiting next to him. Sitting up, he sipped the tea, dipping the bread into it and looked around. A bare room with little indication to its inhabitants, suddenly he heard a stool scrape the floor, and the old man came in.

"Oh, you're awake, good, lay and get refreshed, I will get you away from here, to escape."

Hye-Jin nodded, wondering where he was.

The old man spoke again, "I cut trees and found you lying outside the prison; you looked dead. You are safe here, but tomorrow you must go, as they may check my house!" The old man smiled a toothless grin. "Don't worry we will get you away so that you can get strong. There is a place, not too far away in the forest! Though, I must be about my work in case anyone notices.

Sleep on and get rested."

With that the old man disappeared and Hye-Jin was alone. Later the following night, he was taken by an old woman into the forest. Everything was done with gestures and hand signals, in case anyone was listening. But silently, he followed the woman through thick undergrowth. It was a lengthy walk, that came out onto a plateau that surrounded a hilly area. Exhausted by this time and with bleeding feet, Hye-Jin wondered if he could carry on, but slowly and steadily they walked on, a miracle for Hye-Jin.

Not stopping, they continued up to a higher elevation, with rocks and boulders everywhere. This was harsh terrain, mountainous area and Hye -Jin hesitated, but his guide motioned him to continue, this time on to a steep, rough pathway. Numerous caves surrounded them here, where it was quite high up as the morning light started to break through the sky.

Hye-Jin exhausted by now, followed his companion, as they climbed onto a narrow steeper pathway higher still. Eventually, they turned into a cave, with a hidden opening that was spacious inside. It was inhabited, and had various areas for sleeping, cooking and eating. Once inside, a friendly welcome awaited them and Hye- Jin sat on one of the benches and put his head on his hands. A man came over after a few minutes, he brought water and food and welcomed Hye-Jin.

Meanwhile, his companion was in deep conversation with the old man. It seems they knew each other well and after talking, he eventually bowed low to her and gave her a package of food. She came over to Hye-Jin and took his hands in hers, smiling she bowed to him, and then departed. The old man came over and sat down next to Hye-Jin and started chatting. He reassured Hye-Jin that this was a safe place and he must rest once he had eaten.

Hye-Jin gazed about him; where exactly was he? The cave was huge, and it had many areas, including wall recess's with sleeping pallets in them, some on high shelves. Coats were hung up, and everything seemed very orderly everywhere. Then he stiffened, what was that, at the end of the cave, deep inside, a wooden cross hung on the wall? What was this place?

The old man came over, once Hye -Jin had eaten and ushered him to a pallet to lie down on and rest, and then took out ointment from a cupboard. Taking Hye-Jin's feet into his hands, he tenderly washed them and anointed them with the soothing balm. Assuring the young man, he was safe, he then gave him a blanket and left him to rest. Hye-Jin was so tired, but before he drifted off to sleep, he wondered about so much, where he was, and who lived at this place? Quite disturbed, his mind was befuddled…feet washing, a cross, his thoughts confused him. Could this be something his father had talked about, the Church. He thought whatever it is, it must be a "Jesus" place. Tomorrow he must ask more about where he was, but for now, he was safe and secure without the dreaded roll call in prison, and life felt wonderful. The leader gazed at his congregation.

"I am sure you will agree, that this was a tremendous story? An example of how the Church works and functions in exceptional circumstances, just like the people in the Bible. These people are far away in North Korea, but the Church isn't asleep. It is active in that country as well as here. We can be encouraged through this that there in North Korea the Lord is working, as in other countries all around the world and learn lessons. Another story close to my heart, where there is love is in Syria. In that war-torn place, **The Mighty One** is not far away. It is always good to remember that the Lord walks with us everyplace, and we are never on our own! And in Syria, although fear and sadness are endemic, people are still steadfastly showing Christian love in difficult circumstances. Trauma and hate abound, but the light of **The Promise of Heaven** gets through. I call this the church in dust and ashes. A wonderful example that in the future we may need to remember. It's about a little family and the way they cope with their life in a war zone.

The Church in Dust and Ashes

The noise of war was all around them as a family waited in trepidation. It was astounding…listening to the noise of the bombs, wondering what was going to happen today. Fear was in the eyes of the children as the shells whistled over the rooftops and crashed into the wall on the other side. The youngest clung on to his mother and put his arms around her neck. "Mama, mama," he said as tears came down his cheek. The woman gripped him fiercely and hugged her other two children close to her." It will finish soon," she said as they clung to each other shaking. It finally finished, as a shell blew the roof off the top of their building in a mighty explosion! Scrambling across the floor, clutching each other with debris falling all around, they made for the stairs.

Impossible to see the stairwell, the woman dragged her children, hoping it was there. The dust made it difficult to breathe, and the mother used her shawl to hold on to the little one and clutched the others close to her. The family managed to reach the ground, amid the screams and smoke, suffocating all around them. Emerging, they climbed out of the hole that was the doorway, which lay in pieces on the ground. Coughing, trying to get their breath, they gasped as they inhaled the clean air and shielded their eyes from the bright sunlight. Alabo, her husband rushed over to the family from the other side of the road. Putting his hand on the heads of the children in reassurance, he took the baby out of his wife's arms. He had a bandage on his head and was covered in dust and motioned his family away from the area.

He manoeuvred his wife forward through the rubble, as she grabbed the hands of the other children and the family tried to move away quickly from the chaos all around. Clutching the child close to him, Alabo put an arm around his wife and tried to shield his family from all that was happening. An ambulance rushed past them, people injured screamed, it was a terrifying sight, as the family tried to get past, climbing over rocks scattered everywhere.

Noise, confusion and the fear of missiles, was everyplace in the area. As the little group tried to get away, it was a matter of climbing over debris fallen from the buildings that had made walking perilous. Their aim was to reach a peaceful area on the other side of the city, to escape for a while the turmoil all around them. With their home gone, they needed a place of sanctuary. All around, people lay injured on the ground being tended, surrounded by rubble and roof debris.

All of this made it difficult to walk, while overhead the torrent of missiles whistled by, finally landing with a terrifying crash, making them cringe. They had lived on this street a long time, and now the area was a bomb site, that had once housed their friends. They turned a corner and found a vehicle lying in the road, surrounded by people and stretchers. The stench of a putrid aroma hung in the air, as Alabo motioned his wife quickly forward, past the chaos surrounding them.

Hurrying on, through the mayhem that seemed to be everyplace, they walked for miles, passing many bombs sites, with the occasional vehicle rushing past. After hours of walking, Alabo gave the baby to his wife and carried the children because they were tired. Recognizing that they all needed to rest, Alabo eventually turned down an alleyway, looking for shelter.

This part of the city was a bombsite, but quieter as the sound of missiles had become less evident. Searching, they eventually found a building that had little bomb damage and climbed up the steps. At the top of the steps, they almost fell over a man sitting near the door, surrounded by rocks and bricks. Helping the children over the debris inside the door, he held out his hand to his wife as they entered the building. In the gloom inside, they realized others had sought sanctuary here too, sitting on the ground or on seats all around. The family stood, not wanting to mix, wondering where this was and who was here.

A man came up and greeted them in Arabic, motioning them to take the children inside where there were rugs on the floor. Alabo walked forward inside with his wife, who lay the baby down on one of the large rugs, deep inside the building. Further on, other little ones lay asleep, some with their mothers, nursing them. The little one had fallen asleep as they travelled, and the other children hunkered down on the rugs next to him, tired from their trek.

Alabo crouched down next to his wife and looked around. It was a massive building, and he suddenly realized what it was, a disused church. He frowned this was not the place that a Muslim wanted to find himself in. The man who had spoken to them when they arrived brought them a tray of drinks and offered them to the children. The children looked at their father; they would not dare take anything unless he gave his agreement. Alabo smiled his thanks to the man and nodded to the children. They were thirsty and drank quickly, as did Alabo and his wife. It did not take long for the children to sleep alongside the baby, while Alabo whispered to his wife.

After a few hours, the children awoke, while by now the baby had been fed, but the children were hungry. Joram, the man who had welcomed them, spoke to Alabo and told him there was a little food for them all in the building next door. Alabo thanked him, and the family moved out to the building next door. Opening a big door, they were surprised to see many sitting down and eating, families in a similar state to themselves. Joram came over to talk to them as the family sat down and were offered food by a server.

It seems he was the official here; it was a Christian group who were trying to give out help in the area. The man Joram had injuries similar to so many and walked with a limp. He told Alabo they were welcome to stay as long as they liked. The area was a haven, a place where they accepted anyone who required help, explaining that after everyone had eaten, he and his team moved everything around for people to sleep.

Later Alabo lay with the family thinking of their options; they needed to escape from this melee of chaos. His children deserved peace and safety which was not in his homeland at this time; the war was all around them. It must be time to face the future elsewhere.... meanwhile how welcoming this had been, just a few hours respite from the chaos of the world.

A church who would have ever thought it, mused Alabo? He looked over at the cross, a picture of love in the midst of turmoil and hatred in the world. Yes, there are certainly many ways to show love, and this was one of them, an empty cross, holding out its arms to a needy world, who would have thought it?"

At the church of today, the leader paused, moved around the room. Speaking quietly, he said, "As we all realize people, this is not a great work that many will hear about, but a hand of love and kindness to needy people. It was just a drink and a little food, but tangible evidence of people who cared. How hard it is to stand for righteousness in the face of darkness and war. It is using our hands and feet, our giftings, as **The Beautiful One** expects us to. Reaching out to others, shows we care.

There is one other story I want to speak about tonight, set inside a busy city. Everywhere there is the hustle and bustle of people, but many are the forgotten ones sleeping rough on our streets. In the United Kingdom, a small ministry has developed, where a man shows tremendous love. His story is entirely different from the others but unique, built on love, and a desire to help those who had found life hard. I called it the serving church.

The Serving Church

In a slum area in England, a man is working industriously to get a lot of food prepared.

A man outside shouted to him. "One out here Boss, half cut."

"Bring him in Gordon and put him on that chair," said the man fixing a huge pile of food at the cooker. The room was apparently a kitchen in a doss house and reeked of many strange smells, some more palatable than others. Through a doorway, there was a corridor leading into very sparse bedrooms. Here an assortment of men in a variety of clothing moved around finding a cot for sleeping on. In the other direction a dining room, with many different tables surrounding a huge trestle table. The place was buzzing with noise, movement and the distinct smell of people! The smell of cooking started to permeate everything, overriding the smell of bodies, which was good. The aroma was possibly a dish of chicken and undoubtedly mashed potatoes which lay inviting in a large pan.

The man cooking had a considerable belly, a big toothy grin and a big apron covering all. He shouted down the corridor, and another big guy came in, younger, and also sporting a large pinafore.

"Joe, round up the men and bring them in for grub!"

The younger man grunted and went outside into the hallway. He had a big gong in his hands which he bashed with sheer delight and then hollowed into various rooms that food was out. All of this was met with grunts of approval from the men in their rooms, who started to drift out along the corridor.

At the same time, Gordon had emerged through the doorway, bringing in a bundle of rags, that contained a very dirty intoxicated man. No one took the least bit of notice, as they went past and piled in for their meal. Gordon, once in the kitchen, pulled the man down on to an armchair that was nearby. "He was lying in the gutter, surrounded by rubbish, and he's got a cut on his arm," he said in a very flat voice as if he was giving a lecture.

"Get some coffee in him," said the pot-bellied apron, still organising the food.

"There's plenty in the pot," he nodded in the direction of a container on the side. "It's hot but not scalding; it should help to sober him up!"

With that, he walked into the dining room with various dishes on the trolley and started to serve food. Around about, there was a distinct sound of scratching of chairs on the wooden floor as men got up and crowded around the serving trolley. Added to which the clatter of plates resounded, as everyone was served a portion of the hot food.

In the kitchen, the drunk was given coffee by Gordon who held it to his lips, and the man managed to gulp some of the hot sweet liquid down. The dining room was beginning to get a little quieter, except for the scrapping of plates. Although soon, in the corridor another group of bedraggled men came through the door and headed straight for the dining room.

The chef at the trolley, bellowed out, "Hands men, get the grime off your hands first," and a small grey-haired server, ushered them into the facilities, where they got soap and a small hand towel. Joe got out plates and sorted out forks, for the new arrivals. Once the desired hand washing had been finalised, they came through to get their food, forming a queue at the door as more arrived.

"Gordon bring the other pan," shouted the white pinafore, to the kitchen.

At this Gordon broke off from supporting the bundle of rags on the chair and picked up the pan on the stove. Shoving past the men, who made way for him into the dining room, he deposited the food on the trolley.

"Full house and more Boss, are you going to have enough?"

Boss grinned at him, "Don't you worry old boy, I will keep enough for you!"

With that Gordon headed straight back to the kitchen to bring in another pan.

"Get those other chairs out of the cupboard and put them down on the other side!" said the big apron, or the Boss as Gordon called him.

"We won't have enough room unless you bring them, and this lot can seat themselves there," said the Boss gesticulating to Joe.

Joe and Gordon brought twenty additional seats into the room and lined them up against the wall and window, ensuring that they all had a place by the time they got their food. Gordon then resumed his task of sobering up the man in the kitchen. After much coaxing, the man now drank the coffee and looked more like a person than a bundle of cloth. He held the cup, and Gordon heard his deep muffled thanks as he finished the drink.

"We have food in the dining room, why don't you go and get yourself a plate, it will do you good!" said Gordon pointing in the direction of the men eating. The bundle got up and staggered to the doorway, "Best if you wash your hands, I will show you where." said Gordon and beckoned to the man at the door. Once all of these rituals were out of the way, the man staggered to the chef in the dining room for food. The Boss was getting to the end of the queue as the man from the kitchen arrived.

"You ok mate?" said the chef.

The man grunted and nodded as the Boss filled a plate for him. Putting him on the end of a table with other men around him, he nodded to one of them.

"Look out for him John; he's not been around these parts before!"

A cheery guy in a red beret looked up from his food and smiled.

"Hi, I'm John, what's your name?"

The man nodded back, "Jack."

With that he started to eat; apparently, it had been some time since he had done so, and he ate ravenously. The Boss then went around the table, filling up plates for all who wanted more, while Gordon and Joe took around cups of tea. There was a tray of bread pudding that also circulated, and the men took the large lumps, some putting it into their pockets for later. Once everyone was fed the room relaxed, and the boss got on to a small stand at the other end of the room.

"Good to see you all here boys, we will be putting cots in here tonight for latecomers. However, before you go to doss down, I want to tell you about a friend of mine. Many have heard this story before, but it's worth repeating. Twenty years ago, my life was a mess, I lost everything; I had a problem, I couldn't keep off the booze. An old girl saw me in the gutter, took me to her house, although I'd never seen her before. She gave me food and a bed and helped me when no one else cared. I was in a desperate place. I'd lost family, my job and I was, on my own. Her kindness made a difference, she didn't have much, but she cared. She also introduced me to this. The man lifted up an old wooden cross. She didn't ram it down my throat but just told me this true story.

It started years ago, the Bossman who owned the whole

universe wanted to help people here in the world. He saw the mess we make of our lives. He had a plan; He would allow His Son to come to Earth as a gift, to save people, His Son was like Him, special. All that happened precisely in that way, His son came to Earth, but people saw His power and were jealous and hated Him.

The people then concocted a plan and decided to get rid of him, kill Him off, which is what they did. They killed Him, but they forgot about the power He and His dad had. His Son's blood was like gold; one-touch would save you. So, His son Jesus' death became a gift to the whole world! He was so pure; He came back to life and His power works in your life, if you invite Him to help you each day. Like you have to turn a tap on to get water. It's like this boys, He is not just a powerful man, He is someone who saves, and it's a freebie, the only thing to remember is that you have to ask for it!

So, this bit of wood, this cross they nailed Him to, and left Him to die on, became significant. It's incredible but as I said, it's because He was the Boss's Son, He also became the one who saves people, because He loves them.

Boys, me, I was broke, no one cared whether I lived or died; they'd all given up on me. But when this old biddy told me about Jesus, the Boss's Son, who died for people, I wanted to believe it

She made it quite simple, it's all about feeling sorry here, (he thumped his heart!) and talking to the Boss (he pointed to Heaven). So, one day I spoke to Him, told the Boss I was sorry for the mess I'd made with my life, thanked Him for the gift of His Son.

I know He heard, I changed, drink and the bottle, it just wasn't important anymore. I wasn't a nobody; I was a somebody, and I was different. This cross signifies it, and as I pass it around, remember boys to thank Him. He loves you." After saying all of this, he got down from the podium, gave the cross to one of the old boys and went out to the kitchen.

The "boys" eventually got up from the table and some went down to the bedrooms for their night's sleep. Some cots were then put out for the overspill, but soon the dining room was empty apart from dishes. The boss in the kitchen started to heat food for the helpers, while the others started the long haul of dirty plates.

Quite soon he called them, "Come on fellahs, time for our grub!"

The three of them were joined by the chap on the outside door and started to eat.

Gordon spoke first, "You know boss that story is it true and did it make a difference to you, after meeting her?" Boss laughed.

"Well old fellah, how long have I known you, ten years, why didn't you ask me before now?"

Gordon laughed, "It all seemed to be too good to be true, I thought you just were a do-gooder Boss," said Gordon.

The boss scratched his head, "Oh, I couldn't run this place, get food for them and care, I am a miracle, and it is all to do with that!" He pointed to the cross.

"I know the miracle man, I know Jesus, the Boss's Son, but more than that, He knows me. Oh, Gordon," at this, the big guy started to weep.

"He is real and so full of love and accepted a worn-out old reprobate like me, oh yes I know the Son!" He rubbed his face with worn out hands, and as they started to eat, he smiled. "Oh, yes I know the Son!"

Gordon smiled, "Well Boss, I guess this is the church?"

Boss just smiled and went on eating.

The leader smiled at his people and said to the congregation, "Wow, quite a testimony wasn't it? A powerful ministry of love, to those who will most probably never reciprocate or acknowledge the sacrifice made. These are all real people sharing God's heart in a needy world, and the man Gordon was right, it is the Church.

These are all lovely stories from different worlds, unique people, doing the same thing "doing church." Undoubtedly hearing these great examples of people showing the love of Christ, and using the God-given talents, that they have been given must be an encouragement to us all. A question tonight might be, the talents that you have been given, what are you doing with them?

The Church is the people of God, loving and providing for all, the Lord Jesus' hands and feet! These stories are mere examples of people using their giftings, their talents! Whatever happens in the future remember all that you hear and have been taught, as our future will be challenging.

In the book of Revelation, it tells us to be ready as the judgement of all people will happen, even as the surge of darkness increases. It is realistic and necessary to understand that supernatural powers do not sleep and will endeavour to cause havoc, to infect society and get forces ready to fight the last battle. Evil powers intend to put off Jesus coming to reign in any way he can, the only thing to focus on and remember, is that the battle was won at Calvary!

Throughout our lives, we must be prepared to face

difficulties, also reminding ourselves that we are on the winning side. The battle has been won. These are just the enemy's tiresome skirmishes! Remember church, for all of us, the book of Revelation is to be read, because the last battle is on the horizon and we must be willing to live or die for Christ. We must all be ready!"

Blackened and the Mob

Wap glanced at his leader and snarled, "What have you got us down here for Master!"

The word master was used in a sneering sarcastic way as Blackened summoned his troops around him. They had gathered together, hundreds of beings, of all shapes and sizes that were under the rule of Blackened. Some gave the appearance of being quite jolly until you saw all that they carried. Witchcraft spells, even religious icons were in full view and all around was the smell of death.

A section of them had names emblazoned on them, badges, distinguishing their seniority and showing the spiritual strongholds they represented. These mighty beings had heavenly areas designated to them, huge strongholds, power structures with thousands of spirits attached to them, their power was phenomenal.

Elsewhere there was quite a lot of pushing and shoving between other minor demons as they contended for places next to the elite force of devils. Different languages could be heard at the gathering, although everyone spoke a universal language of evil.

Some carried symbols of the nations that they had power

links to, while spirits of pornography danced all around. Meanwhile warring spirits with eyes bulging, bashed whoever was in their path. In all, it was a ferocious army of darkness assembled.

There was no disguising their uses; warring militant angels amassed together, glaring, as they invaded each other's territory. Anger pulsated around the mass gathered, as the fiends of darkness listened to Blackened.

Our master is arriving and wants to know why we haven't taken more ground for him? His voice was deep and penetrating, "Listen, we had a few slight setbacks over time, nothing too tricky but we have had to increase our workload and become more subtle. Our strategy is significant, smooth and entirely manageable, but the end of the age is coming closer, and he requires a bigger effort. Which is why you are here."

Suddenly, the air was filled with a cloud of dark sulphur, as Satan arrived with a huge entourage of evil beings surrounding him. He snarled at those around and nodded to Blackened.

Screaming abuse at those who got in his way, he sat on top of a mountain and gazed down at his troops. Speaking very calmly he addressed them all.

"I need more control, and fear is a great way to control all, an essential element to engulf people," he sneered. I want them to dread the future. Make them fear what is coming and detest all leadership; use key people and ensure they are indoctrinated and work for us. We have achieved great gains with the people we have enlisted. Leaders who want power at any cost, are fuelling the right evil pursuits, we have taken over their minds, and they are now under our complete control. We have powerful spirits of lawlessness, who are working well in some areas overwhelming governments, that are now in confusion."

A cheer went up, from some of his minions as he continued.

"Revolutions have started, and leaders are locking up all Christians and banning churches. Anarchy, and violence are endemic in many countries where revolutions are bringing everything into chaos. It's just wonderful how you can make people do your will!" Satan spat out at those around him.

"Huge musical festivals are proving useful, as sex, drugs, and evil is indoctrinated to vast crowds, and many are controlled by us. Computers, and the media are being used to feed violence, death and all sorts of fake news, but I require more…We have many on the inside working on news channels, that are completely under our domain; they do what we want, and nations are fed and governed in this way. Although, we must increase our hold in this area, by ensuring that all media is taken over by us, that violence, and evil in all forms, is fed to the masses, especially the younger generation.

Deviants, of all kinds are required, perverted warped minds, that will do all that we want. We are successful in many areas as, communities, churches, schools, universities are now powerhouses, hotbeds of evil, it has taken time, but we have done it. However, I require more effort to ensure marriage becomes a thing of the past and focus on all sorts of perverse relationships. It will take time although many are embracing that way now, but we have accomplished much and will continue to do so.

Democracy needs to be thought futile, and give strength to every means of darkness, spirits, work together on this. Get all the do-gooders locked in jail, but leave nothing to chance and his voice lowered, don't get near to any of the Holy Spirit stuff; it will kill you off quick! Society must not be allowed to acknowledge the power of…. **The Breath**, at this, many fiends gasped!

Be extremely subtle in every approach, and ensure all deception appears utterly harmless on the surface and we've got them! Powers and governments must make war between themselves continuously and involve other nations. Make sure no leader goes safely, trip them up, especially the religious ones, let deception reign! Work systematically, so that evil is the new norm, as we have over centuries. There is a time frame with all of this, and it needs to all be in place fast. Poverty, lust, violence, hate and despair must be fed into every society, and ensure un-forgiveness is high on the list."

Muffled cheers all around as Satan's voice droned on directing the evil beings. "I have noticed some of you are languishing and I am very unhappy with this lazy attitude. Why allow so-called 'important people,' if you get my point, being allowed to sow their Christian seeds? Those who have not been doing their job will be hearing from me; I will certainly be giving you a visit. Evil in all forms must prevail; I do not want excuses." With that, his voice went up a decibel, and his cheeks bulged as he spat out at those nearby, his yellow lips curling into an evil smile.

"Fortunately for us, many are busy calling up the spiritual kingdom in séances."

All around him great cheer went up, and sneering laughter cut his words off.

"As I was saying they are doing us a favour, they are increasing our numbers, as the witchcraft spirits are doing. People think they are in control and call up these unclean spirits, and they join us, so wickedly helpful!"

Another cheer went up.

All scandalous and good, increasing our numbers very significantly, make sure the new ones learn well! We want them to be as filthy as us!"

Another long cackle of laughter heard in the background from the demons.

"That is it; I will let you know when I need you all to come again, get out and go fight, and make sure it is filthy!

Watch out for those who have faith; they will discover you and kill you off, don't let it happen. That 'book,' and his voice went quiet, is poison to us, don't get near it, the contents are what they call holy! Keep your distance from any of this 'call to worship' it is nasty holy stuff that you will not be able to fight. Keep away from all the words of....and his voice went so low it was hardly audible....... Jesus, and..... the blood, you cannot succeed against it!"

A screech went up as the whole group cringed at the name spat out and Blackened laughed as Satan continued.

"We are out to destroy the enemy and to take back power, and that's what we will do. Get out now and do your worst, remember...I will be watching you! I want territory, nations and governments everywhere to fall into our hands, that is what I expect. Now go and dominate all society, time is getting short. We do not have long before the end."

Quickly the army sped away. Over lands and seas intent on getting the job done. It was the darkness of evil, endeavouring to try to bring Hell to Earth! Quite soon the last battle was to commence when all of creation would be affected!

Reflections on the Finale

In the world of the supernatural and the unseen world of imagination, extraordinary things happen. Within this world, we must recognize that preparation for the finale of life is progressing, much of what is known as the battle of the Last Days. Unseen but reposing, all amassed, waiting for the future to tip over to the present, many gather, waiting for the anticipated events; to accede. It is a battle, and it will happen! As in all conflicts, possibly stanzas will flutter over troops, in readiness to defend their cause. Which stanza will you be standing under is a question all must ask themselves.

The flag of righteousness, it is cross-stained with blood, declaring holiness and truth. Next to it, a flag of life with the signs of the world, war, finance and power. Lastly, a standard of evil clothed in the blackness of the night, with forces of all kinds depicted on its surface. It all seems so simple, but analysing where our heart's desire is centred, is vital. These are three stanzas that boldly declare power, but only one was to be the victor, and His name was **The Mighty One,** God!

The Beginning and the End

When a story begins, it requires an ending or at least a satisfying conclusion. The reality is that this is not just a story; it is the life's journey of a mighty Creator and evil supernatural power. The progress of truth within all this is a remarkable adventure that culminated in **The Promise of Heaven,** the giver of salvation. Much time has elapsed since the tremendous sacrifice. It is time now to scrutinise how the world honored the gift and bring judgement. It was to be the time when the author of evil was made to account for his actions. Weighty and deliberate, all planned by **The Mighty One** long ago, although the exact timing was His alone to know.

Righteousness, far searching contemplative was to deal with sinfulness. The actual scenario was to be played out on the world's scene, for all to witness, the demise of the enemy. In reality, it is a hidden war continued from creation, glossed over, or forgotten; in an attempt by the powers of darkness to work in subterfuge. It is an extraordinary battle of truth and righteousness, between holiness and Hell. Once the world of creation open and transparent, full of great promise, became corrupted, it changed, deviated through sin from its original purpose. All understood and known by the Creator, who recognized the frailty of human nature and the cunning of the enemy.

The plan to use special people to unfold His will was unique and significant. He knew that one day closure would come and then He'd deal with the enemy forcibly. To accomplish this necessitates a finale. Moreover, as the Revealer of truth in all circumstances, He is a dynamic power, vast and complex, with plans that were astounding, yet to be revealed to the world.

In the beginning, He desired to create a people He could relate to, a relationship born out of love and humanity, an elaborate plan that was a fantastic feat. It required trust and love, ensuring humanity reciprocated His love in obedience, but not a compliance with the law, but of righteousness, love and free will.

Within this plan, **The Mighty One** had legions of angels that worshipped and adored their Creator. One of these, a beautiful heavenly individual named Lucifer, had succumbed to pride, endeavouring to elevate himself above **The Mighty One**, if that was ever possible? It was allowing this boastful spirit freedom to associate with created beings who could make choices, that the real test became apparent.

Once created, the human beings had free will to decide to go the way of righteousness and follow their Creator or be wooed into a friendship with darkness. Freewill in this relationship was of paramount importance. Not a robotic force, but creatures who loved and acknowledged their Creator. Of course, one could say this was a gamble, but **The Mighty One** understood the future. He realized that many would succumb to a way of unrighteousness, embrace sinfulness; snared into Lucifer's web, as evil was allowed to prevail.

Consequently, He made provision to protect the world from darkness and arranged for a Savior to achieve this. This gift of salvation was demonstrated to all, when **The Beautiful One** arrived, the Savior of humanity, for those who accepted his gift. The sacrifice foretold down the ages, through the Law and prophets was announced as a future event, the start of the birthing of holiness for people. All systematically worked out in **The Mighty One's** plan, to ensure that all had a way to escape the grasp of evil.

This terrible evil, that was far-reaching, significantly impacted world domination and had to be eradicated. However, people must take responsibility, as to how they live.

God's desire was that people would honor the giver of the

gift and walk in holiness, realising that evil of all kinds was wrong. While judgement was on the way for all people, the cost of following a pathway of righteousness or evil would reap its own rewards. Watching closely all that was happening, the enemy of all stood on the Earth, determined to use his strategic supernatural forces to win the final battle. Satan's focus was clear, to usurp **The Mighty One** and to use his own powers of evil everywhere.

The New World Order

In Heaven the angels watched for the signal, ready to deliver the finale. Poised and alert, stood myriads of warring angels; prepared to serve and to fight to the death! The enemy of holiness, evil, was going to be finally eradicated finished, the victor was always going to be **The Mighty One**. Also gathered in readiness together, were horses and riders ready to do T**he Mighty One**'s will, prepared to fight to the end.

On Earth, the Church, the soldiers of Christ, were in disarray. Required to be the front line of defence, for supporting society in holiness, they were proving weak. **The Breath** was there, but many did not receive the power of the Holy Spirit, duped into thinking it was irrelevant. The modern world had laughed at the old world of Church, as science had taken over.

A new world order had begun, where the sanctity of life was sneered at, as the rise of power escalated. Some were into black arts and worshipped idols, encouraging society to make laws to enforce these pursuits. Others put their trust in objects of science and power, as they adopted a way of life that was self-centred.

While a war to eradicate holiness, severe, and unyielding was everywhere, its main desire, never to retreat until it attempted to achieve its end. **The Mighty One,** conscious of this, realized that all had been given through The **Beautiful One's** gift of salvation given for all.

"Behold I stand at the door and knock if anyone hears my voice I will come in and stay!"

It was an invitation to all people to accept His love, just as it was also victory over sin. Ridiculed as old-fashioned "bumpkim" these words mostly fell on stony ground. People enticed by other things ignored the call, and corruption was woven into the church cleverly, as science was elevated, and God thought as trivial.

Truth had been given over to the schemes of the enemy, contrived and manipulated cleverly, to try to make the Church of little value. Although, some leaders taught about the requirement to walk in the way of truth and holiness, still others found it difficult.

The enemy was buoyant. While all of Heaven watched, as Christians slipped further into apathy, as the requirement to consider End Times prophecy seemed irrelevant. The fact was that many were confused about the End Times. What was apparent, was that no one was entirely sure of what he or she should do. Many had envisaged this period in the world and discussions developed on how radical they should be? Sadly, many fell further away, caught up in the deception and evil practiced all over the world. **The Mighty One's** truth exchanged for a lie. Miracles accomplished in the name of righteousness conceived in Hell. Discernment was not used and finding the real truth, became difficult for people.

The body of Christ became even weaker and ineffectual. A

self-centred deluded world absorbed in all kinds of powers had taken over. It was the time for the strategy that God had organised to be put into effect, the battle of the ages.

The gift to mankind of **The Promise of Heaven** had given people a way back to holiness. Kicked out the enemy's rights to keep people in death. Knowing this, Satan was not going to sit quietly by, but continued to fight on furiously!

As an omnipotent powerful creator, **The Mighty One** was always prepared and knew all that was going to happen and was taking action. He watched the enemy put his schemes in place, to corrupt society in every way, confident of His plans for the future. Silently working behind the scenes, a supernatural power of evil systematically wooed nations, families, and media, in an endeavour to achieve its goal. In fact, it was merely a web of evil intrigue, of supernatural proportion, fed to a relatively unsuspecting world.

Power was revealed to be in the hands of evil men, such as the man of Perdition. He was no ordinary person, versed in the art of black magic, he became stronger and stronger. This man of darkness deluded the world, mocked holiness and **The Mighty One**.

Humanism, deception and lawlessness reigned, vying for supremacy in the world. Consequently, the dictator put extraordinary plans in place, with allusions to deceive and woo all. He amassed an army of robotic forces, so human in appearance that many were deceived. These forces were programmed to dominate and control, while the use of holograms to bring fear made it difficult to know the difference between reality and deception. In fact, deception became a fundamental way of misleading the masses and was used in every possible way, with science and pseudoscience, especially encouraged by the dictator.

World leaders duped continuously into a feeling of peace, not realising the incredulous strategies of power, cunning and deception fed to them. As time went on things became worse, with turmoil everywhere, as shortages of food became a daily occurrence. Although continually, Denton and Heaton with many other angels tried to support people everywhere.

Virtual reality was endemic, holograms and a view of the global leader demanding allegiance, beamed over the sky, a great control mechanism. So many deceptive techniques in science executed, making people on the verge of hysteria. Fear of the "Big Brother" syndrome everyplace, with few voicing opinions. Society was cowed, intimidated as they recognized they could not escape surveillance. Christians were put in prison for their faith regularly. While the apocryphal was happening as a mighty force of darkness became evident.

Mentioned in the book of Revelation, as the Beast, this potent force of darkness appeared. It was a correct description, as the thing, a massive being, made his way over nations to take control. He had mighty powers of evil and killed and desecrated all in his path, moving through land and sea, taking no captives. He did miracles to enforce his hold on nations, and many were jubilant at his dominance. Hailing his leadership as mighty and his power to annihilate nations, especially in the Middle East. He aimed to denigrate every part of holiness, bring evil to the fore and kill as many of Christ's followers as he could. Although the Church did not give up, it struggled, and many members went into hiding!

Decrees were now repeatedly issued, by this duo of

darkness, ideas and thoughts from the pit of Hell, to control the world in every way. Quickly, they enforced control through laws to dominate their power over buying and selling. This order ensured that the world government was able to control finance in every way. It was one of the many dictates by "the man" this global leader, that gave him complete power to own and dominate people. With no one challenging his actions, and the Beast working with him, it was a dark time of persecution. Philosophic theories raged, and Christian leaders secretly embroiled in discussions over the 666 question and the postulate instead of looking to **The Mighty One.**

Approaching things differently, concerned with the, shall we, shan't we have the "Mark" controversy raged! It was a great ploy, to use evil over people, to control the individual. A device inserted, ensured that each person's movements were watched, and noted. It was an excellent mechanism to ensure compliance and conformity. Through this and other strategies, the government could control in every way.

Total submission was required, to do the will of the dictator by all people. It was a way of the state owning and governing the individual. The Mark was filthy, straight from the pit of Hell and made the person into a commodity or "trade good" and not a created being! Once it became the norm through a meek acceptance, it was endemic in a society easily swayed by the government.

The procedure enforced, in the guise of financial safety and protection. Buying and selling constrained to those involved, guaranteeing that the person became a bartering commodity. Families were then torn in two, as some decided it was acceptable to receive the stitch. While others resilient, pointed to God's Word, as to the reason for their decision and stood firm against having it.

Many in church leadership, torn by family pressure, sat on the fence and waited. Sadly, the prophetic word seemed limited and Christians were frightened.

Once the law decreed it, the process became obligatory for everyone in the world. For those who would not have the Mark there was an enforced penalty of death. It is evident that what you obey, ultimately you become its slave. In one court, the judge turned towards the couple in front of him and spoke in an even voice.

"The Law of the land is final, for you to eat and live and to give your allegiance, it will be necessary for you to have 'The Stitch.' It is a minor thing and should not cause harm to your skin. It is a mark that will be completely hidden, and I am surprised that people of your calibre cannot accept, that to have an orderly society, we must enforce it. The government desires this to be done, as a sign of allegiance, and the only way to live, any questions?"

The man smiled at his wife and in a very steady voice said, "I respect your words president-elect, but it states in the Bible that we must not allow this on our person. Therefore, we will not have the operation, and we will not have the Mark, or Stitch on ourselves, to do so turns us into a commodity, and we are created people."

"Put them down," said the judge, and the law enforcer, opened the door of the cells and the two walked down into the darkness.

"Next," said the judge as another individual was led out. Denton and Heaton, their two angels, watched the events with interest as they were there to care for the two who had been locked up. They had seen power established all over the Earth as evil, dressed in an appropriate dress of respectability, take hold and sweep over everything in its path. They had endeavoured to guide their charges, trying to open their minds to the reality, of a world government that was evil. Encouraging them to see the truth in **The Beautiful One**, the Savior of the world, and now they would be with them on their last journey from life.

Much of the future foretold had allowed people the opportunity to analyse truth, although many chose to ignore the message. Possibly the old colourful language was too challenging to absorb, that made many ignore the book of Revelation. Fascinating stuff, written down for all to read, the book of Revelation, is an exciting book to decode. The prophetic spoken about, announces that the Savior will return in the sky, for all to see, as the overcoming Ancient of days. An awkward analogy to understand, again discarded by many as hazy claptrap. What is important to stress, is that nothing happens by chance, **The Mighty One** has a plan, and He is the winner!

"I am the Alpha and the Omega," says the Lord God, "who is and who was, and who is to come, the Almighty."

Everything established all in good order, nothing forgotten, and at the right time, it will all take place. Included in this, was a strategy that concerned The Breath, the Holy Spirit, the helper of the people. God had decreed that through the evil in the world and the end of the age **The Breath** was to be taken from the world. Not an elaborate plan, just a way of dealing with evil and people in fairness and love. In the heavens, waiting patiently, were myriads of angels amassed together for the final battle of the age. Waiting in readiness, planned for a future time, were the spirits of **The Mighty One** who would start the judgment call.

The plan had always been to allow people the opportunity, to turn away from wickedness and accept salvation. If they ignored this gift, then destruction will arrive in a variety of ways. Much was still a mystery, but a detailed part of the plan was the matter of two influential people arriving from out of Heaven. These extraordinary men were appointed as God's witnesses, to prophesy for 1,260 days, clothed in sackcloth. They are called "the two olive trees" or **The Mighty One's** lampstands, unique as "they stand before the Lord."

This impromptu miracle will suddenly happen in the Holy Land, as the two will appear in the street, and stand as witnesses to **The Mighty Ones'** goodness. Standing publicly for all to see them, robed in sackcloth, the two beings, promulgate God's power. Powerful, righteous and resolute they declared truth without compromise. At this miraculous event, all the world will be intrigued, as the media waves beam the news over nations. Astoundingly their ministry be characterised by four great miraculous powers given to them. These mighty beings, with unusual abilities, can breathe out a fire to kill their enemies, bring plagues on the Earth, turn water into blood and withhold rain for three and a half years.

At this time, the holy men make a declaration about the conduct of evil in the universe, as **The Mighty One's** ambassadors. In boldness, they speak the truth, announcing to the world, the necessity to look to God. Hate for these two mighty ones is endemic because they are holy, **The Mighty One's** men!

Although about this time, another matter of significance occurred, as an unwholesome evil declared war on **The Mighty One**. In the city called the Holy Place, in a sacred area, the man of Perdition comes and ravages it. He set up his image in the Temple, proclaiming himself as God! A wholly vile and heinous act, endeavouring to discredit and desecrated the holy place of God! It is spoken of in the Bible as the "abomination of desolation". This act declared war and is a significant gesture of evil. At this time, God **The Mighty One** declares His power and disgust at Satan, the "Accuser of the Brethren" and forbids him entry to Heaven, ever again. Prohibited also to accuse Christians, a stance he had been allowed, through **The Mighty One's** integrity in the past.

Once the two witnesses arrived, they stand in the city and condemn the actions of the man of Perdition, declaring **The Mighty One's** power and holiness. Influential leaders view events with interest, ridiculing the men and demeaning them, although wary, realising their power.

The two men continue their posture of witnessing, to the world, declaring **The Mighty One's** authority and power. **The Beautiful One.** Anointed by the Holy Spirit, **The Breath**, the two do not deviate from their task of proclaiming the truth, as **The Mighty One's** ambassadors. The world's leaders, irritated after watching them for two years, initiated their death by the Beast of darkness.

Lying dead in the street, people celebrated, stating that **The Mighty One** was powerless and these men had been nothing, but annoying beings! At the time, governments congratulated each other and send gifts to each other, bragging of their superiority! Locally, people walked past their bodies, and the media lauded the event as the news travelled the world. No one ventured to do anything, about removing their bodies, making a mockery of them, so they lay there as people walked past them.

After three days, suddenly, a remarkable thing happened.

The two men came back to life and stood once more in the street, boldly declaring the truth of Christ. For them to come back from the dead was a shock, it was powerful…and frightening, society wondered at the repercussions of this act. People were fearful, amazed at the miracle, wondering what was to happen next.

This was a demonstration, by **The Mighty One,** to give people the opportunity to change and see His power. Shortly after this, abruptly without warning, just as suddenly as they had come, a voice from Heaven called to them!

"Come up here."

The two witnesses went up to Heaven in a cloud, while their enemies looked on. All confounding, perplexing and fearful, a significant act heralding the future, as time got shorter for judgement to come. Prophecy tells us that the future will be overwhelming in its complexity, with many things about to happen. Fortunately, **The Mighty One** is in charge and focusing on that truth will remain vital when everything seems challenging.

Sometime in the future, the return of The Lord Jesus will occur, **The Beautiful One** will appear in the sky, for all to see. This will be totally incredible, a breath-taking event, as He returns for the Church, the bride of Christ. His return will also be with millions upon millions of angels with Him. The Bible says it this way!

"He is coming in the clouds, and every eye will see him, even those who pierced him."

The Beautiful One, crucified for humanity, Savior of all, has won the keys to life and death. He is a most formidable power, a mighty fantastic Savior whose sacrifice, was unique! In time He will also appear as the Ancient of days, a powerful advocate. He has won the right to open the books in Heaven, that show who have given over their lives to Him in exchange for His sacrifice. At this time all of creation will face judgement, every person who has ever lived upon the Earth. This is all very difficult to comprehend, unless you understand the power given to the Lord Jesus Christ and appreciate how mighty He is as God's Son. One day, all will have to answer for the way that they have lived their lives, which is a sobering fact.

At this time incredible signs and wonders will occur over the Earth. It is a time of devastation, culminating in a mighty battle of fantastic proportion. It is a time of great turbulence, as evil tries to exert power to fight holiness in every way. But the end draws near and **The Mighty One** enforces judgement on the world. In this era, another surprising occurrence happens in the world. A nation who in the past had denied **The Promise of Heaven,** recognizes their error and declares the truth everywhere. While in Heaven, all is waiting in readiness. As the angels commissioned to deliver the plagues of punishment on the Earth and the horsemen positioned to do God's will wait in readiness.

At this time, it is an opportunity for people to turn to God in repentance and recognize their sinfulness. He waits longingly for them to repent and to call on His name and tries to encourage them to do so. Some at this eleventh hour do seek Him and called out in repentance, others arrogantly send up profanities against Him.

All of Heaven was ready, just as they'd been at creation, for the war to begin. A battle for holiness that was far-reaching, and prophetic. **The Mighty One** had overlooked nothing. The heavens were filled with a glorious array of light that gleamed and shone out announcing the final battle in the world. While the Lord Jesus was poised to play His part, as the Ancient of Days.

"You are worthy to take and open the scroll," millions of angels cried out in praise to Him, as they waited for the end to come.

Silently and powerful judgement was coming, and the people were still playing, disregarding truth! All of this is explicit, real, no imagination; this is what will happen, and there will also be twenty-four unique holy elders, seated as witnesses to everything. A quality of legality that is wise and honorable. These are the mighty ones around the Throne in Heaven, fearsome unique and powerful.

Prophecy has foretold it, and now the Battle of Armageddon was about to happen. It is like Sodom and Gomorrah when judgement fell hundreds of years ago. At that time many thought that they still had time to live in any way they wanted. The reality was that justice was about to be declared to all. It was the end of the age, and the judgment spoken of down through the ages, was about to be given. **The Mighty One** had said so, and He was always right!

So much was positioned, ready to be disclosed to the world. **The Promise of Heaven** was arriving in power, when every eye will see Him in the sky with thousands of angels. This was the time He was going to bring the Church, His faithful followers, home to the safety of Heaven. Other mighty and fearful things will occur: plagues, mysteries, judgement and death, the conclusion of all things was about to happen!

A mother tucked her small child into bed and said, "The Bible said it, and it will happen, all we have to do is to remember, God loves us and will always take care of us because He is also

The Promise of Heaven, the winner!"

Ezekiel said we are watchmen, watching out at the End Times, let us be mindful that in everything we have to play our part.

The Seventh Trumpet

The seventh angel sounded his trumpet, and there were loud voices in Heaven, which said: "The kingdom of the world has become the kingdom of our Lord and his Messiah, and he will reign forever and ever."

Also, the twenty-four elders, seated on their thrones before God, fell on their faces and worshipped Him, saying:

"We give thanks to you, Lord God Almighty, the One who is and who was because you have taken your great power and have begun to reign. The nations were angry, and your wrath has come. The time has come for judging the dead, and for rewarding your servants, the prophets, and your people who revere your name, both great and small and for destroying those who bring corruption upon the earth."

The Mighty One smiled and declared to **The Beautiful One** and **The Breath**. "Victory has been won for all; the story that began in the garden is now completed."

"Maranatha, come Lord"

Printed in Great Britain
by Amazon

10078039R00149